THE WRATH OF SHIVA

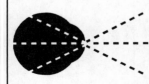

This Large Print Book carries the
Seal of Approval of N.A.V.H.

AN ANITA RAY MYSTERY

THE WRATH OF SHIVA

SUSAN OLEKSIW

THORNDIKE PRESS
A part of Gale, Cengage Learning

Detroit • New York • San Francisco • New Haven, Conn • Waterville, Maine • London

GALE
CENGAGE Learning®

LIBRARY OF CONGRESS CATALOGING-IN-PUBLICATION DATA

Oleksiw, Susan.
  The wrath of Shiva / by Susan Oleksiw.
    pages ; cm. — (Thorndike Press large print mystery) (An Anita Ray mystery)
    ISBN 978-1-4104-5304-4 (hardcover) — ISBN 1-4104-5304-9 (hardcover) 1. East Indian American women—Fiction. 2. Americans—India—Fiction. 3. Missing persons—Fiction. 4. India, South—Fiction. 5. Large type books. I. Title.
PS3565.L42W73 2012b
813'.54—dc23   2012031613

Published in 2012 by arrangement with Tekno Books and Ed Gorman.

In memoriam
B. Kunju Lakshmee Amma
d. 9.7.11

ACKNOWLEDGMENTS

I want to thank Usha Ramachandran, who kindly answered my many questions with patience and humor. I am also indebted to Charlene Allison, PhD, who read the manuscript and pointed out many errors and lapses. Any errors that remain are entirely mine.

NOTE TO THE READER

In Nayar families, the oldest woman is called, out of respect, *Muttacchi*. A mother's younger sister is called *Elayamma* (little mother), often with the personal name attached, as in Meena Elayamma. A servant refers to her employer as *Amma* (mother), and may refer to other ladies of the household as *Amma* or as *Chechi* (elder sister), depending on their age.

The *salwar khameez,* a popular traditional Indian outfit for women, has three parts — pants, long overblouse, and a light cotton shawl called a *dupatta.*

The end of a sari is often elaborately woven or decorated; this part of the sari is called the *pallu* (in the North) or *mundaani* (in Malayalam, the language of Kerala). The *choli* is a small blouse worn with a sari.

The *lungi* is a plaid or colored cotton

9

sarong-like garment worn by lower-caste men and women. The *mundu* is a white cotton sarong-like garment with a narrow colored border worn by both men and women of all castes, and is considered more formal than the *lungi*. Women wear the *mundu* as part of a two-piece sari; the top piece is called a *nerid.*

ONE

Anita Ray rested her arms on the balcony railing and gazed down at the few remaining diners on the terrace below. Of the eight tables spread across the sandy ground, only two were still occupied, the foreign tourists shaded from the harsh midday tropical sun by lush, overhanging palm trees. Beyond the white picket fence waves thundered onto the rocks, and a single fisherman searching for mussels gathered up the day's catch, balanced the full basket on his head, and scampered across the rocks, on his way to the village market.

Lunch at Hotel Delite was almost over, and Anita was growing more and more impatient. She tugged at the light cotton shawl draped over her head and brushed a lock of hair behind an ear. Her cousin-sister Surya was due to arrive today, or rather early this morning, and Anita was eager to see her. The women were almost the same age, and Anita thought they had been more sisters than cousins, sharing everything in their lives no matter where each one was living, in Kerala or London or the States. Their last visit seemed ages ago, and they had a lot to catch up on. Anita had been keeping a short list — tacked to the wall by the mirror in her small flat — of all the things she wanted to tell her. Reading over the list was like running through the carnival of emotions her life had been over the last few years.

The sound of a plane separated from the rumble of the ocean waves, and Anita looked up, searching the sky. A tiny silvery capsule emerged from a cloud and moved across the blue expanse. This was most likely the plane from Mumbai — the first morning flight out of that airport to Trivandrum, the best connection for flights arriving in the dead of night. Anita had taken it often enough on the way home from visiting family and friends in the States — the last leg of an exhausting journey to South India. Anita immediately felt a rush of excitement. That could be Surya's flight, she thought.

After watching the plane circle far above the beach resort and begin its descent to the airport, she turned again to the terrace below. As soon as the terrace was cleared, Anita could get on with her business — doing errands, opening her photography gallery for the evening, and rearranging her schedule for Surya's visit.

A man and two women, tall and light-skinned despite their tans, joked and waved to the waiter as they headed up the stairs to the main floor of the hotel. Built into the rock face, Hotel Delite had originally been a private home on three levels. With its eight rooms and small private dining room for guests, it was one of the smaller hotels at the resort. The hotel was always full, and the terrace restaurant especially popular with guests staying at other hotels.

The only table on the terrace still occupied was the one closest to Anita — seven women who had come for lunch and a tour. They had arrived on the cruise liner now anchored off the nearby harbor; they would stay a day or so and then depart. In a few days another ship would arrive, with another group of foreigners for short or longer stays. The white ship glistened farther down the coast, just near enough so anyone could see small launches traveling back and forth from the coast, but not much else. The ship looked so picturesque bobbing out there on the waves, like a toy, that Anita could almost enjoy the sight of it. Almost.

The short stays of the cruise liners brought guests with their own set of problems, and for some reason Anita's Auntie Meena, owner of Hotel Delite, had decided that Anita was the one to deal with them, so Anita arranged tours and quick visits to major sights and a crash course in the history and culture of Kerala that always left her feeling exhausted and slightly tacky. There was something unsettling about reducing the history of a glorious and ancient culture to a one-hour talk delivered while walking backward.

The women's voices grew loud as they pushed their chairs back and stood, calling out reminders to each other as they gathered up their purses and sun hats and headed for the stairs. A small van was waiting for them in the parking area, with a tour guide and a plan to occupy them for the rest of the day and into the evening. Their voices faded briefly in the stairwell, but then the women burst almost as one through the main entrance to the hotel. Laughing and teasing each other, they climbed into the van, slammed the doors, and drove away. Anita sighed with relief. They were gone, in the capable hands of a guide and a driver. She was free for the rest of the day.

■ ■ ■ ■

Lighthouse Road rose steeply from the rocks and the water, a challenge to the three-wheeled autorickshaws whining up the hill with their passengers and to tourists fighting the heat and humidity on foot. Anita smiled at the bright red faces she passed as she walked down the hill later that afternoon, before turning down the narrow lane leading to Hotel Delite. She had a bundle of new photographs to examine and was looking forward to a quiet hour. She headed into the hotel for a bottle of water and the day's gossip, greeting Ravi, the desk clerk, with a genial nod.

Drifting through the office doorway came the familiar sound of Auntie Meena on the telephone — *shari, shari, shari* — an active listener if ever there was one, filling her end of the conversation with the soft sounds of agreement. Her voice rose and fell in a range of emotions while her vocabulary remained one single word. Meena's use of the word *shari* was virtuosic. But before Anita could disappear down the stairs to the terrace below, Ravi hunched over the registration desk and slid farther away, out of sight of Auntie Meena inside the office.

Curious, Anita paused at the top of the stairs, then moved back to the front of the desk.

"What has happened?" Anita whispered. "Who's she talking to?"

"To Punnu Chellamma." Ravi glanced over his shoulder, but when he heard the telephone drop into its cradle, he drew the registration book closer.

Surya's grandmother? "To Muttacchi? Hmm," thought Anita, frowning. "What a lot of drama for so early in the evening."

Anita was used to her aunt's displays — the wild swings of emotion and the melodrama of her life. When Meena Nayar's husband died unexpectedly some years ago, leaving his widow with a modest hotel and a daughter in school in the States, Anita had volunteered to stay with her for a while to help her out, thinking it would be a lark to live in a hotel. It was. But a few months turned into a year, she entered university, she finished university, and, well, here she still was. Anita leaned into the office doorway.

Meena Nayar, owner of Hotel Delite and a perpetual sufferer of life's iniquities, was staring at the old black telephone, her expression pained and sad. It was not an unusual expression for her, Anita felt;

16

Meena was a woman in her fifties who often said she had been born into her fifties, meant to be fifty-something all her days, a drab age that promised nothing of the exuberance of youth or the respect and ease of old age. It seemed an injustice to her, she told Anita. Meena leaned against the desk, her hand still on the black receiver. She closed her eyes, took a deep breath, and exhaled. But since this display of despair was for Meena herself alone, Anita took it seriously.

"I thought you went to welcome Surya. But you were talking to Muttacchi. What has gone wrong?" Anita asked as she came into the room.

Meena shut her eyes tight. "What always goes wrong?" The older woman sighed, but her breath caught. "She did not arrive."

"Oh, Auntie. That's too bad." Anita felt a wrenching and for a moment looked away. Well, she should have expected something like this. She had so wanted to see Surya, but her cousin was famous for being erratic in her arrivals. Anita took a deep breath. "Muttacchi must be very disappointed. She adores Surya — she's been looking forward to this visit for some time. Did Surya say why she couldn't come?"

Meena shook her head, her face tight as

she tried but failed to conceal her feelings. "Not a word. Not a word to her dear old grandmother. Not one word! And after all those warnings! Is it any wonder Muttacchi is distraught?" All of a sudden, Meena swung toward Anita. "Don't you ever do such a thing! Never! You will always tell me what you are doing! Promise me!" She slapped her forehead. "Oh, what am I saying?"

"Yes, Auntie, what are you saying? Usually, you're ordering me *not* to tell you what I'm up to." Anita stood with her hands on her hips, a mischievous grin on her face. She believed most of life's ills could be eased, if not solved, with humor.

"This is not funny, Anita. Not funny. It is very distressing."

"Yes, I can see that. What did you mean about the warnings?" Anita asked. "You said, 'After all those warnings.' " She pushed the *dupatta* off her head and let it fall down the back of her *salwar khameez*. Saris seemed much too hot in this weather, and the light cotton blouse and pants made heat tolerable. The dupatta, or light cotton shawl worn as a headscarf, gave some protection from the sun.

Meena waved away the question. "I am upset. I can only spare a few hours to attend to things, and then I must go. Tomorrow we will put all this distress aside for her."

"We? Do you mean me? I'm going also?" Something else that was different. Whenever there was trouble, Anita thought, Meena usually took the opposite tack and did everything in her power to keep Anita out of it.

"Yes, you. I am relying on you to let Muttacchi understand this is a small matter and Surya will soon appear. There is no worry. You will make her see there is no reason to worry. We will find other things to enjoy at this time. We will distract her. We will go up tomorrow morning. Tonight I must attend to some hotel business." Meena looked like she was ready to say more but decided against it.

"Maybe Muttacchi got the dates mixed up," Anita said, knowing it was unlikely. The old woman had ruled a large family and managed a larger estate for years; she didn't get little things wrong.

"Yes, yes, maybe so!" Meena was buoyed by the idea of the whole thing being a mere mix-up of dates. "I called Surya's parents in London. They are saying she is calling them last night from Dubai, when she is between flights. So, she has decided to go elsewhere."

She grabbed her purse and stamped it once on the table. "So inconsiderate she is." She gave Anita a woeful look, then turned and left the room.

"Well, well, well." Anita went out to the registration desk and stared through the open doorway. Even though the afternoon was waning, the sun hit hard on the potted plants lining the walk around the side of the hotel; a maidservant passed the open window with a broom scratching the ground, crows swooped and alighted and flew away when the broom threatened them, cars honked on the road nearby. Tourists were straggling back after a day at the beaches, shopping, a trip to a nearby temple, or perhaps to Kanya Kumari. January in South India was the height of the tourist season, and in Kovalam was absolute perfection. Everything was as it should be. Except for my relatives, Anita thought.

At this time of day Auntie Meena should be in her office, bemoaning the tribulations of running a hotel and catering to a group of people who made no sense whatsoever, the rising cost of fuel, the difficulties of providing adequate water, the plans of government that would put them all out of business, and whatever other disaster she could conjure up while going over the accounts. Auntie Meena lived for her worries, as long as they weren't too immediate.

Ravi grunted and turned the page of the registration book, made a notation in red pencil, and began to stare at the page again.

"She's quite distressed about something, but she's afraid to tell me the truth. It can't be only that Surya canceled a visit at the last minute." Anita leaned against the desk.

Ravi glanced up at Anita. They were about the same age, and Anita considered him something of a younger brother — sweet, easy to push around, a delight to banter with, and an all-around good sort. "Why not?"

"When have you ever known Surya to be reliable? She barely knows what year this is. If it weren't printed on the front cover of *Vanity Fair,* she would never know." Anita studied Ravi, who in turn was assiduously studying each page, leaning closer to each block. "What are you not telling me?"

"Why do you think I have something to tell you?"

"Because you won't look at me, that's why." Anita tapped the countertop. "Perhaps I should tell Auntie Meena that you are longing to be married."

Ravi gasped. "You are cruel to me." He looked so pained that Anita almost regretted her ploy; when Auntie Meena learned his mother died when he was a child, she had promised to find him a wife when he was ready, to his dismay. "She will hound me to look at this girl and that girl, and soon she will force me to choose, and then I will be burdened with a wife and then a child. And if I am discontented, I cannot leave — society will not accept me if I leave — and if I stay I will never know peace of mind. Only the temple is my refuge."

"Are you sure you aren't already related to us? You and Auntie Meena are perfect catastrophizers." Anita sighed. "Just tell me what you are withholding."

Ravi looked over his shoulder, then set his elbow on the counter and leaned over. "You are cruel to me." He rubbed his fingers along the edge of the counter. "Yesterday hotel is receiving a telephone call. Already Muttacchi is knowing that Surya will not arrive. There were omens, she said, last month. She calls to tell us this." Ravi leaned over and whispered. "Your auntie is worrying the omens are true."

Anita settled herself on a stool. "She never mentioned any of that to me. You overheard all this?"

Ravi lowered his voice. "They discussed premonitions. Omens. Warnings, Muttacchi

22

calls them. Your aunt asked if she is frightened."

"And that means Auntie Meena is frightened." Anita turned on her stool to gaze at the now-empty office. "But of what?"

Anita dodged past two European women haggling with a salesman at the door to his jewelry shop. It was early evening, and shopping was picking up. The sidewalk hawkers unfurled brightly colored *lungis,* or sarongs, bamboo mats, and maps of India. Younger ones tapped small drums among dozens hanging like giant beads around their shoulders and down to their legs. Village children played around neatly wound and piled nets near black, wooden boats, *vellams* that braved the violent waves year round.

Anita loved the bustle of the resort, the mix of nationalities and locals, languages and foods. She paused to gaze at a shop window, at the brass pitchers and images, shiny in the sun. Business must be improving, she thought. These goods are better than last month's cheap trinkets.

Anita turned down the alley leading to her photography gallery. This was high season, and she had planned on keeping to a regular schedule with her shop — at least to the extent she was capable of keeping anything on schedule. But with Surya's sudden change in plans, Anita saw her own good intentions evaporating. She grabbed the handle to the corrugated shutter and tugged, sending it sliding upward.

"Ah! You have decided to work today?" An old man, with a tape measure draped around his neck and straight pins stuck along the edges of a shirt pocket, stepped down from the shop next door, shuffled along the lane and waved his gnarled hand in greeting.

"Did I surprise you, Chinnappa?" Anita gave him a warm smile and began to set up her easels. "I'm only here for today," she said. "I have been summoned."

"Ah! Summoned." He nodded, his white hair staying neatly combed. "And who is the one who has such power over you?"

"My Muttacchi, Punnu Chellamma. She is my mother's aunt and very old." Anita unlocked a closet in the back and stood in the doorway just long enough to enjoy the cold air-conditioned air, then began pulling out boxes of photographs, framed and unframed. "My cousin Surya was supposed to fly in last night — actually, very early this morning — and she didn't show up. And she didn't come in on the plane from Mumbai either." Anita gave him a conspiratorial

24

look. "She is becoming more unreliable the longer she lives overseas."

"So, she forgets her duty." Chinnappa clucked and lowered himself to sit on the raised stone platform that was the gallery floor. "It is the way, isn't it? Off to the West, off from duty."

"No, it is not, Chinnappa." Anita pushed a large wooden box on rollers across the floor and ran her hands over the matted and shrink-wrapped photographs. "My mother lives in America and she is a dutiful woman."

"Ah, but she is a Nayar lady though married to an American, isn't it? The man who loves trees."

"He's a forester," Anita said, deciding not to tell her friend for the umpteenth time that her father was a forester advising foreign governments on how to restore growth in certain areas, to hold back deserts. Trees had brought him to India in the first place, but it was a young Nayar woman who had made him stay. Anita stopped her preparations to take a good look at the old man, wondering if he was just trying to get her goat. "He doesn't simply love trees — that makes him sound silly."

"Ah, even so." Chinnappa winked at her.

A young boy about twelve years old came

running down the lane, calling out, "I am here. I am here. Am I not here?" He arrived at the gallery, panting and sweating.

"How is it you know when I'm opening up, Peeru?" Anita smiled at him.

"Does a dog not smell meat?" Chinnappa snarled at the boy.

Since the boy's arrival one day with an offer to work and looking as hungry as she had ever seen a child in Kerala, Anita had taken him on as a general helper. He rushed to the closet to set up the remaining easels and photos.

Anita pulled out a table and chair and set up a cash box. "There's another cruise ship in the harbor. We had a small group come for lunch and a tour." She pulled out the chair and sat down sideways, crossing her legs and leaning her arm across the back. "Do the ships interfere with the fishermen?"

Chinnappa shrugged. "Does it matter? Government pushes them off the beaches, off their land, out of their harbors. And now, out of the sea."

"You are a cynic, old man!"

Chinnappa laughed heartily, his few remaining teeth glistening in the sun.

For the next couple of hours a steady stream of tourists wandered through the gallery, some gazing in from the walkway instead of struggling up the one steep step onto the platform, others staring for long minutes at a particular photograph, still others flipping idly through every matted picture in the two bins, finding nothing of personal interest.

If someone did find something they liked and asked about the price, Anita made one up on the spot. Pricing was not her strong suit, and she refused to spend more time on it than absolutely necessary. Besides, it was something of a game to see if she guessed well for the prospective buyer. She sold one photograph, to a German man who looked so grim during the transaction Anita was surprised that he actually handed over the wad of rupees.

"I got your message," a young man said.

Anita turned around at the sound of his voice, felt a tingling down her chest. Anand Nambudiri, with his black wavy hair curling around his ears and his bronzed skin shiny against his white shirt and white slacks, jumped onto the gallery floor. He was about Anita's age, but unlike her he took his work, for a high-tech company, very seriously. "Thank you, Peeru." Anand took the chair offered and set it near Anita's. "Too bad about your cousin. Where is she?"

"Don't know," Anita said. "She called her

27

parents from the airport. Auntie Meena called their mobile and it rang while they were at a concert in London. Surya talked to them while she was marking time in Dubai. I guess she was tired of shopping." Anita was trying to give her cousin the benefit of the doubt, but was having a hard time denying her frustration and annoyance. "I tried her mobile a couple of times but got nothing." She shrugged.

"So we're off for the foreseeable future, eh?" He crossed his legs and winked at Peeru.

Anita's annoyance bubbled up as she contemplated the complications Surya's nonarrival had created. Anita would have to reschedule her plans with Anand and making them in the first place had been hard enough. Auntie Meena took her responsibility for Anita while she lived in the hotel very seriously — more seriously than her own mother did — and wanted to vet and approve every man who came to the hotel if he wanted to speak to Anita.

Really, Anita couldn't understand why her Auntie Meena disliked Anand so, but she didn't try to hide it. She looked grim when he came by the hotel for any reason and whenever Anita mentioned his name. Whenever she talked about family marriages that had gone bad, Auntie Meena had taken to slipping in some minor comparison between Anand and the disappointing husband or suitor. If Anita protested, Meena said only, "He is unsuited to you, unsuited in every way." But Anita didn't think he was unsuited at all. Anand Nambudiri suited her just right — unattached, out for some fun, and the son of crazy parents who thought Anita had found the secret of life — unlike her own relatives who were convinced Anita was heading for disaster every time she walked out the door.

"How about a little snack?" Anita pulled out her purse and handed Peeru a wad of rupees. "Four coffees?" Peeru ran off with his order. "I'm gaining strength for the visit to Muttacchi's. Every time I see her she wants a report on my life, which she doesn't think well of."

"She and your auntie Meena are of one mind," Anand said.

It was a minor annoyance to Anita that almost every relative she had was out looking for a prospective husband for her — anyone and anything to get her away from singlehood and hanging out in a photography gallery. Anita turned her attention to a gaggle of women tourists coming down the lane, a tour guide in the lead. "Oops! Collisions are coming."

Anita steeled herself for another series of complaints from the tour guide who was driving Hotel Delite and its staff crazy. But to Anita's surprise, Sophie barely glanced her way as she led her charges down to the beach walk.

"The snorkeling is one hour with a diver who will take you out in a canoe in the morning. Is over there." A bright pink silk wrap was tied across her chest, falling to her knees. She pointed across the beach, and the group disappeared around a corner.

"That's a lucky miss," Anita said.

Two

The following morning Joseph, the Hotel Delite driver, jounced down the driveway to Muttacchi's estate, where she lived in near-regal isolation among the remnants of a once large family property. The driveway ran straight before ending in a sandy yard in front of the main wing of the house. Joseph pulled up to a thicket of trees, careful to park in the shade, and turned off the engine. All that was left of the old family property were a few buildings and a small portion of land, but it was still impressive to Anita's eye.

Standing by the front doorway leading into the courtyard was a bright red motorbike, so painfully new that a white label on the back fender wasn't even dirty yet.

"For Surya?" Anita said to Auntie Meena, sitting beside her in the back seat.

She nodded. "To make her feel at home. To make her visit enjoyable for her. To tell her how much her grandmother loves her."

"I wonder if Surya's ever ridden one," Anita said mostly to herself. This business with her cousin was beginning to worry Anita; Muttacchi was devoted to her granddaughter Surya, but those who knew the family well knew the old woman's feelings should never be taken for granted. Surya's trip last year was a series of flighty jaunts around the countryside visiting relatives, dropping in here or there, and then rushing off. Muttacchi had been courteous, but Anita could tell the old woman had ended up exasperated with Surya.

"Remember, we are here to comfort Muttacchi, not upset her."

"I'm surprised you brought me." Anita reached for the door handle.

"That's what I mean, Anita. You must be sensitive to the situation. We are so close; it would be hard to explain to Muttacchi why you could not travel even from the hotel to offer your concerns. And another thing. Do not sound foreign."

"But I'm not foreign."

Meena sighed with a certain frustration. "You know what I mean. Do not call me Auntie. I am your *elayamma*." Meena turned to the door on her side of the car.

Anita opened her mouth to protest but

thought better of it. Using the term *elayamma,* little mother, came dangerously close to giving Meena more authority than Anita wanted her to have.

"So, come."

Anita and Meena climbed out of the car, passed through the entry, and headed for the courtyard while Joseph found someone to take the luggage.

"Here we are!" Auntie Meena waved to Muttacchi at the other side of the yard. A table beneath the pergola at the far edge of the courtyard was set for tea, and the old woman appeared to be deep into the morning ritual, with teacups and plates of snacks spread around her.

"Come, come, come!" Muttacchi reached up her arms to welcome the other women. "You are just in time. Sit, sit." The old woman patted the arm of a nearby chair and then pointed Anita to it. "You will cheer an old woman."

Meena pulled up a chair and began to inspect the plates of food. Anita left her aunt to her personal business, the trap of the hotelier — mentally calculating the ingredients in each and comparing them to her own offerings. Satisfied, she took a chair and offered Muttacchi sympathies on the failed visit of Surya.

"Acch! It was not to be. But another time, yes." Muttacchi fussed with the plates and cups but avoided meeting anyone else's eye. "Now, here is my difficulty. Shall I call my daughter and complain she has let my granddaughter become too modern, or shall I join the ripple."

"Eh?" Meena frowned.

Anita looked blank, then grinned. "Go with the flow, Muttacchi."

"Ah, yes, of course. My daughter doesn't like fuss."

"I spoke with her," Meena said. "Surya called from the Dubai airport but she only mentioned her later plans, so her mother didn't know if she was changing plans or not. I shall call her again, to get Surya's new mobile."

"Oh dear," Muttacchi said, looking past them. Anita followed her gaze. Farther down the path, after it turned from stone to sand, Anita saw only a maidservant with a broom, going about her daily chores. Anita raised her eyebrows and turned to Muttacchi, but the old woman nodded and waved her hand in the same direction again. Anita turned back to the maidservant.

"That's Gauri, isn't it?" Anita said.

"Indeed it is." Muttacchi sighed and snapped the end of her sari in annoyance.

The maidservant swung the reed broom out and around, holding the rough coir rope banding the reeds with her muscular fingers. Then she grabbed the reeds in her hand, tapped the ends flat against her right hip, and with a flourish swept the broom down and along the sandy path. The broom brushed along, rose, and dipped again, scraping, rising, falling, scraping. Her left hand, fingers lightly curled, rested on the small of her back as she leaned over her work, moving forward a step at a time, like a dancer gliding across the stage.

"Is there something wrong with her being here?" Anita turned her attention to Muttacchi, who seemed both resigned and annoyed at the sight of Gauri. But the maidservant was a longtime family employee, joining the estate when she was a young girl. Now in her thirties, she was feisty, independent, and thoroughly reliable, though you wouldn't know it from Muttacchi's expression.

"It is such trouble when things go awry." Meena folded her arms on the table and watched the maidservant sweep, her rhythmic passage across the path almost hypnotic. "So hard to get good servants." She launched into a tale of a maidservant at Hotel Delite who couldn't work longer than an hour without breaking into woeful tales of her family troubles. Meena once found her, sitting on an unmade bed, wailing away to a hotel guest.

Anita looked from one to the other, not sure what was going on. She was even more confused when Meena took up the conversation again.

"Do you request such prognostications of her?" Meena asked, changing the subject.

"Of course not." Muttacchi snorted in mild disapproval. "I have my astrologer, do I not?" She tugged on her sari, pulling it farther up her shoulder. "But she is with us so long. Of course she wants to warn me."

"Is this the source of the omens I have heard about?" Anita asked.

Meena gave her a blank look, then sighed. "Ah, Ravi. Yes, he overhears everything. I wonder if I can —"

"No, Auntie Meena, you can't," Anita said. "Meena Elayamma," she said when she caught Meena's warning look.

"Can't what?"

"Whatever you were thinking of about Ravi," Anita said. "So, is she?"

"Yes, she is the one." Meena leaned back in her chair, a little pout on her lips.

"Gauri came to me well over a month ago and said Surya would never visit me again."

Muttacchi's words caught in her throat, and she gave a little gasp. "That was all she said. Then she walked away. I was deeply hurt."

Indignant at the apparent insult to her older relative, Meena straightened her shoulders and turned to scowl at the maidservant. Muttacchi tried not to look annoyed or injured. Curious, Anita leaned forward, watching Gauri more closely.

Gauri moved along the path, sweeping leaves fallen from overhanging branches, from the *champaka* shrubs past their bloom in clay pots lining the path, the occasional twig, the pile growing larger and larger, but still not very big — the grounds were clean overall, swept every day. Occasionally the small servant woman turned and swept the path behind her, so that the ground was marked with the curve of the broom and no sign of a footprint on the sand. The figure grew smaller and smaller, her white sari no longer sparkling in the sunshine, the coconut oil on her tidy black hair no longer glistening as she moved into shade.

Without warning the woman's body grew still. She straightened up, her arms coming to rest at her side, the broom falling from her hand. Her fingers grew rigid and flat against her thighs, her head lifted, her neck stiffened. At first almost imperceptibly, her limbs began to tremble, shaking lightly as though feeling a slight chill, then slowed to stillness. Her body began to sway. Standing on the dirt path, her bare feet rooted to the spot, the maidservant swerved in a gentle circle, round and round, legs stiff, arms stiff, neck stiff, but showing no signs of toppling over. Then, just as unexpectedly, her motion slowed and the circular, dizzying motion came to an easy end; once again she stood stock-still. In a moment her head tilted back, her face raised to the sky, her mouth open. And there she stayed, minute after minute after minute.

After some time, her head fell forward, her mouth closed, and she stared straight ahead, her eyes blank and unseeing.

"You see, Meena? Did I not tell you?" Muttacchi turned to Aunt Meena.

"Just as you said, Muttacchi, just as you said." Aunt Meena frowned and crossed her arms. "She is possessed." She reached out and rested her hand on the older woman's arm. "How difficult for you."

Anita kept her eyes on the maidservant. "How long has this been going on?"

"Why are you asking this, Anita?" Aunt Meena gave her niece an appraising look.

"I was just wondering, that's all." Anita paused, still watching the maidservant. "Did

Gauri start having trances before or after she had a premonition about Surya?"

"Before. It was perhaps several months ago she first came to me about Surya." The old woman spoke softly, almost a whisper, looking back and forth between Gauri and Anita.

"And you want to know why?" Anita looked at both women.

"Don't be absurd." The old woman gave her a contemptuous look and shook her shoulders. "She is possessed because the gods have chosen her." Her voice was firm, but her eyes were troubled.

Anita opened her mouth to speak, but thought better of it. It seemed obvious to her that Muttacchi wanted help but simply wasn't ready to admit it; there could be no other reason for Auntie Meena to have brought Anita along with her. If Surya had canceled her visit and gone elsewhere, there was nothing Anita could do about it — but Gauri, now, that was another matter.

"How long does this usually last?" Aunt Meena asked. The sleeves of her *choli* pulled tight against her flabby arms as she pushed herself up in her chair and turned her attentions to the older woman.

"Hours or minutes. No set time." The old woman shrugged. "It is your opinion I

39

wanted."

"Ah! You think she is shirking her duties!" Meena looked eager and relieved. "And you want me to test her. Is that it?"

Anita glanced at her aunt.

"This is something I can judge," Meena said. "I have excessive experience in these matters, Muttacchi. I am having many employees over the years of running Hotel Delite, and you are knowing the difficulties of managing a large staff, and it is even greater in a business. You are right to call on me to look into this matter. Giving up time for such business is no matter, no matter at all. And you are not to worry. I am discovering the falseness here."

"No, no. You misunderstand me."

"You are not to be worrying," Meena insisted. "I will find her out. I have experience, and my staff would never try to cheat me. Never."

"Well, you got that right, Meena Elayamma." Anita smiled when Meena scowled at her.

"We are speaking of Gauri. She is not false, Meena. She is pious." Muttacchi shook her head and little white hairs flew out around her forehead.

"Pious?" Meena glanced at the maidservant stiff limbed and still. "You are certain of this? She is not deceiving you?"

"I have known Gauri since she was a child. Her mother worked for this family, and her mother's mother. She is connected."

"Oh." Meena frowned. "This is a difficulty." Anita thought Meena looked a little disappointed at the loss of a meaty challenge.

"Even so," Muttacchi said.

"What happens when the trance ends?" Anita asked.

"She collapses on the ground." The old woman nodded toward the maidservant. "Like that."

Just as she spoke, the maidservant's head went limp, her hands twitched, and she buckled at the knees, collapsing onto the dirt, falling forward onto her face. She made no effort to throw out her hands to break her fall and landed hard on her left cheek. Anita jumped up from her seat.

"Usually someone is working nearby ready to catch her when she goes, but not this morning." The old woman pressed her palms flat on the table and pushed herself up from her seat. "Come, let us attend." She shouted out for Bindu, and another maidservant, a young woman, came running. She slipped her hand beneath the old woman's arm and led her onto the path.

41

Anita was already at the collapsed woman's side, feeling her forehead, checking her pulse.

Behind her Anita could hear Muttacchi and Auntie Meena muttering over the problems with servants these days, and life in general, their enthusiasms slowing their progress to a standstill. But for Anita, there was no one else but the woman on the ground. Her sweeping had brought her to the end of the path, where the ground grew rough as it approached the little forest on the edge of the property, standing between the buildings and the Karamana River.

This was the *kavu,* the sacred grove of this place.

At the mouth of the small forest was a natural opening that looked wild and unkempt, which it was, Anita knew. This was untamed land set aside when the area was first settled, and it had remained separate and sacred, never entered, never harvested, never touched in any way. No one could enter, and owners were uneasy if non-family members drew too close to it.

The far border of the grove meandered along open scrubland until it turned toward the Karamana River. Directly in front of Anita, the edge of the grove wandered away down to the riverbank. Occasionally in the very early morning, in a really still night, when she had visited, Anita could hear shallow waves lapping the shore when a laden boat passed by.

Anita knew the grove had been trimmed over the years, as more and more land had been sold off to satisfy the demands of family members who wanted to move on, or even out of the country. From a once grand sacred grove of more than thirty hectares, running along the river as well as deep inland, only this small plot remained, less than one hectare. If there were an easy path, Anita could walk its perimeter in fifteen minutes.

Where the jungle had once flourished, modern homes belonging to strangers now stood, neighbors near enough to be overheard on some nights, or even seen during certain seasons when trees lost their leaves and cooking fires burned bright. But if the deity of the kavu was angry at the loss of his home and the encroachment of strangers, he gave no sign. Ten feet inside the opening sat the stone image of Bhairava, darkening with the passage of time, alone in stalwart, splendid isolation, staring out at the mortals who worshipped him. Just even with the opening, on the scrubland, sat a stone oil lamp, and another stone covered with tuberoses.

Muttacchi nudged the maidservant with her foot and called out for a glass of water.

"She will only take it from me," Muttacchi said, staring down at her servant. "The first time it happened Bindu came with water and this one grew hysterical, saying she will die if she takes it. I said nonsense, but she insisted. You need water to live I am telling her, but no, she says, if she takes water from that Bindu's hand she will die. Then you will die if you don't, I tell her. No, Amma, you give it to me, she says. So I give it to her. I alone can revive her, she tells me."

"Is she mad?" Meena asked.

"Perhaps."

"Does she do this every day?" Anita asked.

"No, not every day. But at least once a week now. Sometimes more. Bindu! *Va! Va!* Hurry with that water!"

"And where does she do this? When she's sweeping the pergola? How about when she's working in the kitchen? Does it happen in the bedrooms? Does she go into a trance there?" Anita rattled off her questions as she leaned over the figure.

"Ayoo!" Auntie Meena slapped a hand over her mouth. "Imagine such a thing in the kitchen? Who would eat?"

44

"Never in the kitchen," Muttacchi said. "Never in the rooms. Only on the grounds."

Bindu hurried up to them holding a glass of water in her outstretched hand, and the old woman knelt down with some effort and began to dribble water over the maidservant's lips. Gauri groaned, and began to stir, drawing up her arms until she pushed herself up and sat. She was covered in a light dust of the iron-rich soil. She reached for the glass of water and held it several inches above her mouth, pouring the water down her throat. Dizzy, confused, she swayed and moaned for another minute, then got to her feet. Anita rose also and stepped back.

"Amma!" Still swaying but with her eyes gliding from one woman to the next, the maidservant bent and touched both her hands to Muttacchi's feet and then to her eyes. The old woman managed a wan smile and waved her off.

"Help her, Bindu."

Gauri picked up her broom and staggered away, Bindu close on her heels.

"It is a dilemma, Muttacchi." Meena sipped her tea and gazed at the spot on the path where the maidservant had lain. The three women — Muttacchi, Auntie Meena, and

Anita — were again at the table beneath the pergola. A servant brought a fresh pot of tea, hot and milky, and a thick blanket of flowers filtered the sun above. "Have you tried nothing yet?"

"I have been to my astrologer, of course."

"Of course." Meena nodded her strong approval.

"He knows her, knows her situation, knows our family." The old woman stared up at the yellow flowers of the umbrella tree marking a corner of the open courtyard. "Gauri has been with this family for as long as she can remember — thirty years at least. She came to work first as a young girl, eight years old perhaps, with her mother. Doing little things. I think she helped with my first grandchild."

"Does he think he can restore her to her natural state?" Meena leaned forward. She had absolute faith in her own astrologer, another longtime family associate, and waited expectantly for the words of approval from her older relative.

"That is the desired end, isn't it?" Muttacchi shrugged.

"What started her having these trances?" Anita asked.

Meena stared at her. "Did you not hear Muttacchi? She is chosen."

"Ah, yes." Anita leaned back in her seat. "Is that what Gauri said?"

"No, not at all. At first, it is only *vata* — wind, spirit — that is touching her. Then she understood it to be Bhagavati."

"How many times has this happened?" Anita asked.

The old woman laughed. "You think like your grandfather Rajan."

Anita frowned. "I'm not sure how I should interpret that. I always liked him, the little I saw of him."

"He was a chemist," Meena said. "He could not always understand the finer points of the household." She sighed and lost herself in reverie. "Science was all to him."

"Does she do her own cooking?" Anita asked, persevering. She tried to recall everything she could about Gauri. In Anita's mind there was something odd about a woman who had apparently been ordinary for most of her life suddenly taking to having trances and premonitions, as one chosen by Bhagavati.

"She is a maidservant. She does not live here, but she helps Lata, the cook, in the kitchen among other duties. She eats what she makes for the rest of us." With a tilt of her head, Muttacchi dismissed the topic. Anita continued to frown.

"Has she been sick?" Anita asked.

"She has mentioned nothing." Muttacchi peered at her.

"But she did say at first it was only vata," Anita said.

"Well, yes," Muttacchi agreed.

"What exactly was her premonition about Surya?" Anita hated to ask the question, since the disappointment was still raw, but she knew two people could interpret the same simple sentences quite differently.

Muttacchi's right eyebrow shot up, but she inhaled, pursed her lips, and stuck out her chin. "Yes, I mentioned this myself. Yes, she said Surya will not enter my house again. Never another visit. She will not return."

"Did Gauri give a reason for saying this?"

"Only that it was coming to her as these things do," Muttacchi said.

"She said this after a trance?" Anita said.

The old woman nodded. "Many questions you have." She turned to Meena.

"Yes, why these questions, Anita?" Meena asked, a slight tic by her right eyebrow giving away her discomfort. "We are discussing her cure. The astrologer surely knows what to do. You mustn't ask meaningless things. It's disrespectful." She gave Muttacchi an awkward smile. "Pay her no mind. What has he said, your astrologer?"

"It seems to be more complicated than I thought," Muttacchi said.

"Oh dear." Meena lowered her teacup. "We are not progressing well."

"Not at all." Muttacchi sat up straighter in her chair, looked up at the flowers above her. She was a woman who had run her life and her family's life for almost sixty years — the oldest woman in a matriarchal line, used to deference and accommodation, never doubt or opposition. "I am advised to send her to a well-known *mantravadi* in the north. He is a famous conjurer, known to cure such problems — he has many patients for his mantras and *pujas*. She is to be sent away for at least three months."

"Three months!" Meena's tea sloshed into the saucer. Anita was pleased to see someone else express shock at this prospect. Those were her sentiments exactly.

"Indeed. It is the recommended period of time." Muttacchi didn't sound convinced herself. "And the sooner, the better, I am advised."

"Why so long? This is an exorcism we are talking about, isn't it?" Anita asked. "What's the treatment?"

"It is various, I believe," Muttacchi said. "There are herbs and pujas, of course. And there are other people there who have the same suffering, and they are together."

"That's it?" Anita asked, trying to figure out the role of the mantravadi.

"Ah, no," Muttacchi said. She coughed. "The treatment is complicated — it is hard to bring out one's original nature when a spirit has settled in. They will chain her in a room with other women, or perhaps alone. She will, of course, go willingly, the astrologer has advised me."

"They chain her up?" Anita tried to control her voice but had to stop speaking and swallow hard to recover herself. "Ah, Muttacchi, have you asked Gauri if she's willing to go?"

Both women rewarded Anita's question with the contempt they felt it deserved.

"Perhaps you can leave her as she is, if the trances don't bother her. Yes?" Anita looked from one to the other. Again, she was rewarded with that biting look her female relatives had perfected. Anita had once promised herself she'd practice a suitable reaction for them.

"It is a hardship to lose a good servant," Meena offered, changing the subject. "Three months. If I lost one of my hotel staff for three months, well, a difficult time would ensue."

"Has anyone asked Gauri what she thinks about all this?" Anita pushed her empty teacup onto the table, knowing once again that her question was irrelevant, as far as her relatives were concerned. It was bad enough that her aunt rattled on and on about her, Anita, only being half real because of her Irish-American father, and the shame the entire family seemed to feel because Anita refused to get married to any of Meena's prospects, and refused to find what they considered an honorable career. She could endure all this, but chaining up a poor, sick, helpless servant woman?

"We must do what is best for her," Muttacchi said. "She is dear to us, to me."

"Well, I'm glad of that," Anita said with relief. "So, if you don't send her away, what else can you do?" She hoped now more humane doors were opening. After all, there wasn't anything actually wrong with Gauri as far as Anita could tell.

"I will consult my astrologer," Muttacchi said with a smile. "Something can be done perhaps near to home. I would not like her to leave me."

"Much better idea, Muttacchi." Relieved that the problem seemed to be resolved, Meena poured herself another cup of tea. "Much better. You will not lose a servant for more than a day or so, she will stay under your eye, where she belongs, and gradually she will return to her usual good nature." Meena paused. "She did have a good nature, did she not?"

"Gauri is ever Gauri." Muttacchi leaned back with her cup of tea, a strained smile on her face. "We are used to her."

Anita's two relatives trundled off to their rooms to prepare for the astrologer's visit, leaving Anita alone to ponder Gauri's behavior. Anita had seen numerous possessions over the years — most of them during Onam, the annual festival in the month of Cingam, August/September, when the entire city of Trivandrum turned out to celebrate the return of King Bali to visit his people and reassure himself of their happiness. City intersections were decorated with flowers; images of Ganapati, the elephant-headed god, were everywhere; and in the evening, during hypnotic musical performances, half the city seemed to be lifted into a trance.

No, possession and trances were nothing special for Anita, but Gauri's circumstances suggested something more was going on. First the trances, then the premonitions about Surya's visit. Muttacchi was worried — she wasn't accepting Gauri's behavior as just another quirk among many manifested by her servants over the years.

Anita could feel the anxiety flowing from the old woman — it made Meena nervous and Anita alert. She had never felt so much vulnerability here and wondered if that meant changes in the estate she had not noticed. The buildings looked as they had all her life. She had never wondered about their design and arrangement — until now.

Muttacchi's home was really three buildings of approximately equal size. The first was a long building made up of three rooms in a row; the side facing the street was fitted with small windows, and the side facing the inner courtyard was fitted with doors for each room. At one end a doorway ushered visitors into a small terrace covered by a roof linking the first building with the second one, which stood perpendicular to the first and to the road.

These two long buildings, of equal length, formed two sides of an open courtyard where chairs were set for visitors. Beyond the second building was a group of three small huts, including a small family temple. The area was out of sight and sound of the courtyard and main verandas, shielding the servants' work from view. At the end of the second long building stood the two kitchen rooms back to back. A third building with two rooms and a long, deep veranda stood farther away, and it was here that Gauri had been sweeping. The buildings suddenly appeared vulnerable and unprotected to Anita.

Anita collected her teacup and carried it to the kitchen. Lata, the elderly woman who did most of the cooking, didn't notice her, continued staring aimlessly at food stocks while her fingers tap tap tapped on the side of her leg in an unconscious process of calculation. Nearby, Bindu chopped vegetables for the main meal.

Through the back door Anita spotted Sett, an old man whose duties had always seemed negligible to Anita, giving directions to Arun, a young boy who did odd jobs for the family and was just then collecting *thetti* flowers to deliver to relatives for puja later that evening.

"You are wanting, Chechi?" Lata said, turning to Anita and addressing her respectfully as elder sister.

"The banana *vadai* were excellent," Anita said, placing her dirty cups near the door. Lata lost some of her abstractions and smiled, blinking and stilling her hand.

"An old recipe," Lata said. "I shall write it down for you."

"Meena Elayamma will want it also."

54

Anita leaned out the door. The estate was quiet, with only the *dhobi,* Veej, moving about, hanging sheets on a line near the courtyard. They would dry in an hour, thought Anita, half that time in the hot season, even if they were khadi cloth. Tall and lean, with knees as thick as his shoulder, Veej kept his graying hair and mustache short. "Is it very disruptive, this business with Gauri?" Anita asked as she turned back to Lata, who was by now peering into a metal canister.

"Gauri? Acch! Such trouble." Lata fitted the lid back on and slid the canister onto a shelf.

"Did you know her as a young girl?" Anita moved deeper into the room, signaling she was ready for a chat. "I remember her back then, too, of course. We sometimes played together, but she was older than I am, and she had work to do most of the time."

"She had work to do all of the time," Lata said, her eyes on her canisters. She was a tall, thin woman, with bony arms and feet, her toes splayed wide from never wearing shoes. Her *mundu,* the skirt half of her two-piece sari, never fell all the way to her ankles, and her *nerid,* the top part, was always tied around her shoulder and tucked into her waist, leaving her arms and hands

55

free to work.

"It must be upsetting for the staff to come upon Gauri in the middle of one of her trances," Anita said. She knew Lata would never confide in her — that would be breaking a code of behavior that ran so deep that she probably would never be able to articulate it — but she wouldn't dissemble either.

Lata swung around to face her. "It will be over soon. The astrologer will make arrangements, and Amma will insist, and it will be all over." She rubbed her hand across her bare midriff, back and forth, back and forth, her face contorted in controlled anger.

"And if Gauri refuses?"

Lata's anger collapsed. "Why would she refuse? It is a generous thing Amma does, to tend to her, to offer to help her."

"Gauri may feel Bhagavati is honoring her." Anita wondered that Lata seemed not to feel this way, since most Hindus accepted such behaviors. If Gauri was chosen, that was all there was to it.

Lata turned away, grabbed the small stack of dirty dishes in her large hands, and carried them to the back door. "Sett! Come, useless man! Take these." She shoved the stack at him as soon as he appeared.

Anita glanced out the door; she could feel Veej, the dhobi, watching her as he slung sheets over a line. As soon as she caught sight of him, he turned away and pulled another sheet from the basket, shook it out, and threw it onto the clothesline.

"So even though my Muttacchi is quite worried about Gauri," Anita said, "you are not. You think she may be overworried." She paused. "No one else seems worried."

Lata glanced at her. "Gauri will recover or she will not."

"Meena Elayamma worries about her servants." Anita spoke softly, wondering at the fury in Lata and the undercurrent of tension among the servants.

Lata paused, perhaps touched by Anita's words, to think that her employer cared about her. The cook stood with her hands reaching across the counter and stared out the door. The estate was quiet, with the sheets flapping in a light breeze, Sett rattling dirty dishes in a small bucket, and Arun counting his flowers, losing count and starting over every time Sett swore at him.

"The kavu looks smaller," Anita said. "Is that because Muttacchi is trimming some of it?" If Anita had wanted to get Lata's attention, she certainly succeeded.

"It is not harvesting. No, no, no." Lata bristled, and her face flushed. "We can do nothing about the cows. They nibble here

57

and nibble there, and if the owner does not contain them or rent them to the milk co-operative, then we are of necessity chasing them away. Cows foraging are very damaging." Her eyes sparkled. "But Amma would never, never harvest the kavu. Perhaps she needs to keep a closer eye on it, to make sure no one has reason to say what you just said."

This outburst so surprised Anita that she merely smiled stupidly at Lata, partly as a precaution against telling the old cook how glad she was to see what was able to upset her. She seems devoted to the kavu, thought Anita, as though no one else is any longer.

"What do you think has happened to Gauri?" Anita asked.

"Ah," Lata said. "Bhagavati has found her. What is she to do? She must give Bhagavati what she wants."

"What is it Bhagavati wants?"

Lata shrugged.

"How is Gauri supposed to figure that out?"

"She should go to the mantravadi. So much less trouble for everyone. Useless woman." This grumbly advice came from Sett, and apparently had been given before.

"You are the useless one." Lata waved him off. "Amma will solve this problem," she said to Anita. "Just like she has solved every other problem. Does she not still rule her lands and her family?"

Well, thought Anita, that is a very good question.

THREE

When Anita heard the autorickshaw approaching the house, she excused herself and walked around the side to get a better look at the astrologer whose very word could send a young woman into imprisonment, supposedly for her own good.

The autorickshaw and its driver pulled up and stopped at the front of the house, where cars parked and vendors waited for attention, and after a few words with the driver, the astrologer climbed out and ambled toward the entry, his bowlegs wobbling beneath him. The driver climbed out and began to turn the auto around, as though it were a bicycle. With an oddly formed right leg, as though he'd broken it once and it hadn't been reset properly, he leaned against the auto as much as he pushed it.

The astrologer headed straight for the entry gate and rang a small bell. Without moving to the doorway to speak to him, Sett peered down the path at the entry, and scuffled over to Muttacchi. She gave a perfunctory wave of her hand, and in a moment, the astrologer stepped lightly along the sandy path to the pergola. Greeted warmly, he accepted a cup of tea.

"Yes, Konan, it is a grave matter," Meena was saying as Anita slipped back into her chair.

"And it has grown even graver," Muttacchi said. "Gauri predicted that Surya, my granddaughter, would not arrive and it has happened."

"Ah, what is this?" Konan leaned closer. He was thin and wizened, and next to the well-fed older women, he seemed to shrink moment by moment. "You have heard from Surya? And she will not come? So disappointing." He grew more serious. "And this was predicted?"

"She has not come. The call from her family to explain this will come soon," Muttacchi said. "Probably to tell us she has gone to some other place and will come or perhaps not." Anita felt painfully sorry for Muttacchi, whose sadness at this missed visit seemed to deepen with each mention.

"Ah, yes." Konan templed his fingers, tapping the tips lightly together, and nodded knowingly.

"That is another matter," Muttacchi said. "But for now, we must solve my other dilemma. Gauri. Her trances. Is this dangerous in some manner, Konan?"

Anita said as she pushed herself up in her chair, "How can she be dangerous?"

Muttacchi looked at Konan, but he concealed his feelings, lowered his eyes and hummed a little before speaking. "Yes, your granddaughter — I am very sorry about this." He spoke slowly, and somewhat awkwardly. "I shall consult her birth horoscope. It is perhaps written that she is not coming here at this time. I will consult and advise."

Anita smiled at his diplomacy. He certainly seemed to know how to keep his patrons happy.

"Now, as to Gauri. You must tell me again precisely what she is doing." The astrologer cocked his head to one side, to listen better.

"The same as I have told you before. On the days of her trances she is merely working like any other day, but on such a day she comes near the end of her work and goes rigid, then she collapses on the ground."

The astrologer closed his eyes and hummed. "And is it always the same time of day?"

Muttacchi gave this some thought. "No. Different times."

"The same place?"

Again, she considered the question. "No. But always outside as far as I know."

"Different times, different places."

"Does it mean something?"

"Each part means something."

And that, thought Anita biting her tongue, is as much use as a gardening hose during the monsoon. Muttacchi sighed, and Anita distinctly felt a wave of sadness flowing from the old woman. She loved her servants — they were the same as her family.

"What does it all mean?" the old woman asked. "I rely on you to return serenity to my household."

"This is my only goal, Amma." He bowed his head once more. "It is possible the deity that has possessed her has evil intentions to you and your family, but it is also possible that it is the result of a fault of the girl. Gauri is not without faults, as we know." Konan looked up when he'd finished speaking.

"What faults are you talking about?" Anita asked.

"Shhh, Anita." Meena gave her niece's hand a mild slap.

"It's all right, Meena." Muttacchi turned

to Anita. "She is prone to hysteria. A small matter, but disconcerting sometimes, particularly when she falls to this when we are engaged in social activities. She is also very bossy."

"Hmm, I can see it would be upsetting." Anita settled back, keeping her skepticism to herself. Gauri was becoming more and more interesting indeed.

"Now, Konan, tell me your advice. I have considered the suggestion of sending Gauri to a mantravadi in the north, but perhaps there is another solution, one that would keep her here close to hand. She is after all my family's responsibility, and I feel she should be here, not sent away, if we can do something for her here. I know you can help me. Yes? We can do something here, yes? Can we?"

Konan swung his head back and forth in an apparent effort to not have to say no. After a moment of silence, broken only by Meena's short quick breaths, a twig falling to earth, and the occasional voice coming from the kitchen, Konan raised his head and spoke slowly, softly.

"Nearby is an old temple, little used these days, but the family keeps it up. The land and buildings around it have been sold but the temple remains on family land and the owner comes each evening for puja, his younger brother in the morning. They are very dutiful in their worship. I have known them for many years, and I have known their pujas to be most effective in many ways, particularly for family harmony."

"A most laudable goal," Meena said, nodding appreciatively. "More should strive for this."

"Shh." Muttacchi gave a wave, and Meena blushed. "Please, Konan."

"In some years past a similar situation arose in his family, and a priest was called to help with this. Pujas were performed, a certain rite completed, and the disturbed party was restored to calm and his place in the family." Konan nodded at the satisfying memory, then added, "And he has not been troubled since."

"This is exactly what we are needing," Muttacchi said. "Will this family open their temple to us?"

"They are Nayars, like you." Konan went on to delineate their lineage, which left Anita's head spinning from the effort of trying to follow all the intricacies of the interrelationships.

"Ah, yes, I know them." Muttacchi nodded. "This is good. We will arrange this, with your help."

"There is always a danger . . ." Konan paused.

"Yes, yes, what danger?" The old woman grew stern. Anita thought she sensed a gnawing fear that something might still happen to Gauri.

Konan lifted his hands in a helpless beseeching. "A simple ordinary danger."

"Yes, yes?" Muttacchi grew softer, as though she realized she had just challenged her astrologer.

"She could grow worse. It has happened." Konan bowed his head, but lifted his hands in a gesture of helplessness. "Sometimes someone who is possessed undergoes treatment and the spirit grows even angrier. She could take to speaking awful things." Konan winced as he glanced at his patron, watching for her reaction to this unpleasant, perhaps awkward, even bad, news.

"What sort of things?" Meena looked perplexed, and Anita thought once more how naïve her aunt could sometimes be.

"The spirit may want to harm a member of the household and use Gauri to make accusations." Throughout his explanations, Konan kept his eyes lowered.

"Gauri?" Muttacchi frowned. "No, not Gauri."

"It is not Gauri who is speaking," Konan

66

pointed out.

"Yes," Muttacchi said, nodding. "She says it is Bhagavati."

"She could make wild accusations that might cause hurt," Konan said. "It is a caution to bear in mind."

Meena began to shift in her chair, looking from Konan to Muttacchi and back again. Like most truly innocent souls, Meena was sure there was some sin unatoned for hanging over her head — it fueled her obsession with karma and avoidance of conflict. "Perhaps a small puja and Gauri is kept apart, just in case."

"No, we must not be afraid. We must offer the cure." Muttacchi was adamant, and Meena sagged in her chair.

"Of course," Konan said, his eyes shuttered.

"If the deity does speak through her, we can speak to it and perhaps learn why it is doing this terrible thing to our Gauri." Muttacchi spoke with such heart that Anita could almost believe Gauri was one puja away from recovery.

"As you wish." Konan bowed from the waist in his chair, and managed a smile, but he still didn't look as happy as a man should who has just assured himself of a large commission and an even larger advance in his reputation.

By the end of the midday meal, Muttacchi was yawning, ready for her afternoon nap; even Meena was growing tired of her endless litany of complaints about the struggles of running a hotel; and Anita was getting restless. Every time she had tried to probe more deeply into Gauri's situation, and Muttacchi's experiences with it, one woman or the other brushed her off and changed the subject. Anita was frustrated as well as confused.

"Do you want anything before I take a walk?" Anita offered.

"You have checked the telephone service?" Muttacchi asked, her wrinkled hand reaching for Anita's and holding it loosely in her own.

"Twice. No messages. I'm sorry, Muttacchi."

The old woman squeezed her hand, then let it go. Anita rose, ready to set out.

"Not that way," Muttacchi said as Anita headed off toward the kitchen. "Those are servant buildings now — storage and such, and some rooms for families when they come. Don't go there."

Anita turned around, scanning the grounds for an interesting path.

"And I will know if you disobey me."

Startled, Anita looked down at Muttacchi, who was watching her with a sly look.

"How? Do you see around corners?"

Muttacchi pointed to Anita's feet and her very dusty sandals. "You are the only one in the household wearing sandals. No one wears footwear unless they are leaving the premises."

"Very good, Muttacchi." She gave the old woman a broad smile — sometimes she really liked her relatives. "I can see I'll have to watch out for you."

"As long as I don't have to watch out for you. Now help me to my room before you go."

Muttacchi pushed herself up to a standing position and draped her left arm over Anita's shoulder, leaning hard on her as Anita led the way to the bedroom. Anita helped the old woman up the steps to the veranda, then into her room. The small windows had no wooden bars or screens but a shutter closed tight with a wooden bolt. The top third of the wall had narrow wooden slats to keep out crows but was otherwise open for light and air. "Move that mosquito netting."

Anita pulled aside the netting and helped the old woman climb onto the bed. The mattress seemed as hard as the rock base below it, but Muttacchi sighed happily as she slid onto the sheet. Anita tucked in the mosquito net.

"Close that door and one window and that other door." She nodded to the second door leading to the side veranda. Anita did so and turned to leave. "Wait."

"Yes?" Anita moved back to the bed.

"I always thought Meena was a foolish woman, but she is shrewd." Muttacchi gave a gentle snort. "She has kept you close to her. Now go."

Anita tucked in the mosquito netting, picked up the tuberoses that had fallen from the niche in the wall where the image of Ganapati sat, receiving offerings twice a day, and headed for the door. She tidied up as her relative instructed, then stepped onto the veranda, gazing out at the estate.

It was all the same in so many ways — the older relatives taking naps after lunch, the noise of the road muted by the trees, the servants ready to refill teacups or plates of food, hurrying along with freshly washed sheets or a sari, the fragrances from trees and shrubs. And yet, things felt different — the trees pruned, the estate smaller, the servants older. When Anita was little, the Ganapati in Muttacchi's room seemed huge, and now it seemed tiny. Anita glanced back as she pulled the door shut behind her. It is tiny, she thought, staring at it. The old one has been removed.

Anita paused in the doorway, pleased that for once her advice had been taken. The old Ganapati was indeed old — an antique bronze given to the family in honor of its service centuries ago. But for the family members it was simply the family *murti,* the image of worship every day, the object of all those pujas. Muttacchi had inherited responsibility for it along with the duties of the estate, and she would pass it on, along with the duties. When the history of the image had finally hit Anita, she had urged her mother to speak to Muttacchi. When that failed, Anita begged Meena to speak to the old woman. "The murti is worth all of the estate and more," Anita pointed out. "Muttacchi shouldn't have it lying around in her bedroom."

"It is not lying around!" Meena replied, shocked.

Anita didn't know when Meena had prevailed, but at least she had, and the antique murti was now safely put away.

Anita closed the side door, which squeaked and creaked like an old cart rolling across a

71

wooden bridge — no burglar was going to get into one of these rooms without announcing his arrival first. Out on the veranda the heat of the afternoon descended on her. The depth of the veranda kept off the worst of the sun's rays, but the stone was warm beneath her bare feet. She headed for the side steps but stopped. There, in the sand, was the unmistakable print of the sole of a shoe or sandal.

In a homestead where no one wore sandals unless they were leaving the place, who would be leaving prints? Or, rather, who would be walking up to the side of the house instead of to the main entrance? Anita followed the footsteps along the edge of the veranda to the end, which looked out onto the parking area in front. She walked back and looked at the footsteps again.

Anita took off her sandals and followed along beside the footsteps. It was clear that whoever had made them did not have a normal gait. Instead this was someone who went forward one step at a time, putting out the left foot, drawing up the right, advancing the left, pulling up the right, moving along the side of the veranda as far as the steps. Also, the right foot turned out more than normal, with the weight unevenly balanced on the outer edge of the sole.

Anita followed the trail again, stood by the steps, and understood. From this vantage point the person could see the pergola and the grounds beyond while shielding himself from view by the pillars along the veranda.

Anita turned around and followed the footsteps into the parking area until they disappeared in a confusion of tracks. Again, Anita stepped back and studied the ground. No footsteps but clear tire tracks leading away — three tracks, for an autorickshaw.

She had seen the auto and its driver arrive, with the astrologer in the passenger seat. She had not seen another passenger, just the astrologer. She turned and followed the tracks back to the veranda steps and peered past the pillars. At the pergola Bindu was wiping down the table and sweeping away the last crumbs, Gauri was carrying dry laundry toward the servant quarters. Sett called out, someone answered, the dhobi appeared and took the laundry from Gauri. No one seemed to realize that Anita was there. She turned back to the parking area, then again to the pergola.

"The auto driver was spying on us," she said half aloud. "Why on earth would an autorickshaw driver care about what was going on inside this house?"

FOUR

Anita crossed the yard, stopping at the corner of the second building. The end room had been used as an office in past years but now was shuttered, and the paint on the door was dulled and flaking, small chips mixed in with the leaves that had piled up on the steps; it was obvious that no one had used this entrance in some time. Anita reached down for a chip of paint to show Muttacchi — the estate should at least be kept immaculate.

"Ooh! Lucky," Anita said as she picked up a small mother-of-pearl button. Her hand immediately went to the placket on her salwar blouse, and her fingers rippled down the row of buttons. But none was missing. She slipped it into her pocket as she walked to the corner of the building. Under the shade of a copse of trees stood a small temple, barely the size of a small telephone booth, closed until the evening puja. Anita peeked around the corner. There was Veej, again hanging laundry on a line strung from the house to a tree. He waggled his head in acknowledgment as Anita approached. Veej had been Muttacchi's dhobi for ten or fifteen years, but Anita saw little of him after she grew too old for play with the servants.

"The auto driver?" Veej held a dishrag in midair as he spoke, then tossed it over the line. "Coming here with Konan?" He reached for another rag. On the back veranda Sett sprawled on a towel, but his eyes were half open and he wasn't snoring. Anita found herself glancing at the old man every few seconds, wondering if he had something to say, but he kept silent and still — very still.

"Did you see them arrive?" Anita asked again.

Veej shook his head. "I am not noticing. I am working."

"Yes, of course. I saw the laundry hung out on the other side of the courtyard." Anita moved along the back of the house, checking out the pots left to dry on the long, deep veranda, the stack of kindling leaning against the wall, the plastic water buckets, their bright red and yellow and blue and green a startling contrast to the quiet whitewash of the house and crumpled gray leaves and rust-red dirt of the grounds. "I thought you might have seen something when you were putting it out."

Veej shook his head again and another rag flew onto the line.

"Perhaps you noticed him, Gauri." Anita walked over to the maidservant, who was now sweeping the yard at the end of the kitchen rooms, humming to herself.

"Tee?" Gauri straightened up, and Anita repeated her question. "No, no. I am seeing nothing."

Anita turned at the sound of Sett's grumbling but couldn't quite make out his comments. Annoyed, she almost demanded to know what work he was supposed to be doing, but she bit her tongue. If he was hanging around with nothing to do, that wasn't really her business.

"I was wondering if you noticed anything when you were collecting sheets or sweeping on the other side," Anita said to Gauri. "I think he came to the side of the other building, next to Muttacchi's bedroom, maybe listening in on our conversation with Konan."

Gauri frowned and tsked her disapproval. "This no good, Chechi."

"I agree. That's why I was wondering if anyone here knew him. I thought he might be someone known to the family, someone who took an interest in our welfare." Anita thought that sounded plausible, if unlikely. No one should want to hear an auto driver was eavesdropping on a private conversation.

"This no good." Gauri continued to shake her head.

The cook appeared in the doorway, balancing on the tall wooden sill, her hands resting on the jambs. She scowled at the other workers, as though she were about to demand to know why they weren't working. Gauri quickly repeated Anita's question. Lata shook her head slowly, but her eyes were troubled, Anita noted. So, she doesn't like the sound of that either, Anita thought, but she's not going to say anything.

"Perhaps Sett saw something," Anita said. But just as she walked toward him, he lay down and let out a stentorian snore that ended all conversation.

The household servants, in subtle ways Anita had to admire, moved away from her into their work and their own world, leaving Anita no choice but to move on also. Reluctantly, she gave up on them for the time being — promising herself she'd probe more deeply as she got each one alone. For now, however, she would try something more practical. She collected her camera from her room and returned to the front yard.

Anita studied the tracks where the auto had entered, turned, and driven out, and began to follow them. The front wheel went through a deep rut and over a rocky bump, leaving Anita thinking that the driver wasn't very good. She followed the tracks of Konan's autorickshaw down the driveway to the road and looked up and down. At the moment, there was nothing moving except a dog trotting along the shoulder, heading south. Someone must have seen the auto pass by, considering how little traffic this area saw.

The afternoon was quiet and no car or bike or other transport moved anywhere on the road. This was not one that would ever carry a lot of traffic, but she expected to hear horns throughout the day. Sound traveled in the countryside, so much so that she had a fleeting image of Muttacchi lying half awake through the night, waiting for the sound of Surya's taxi arriving from the airport. It really was inconsiderate of Surya to say nothing. Anita shook off the gloom and stepped out onto the road. About a quarter of a mile to her right stood a cluster of shops, their goods stacked outside awaiting customers for the late afternoon shopping, but for now barely a blouse fluttered in the near-dead air. There should be a taxi stand, she knew, and she headed for the hamlet. As the shops came into focus, she spotted two autorickshaws parked under a shade tree. Anita headed for them.

"Eh?" The auto driver awoke with a start in the back seat of the first one Anita approached. "Where?"

"Nowhere at the moment." Anita peered in as the driver slouched back down in the seat. "I was looking for the auto driver who came to Punnu Chellamma's house this morning." She nodded back down the road toward Muttacchi's family house.

The driver frowned, shook his head and closed his eyes again, then popped them open again in surprise. "Punnu Chellamma? Her house?" He pushed himself up in his seat. "You are Punnu Chellamma's granddaughter? You are visiting from England? You have arrived after all?"

"No, no, I'm Surya's cousin-sister, Anita." She knew she shouldn't be surprised that news of Surya's nonarrival had traveled into town, but the level of interest caught her off guard.

"Ah!" His eyes lit up, and he smiled warmly. "You live with Punnu Meena. Very good. Where do you want to go? You ask. I am driving and we are going now."

"No, no, I just want to know about another driver, the one who brought the astrologer Konan this morning."

"Did not see him. I am better driver." Before Anita could protest, he leaned out the open side and shouted to the other driver. "No, he doesn't know him either. But you are mistaken perhaps. Konan would not come in an auto. He lives Pattur side. I will take you there."

"Why would he not come in an auto?"

"He is taking bus or walking. Pattur is not so far." The driver clambered out of the back and pressed himself into the driver's seat. "Come, I take you."

"I saw him arrive in an auto."

"Konan?" The driver seemed surprised at this, and considered it. "Amma is generous."

"So, the driver?"

"Not seen. Do not know him." He pulled up the starter bar, but Anita again declined. The engine died.

Anita pulled back from the auto, not trying to hide her frustration. She turned to the row of shops and asked the proprietors at the open ones, but got the same answer, a mixture of lack of interest and lack of observation. Stymied, she walked back down the road and turned onto the driveway.

On her right was a thick forest barely half an acre, bounded by the road on one side, and private estates, including Muttacchi's, on the other sides. She didn't know who owned this kavu, but it seemed to be one that was separated from its owner's other property. Nevertheless, it seemed well protected with a stonewall that ran around most of the perimeter. Anita wandered along the edge of it, taking photos while circumambulating the small forest until she came to a clearing where an old, black-encrusted lamp stood, its dozen leaf-shaped oil cups still damp from a morning puja. A few white flowers lay scattered at the base, their petals turning brown. This forest was probably why no one in the estate ever heard anything — it was a perfect sound barrier.

Nature wasn't her first choice for photographs, but kavus were disappearing in this part of Kerala, and Anita thought it might be nice to have a record of some of them. She checked the number of shots on her memory card and kept on walking.

The kavus were home to old trees and lianas and flowers, along with animals and birds, and Anita had never been allowed to play in them. If she had been interested in medicine or horticulture, she might have been more obstinate and rebellious and even insistent, but as it was, she regarded them as just a jungle full of unknown plants. She preferred people and what they wrought in this world.

Anita had grown used to the kavus over the years, and wandering around this one made her feel that nothing had changed. A cow grazed along the edge, ignoring two little boys chasing away a trio of goats farther along. A woman gathering firewood carefully poked a stick at a branch lying half in, half out of the grove in a break in the stonewall. Anita snapped a photo as the woman maneuvered the branch onto the pile already teetering on her head. Two thousand of these small patches were left in Kerala, and Anita's relatives held onto a number of them. Muttacchi was fierce in her protection of her declining lands and kavus, but she was probably fighting a losing battle, her tent pitched between marauding goats and cows and scavengers, on one side, and greedy, westernized relatives on the other.

"Are you sure you don't mind?" Auntie

Meena lifted the mosquito netting and let it fall again, judging its weight and effectiveness. She glanced at the other large bed and then at the rest of the room, instinctively appraising it with her hotelier's eyes.

"I told you, I don't mind at all." Anita dropped her overnight case on the chair and unzipped it. "You warned me we might stay a couple of nights, so I came prepared." She turned around to smile at her aunt. "Both mentally and physically. I have enough clothes for several days." She pulled out two sets of salwars and slid them onto a shelf of the teak armoire. With a quick look down, she stepped over the one-foot-high doorsill into the bathroom.

Anita had been given one of the two bedrooms in the third building, which held two large double beds, an armoire, a small desk, and two chairs. The walls rose eight feet before giving way to narrow wooden slats to let in light and air and keep out crows, as in Muttacchi's room. The bedroom was in fact a wooden shell set inside a concrete frame, raised on a tall plinth to ride out the rainy season. The bathroom was large, tiled, and closed to the elements, with a single wooden tree branch hanging like a swing from the ceiling to serve as a towel rack. She dropped her kit on the sink and draped a towel over the branch.

"But you are so far from the main house," Meena said, looking more and more uncomfortable. "Perhaps you could share a room with me?"

"Muttacchi has assigned you the room of the important guest." Anita thought that was an exceedingly clever way to get Meena to stay overnight and wasn't about to undermine the old woman's trick.

"I am honored." Meena smiled smugly then seemed to think better of it. "Yes, well, you can stay out here if you insist, but you may take my room. You may be lonely out here. And I cannot remain — the hotel is too demanding at this time. I can only stay one night. Tomorrow I return."

Anita closed the closet door and turned to her aunt. "You really don't like the idea of my staying so far away from the other buildings, do you?" She rested her hands on her hips. "I'm all right here, Auntie. I have always stayed here — it's my favorite spot."

"But, Anita —"

"Tell me, what's really bothering you."

"Well . . ." Meena looked around her. "It's just that, well, Gauri is acting so strange. Who knows what she will do?"

"I don't think there's anything to worry about."

"Muttacchi doesn't agree with you."

"Would it really be so awful if Gauri remained uncured?"

"Don't say that! Muttacchi would be very upset." Meena shushed Anita.

"Muttacchi is worried that Gauri is losing her grip on life, not that she's dangerous. She loves Gauri. That's what this is really about — she's afraid for Gauri, not of her."

Meena shook her head, gave Anita a look of doubtful hope, and reached for the heavy wooden door. "I hope you're right." She stepped over the tall wooden sill, disentangling her sari from the doorway. "Tourists are so much easier."

FIVE

The stillness of the night was profound. Anita lay beneath the cloudy white netting staring up into the black of the ceiling, listening to the few night sounds flowing in through the open upper story. Occasionally voices from one of the other buildings reached her, and she imagined the friendly chatter as everyone settled down for the night. But then her thoughts slid to Muttacchi, and she felt again the old woman's sadness.

Muttacchi had been waiting and planning a long time for Surya's visit, and now she was putting the same energy into concealing her disappointment. Was Muttacchi lying awake right now, staring up at her ceiling and calling softly to her granddaughter? Anita rolled over on her side and sent a quiet prayer of gratitude for Auntie Meena's kindness, that unshakable devotion to family hidden beneath her unrelenting crankiness. The night deepened, the silence grew thicker, the air colder. No candles or electric lights burned for the insomniac, no radio or television voices broke the silence. Anita fell asleep feeling suspended from the rest of the world.

Anita awoke to the familiar sound of an animal scratching in sand. She rolled over and reached for her watch — pressed the hour button and watched the face light up: 5:30 A.M. The residents would be up and about soon — washing, worshipping, cooking, eating, preparing for the day. Anita threw off the netting and sat up. She hadn't slept much but she wasn't tired. After a quick shower, she dressed and pulled open the heavy wooden door and stepped out onto the veranda. A cup of thick, milky coffee sat on the table, covered by a net cozy.

"Morning, Chechi."

Anita searched for the source of the voice. "I am here."

Anita walked to the edge of the veranda and leaned over. There, bobbing up and down along the side of the building as she collected kindling for the cooking fires, was Bindu. "Morning, Chechi. I am bringing coffee when I see your light. You are wanting more before breakfast?"

"No, this is fine. When is breakfast?"

"After puja."

"That could be any time between now and eight o'clock." Anita pulled off her dupatta, which had been hanging around her neck like a scarf, and flapped it open, draping it over her shoulders like a shawl.

It was chilly at this hour of the morning, away from the city and among the trees.

Bindu seemed to find Anita's comment amusing because she stood up and laughed, shaking her head and repeating the comment over and over. She picked up a few more twigs and trotted off, still laughing. Anita lifted the netted cozy and set it aside. The coffee cup was steaming nicely, so it must have just arrived. She pulled up a chair and sat down to enjoy her drink. A moment later she heard footsteps and looked up to see Gauri approaching with a small covered tray. She too seemed to be laughing.

Gauri placed the tray in front of her and motioned to it. "Now to eight o'clock!" She shook her head and laughed. "Biscuits." She pulled off the white napkin covering the plate to reveal small cookies. "While you are waiting."

"I'm glad you all find it so funny," Anita said.

"Meena Amma is helping in the kitchen."

"Auntie Meena? Helping?"

Gauri seemed to think this too was funny and sent forth a little stream of giggles. "Ah," she said. "She is there and cook is there, and somehow we will have food very soon. Bhagavati is generous. You eat." She pointed to the cookies.

As she turned to go, Anita called her back. "Gauri! You know, I was here yesterday." Gauri nodded, her smile of amusement unaltered. "I was wondering about what happened."

Anita had expected the maidservant to grow serious, but instead she continued to smile, tossing up her hands as if in exasperation, and tipping her head back and forth. "It is all up to Bhagavati. Who am I?"

"Does it frighten you, when you go into trances?"

The question must have surprised Gauri because she paused, stared at Anita, then smiled sheepishly. She shrugged. "Bhagavati is Bhagavati. Who am I?"

"Do you think there is a reason why Bhagavati has come to you now?"

Gauri shrugged again, still smiling. "Of course there is a reason. It is not known to me, but it is there. Bhagavati always has reasons."

"You're pretty sure she's going to show you when she's ready." Anita was relieved that Gauri didn't mind her probing and was coming to like the maidservant more and more. Until this visit, she had simply been a woman in the background who worked, chatted occasionally, and seemed satisfied with her life. Anita knew this for what it was — her own self-serving blindness that let her dismiss any deeper concern for this particular person.

"Who am I? It is all up to Bhagavati." Gauri's smile was warm and sweet.

"Is this the first time you have gone through this?"

"Yes, nothing has come to me before — not like this. Little moments during Onam, festival time, but this, now — no, nothing like this."

"Muttacchi is worried about curing you. She is talking about an exorcism."

"Ah, Konan has come, yes. Yes, there is a cure. This will happen." Gauri seemed to accept this just as easily as Bhagavati's selection of her.

"And you are willing to do this?"

"Amma has cared for me since I was a child. My mother died and Amma kept me. She cares for me."

Such trust, Anita thought. "And you want to be cured."

Gauri shrugged and smiled. "It is up to

Bhagavati. If she is ready to leave, she will leave." She waved away the problem, then said, "You eat." She pointed again to the cookies, and headed back to the kitchen.

"Today?" Meena's hand stopped midway between plate and mouth. "You can't mean *today* today."

"What other today is there?" Muttacchi glared at her, then shook her head. Her edginess had been evident from her first greeting an hour earlier as she hobbled out of her room and across the veranda. Her smile was more of a scowl, her greeting was barely an acknowledgment, and her body seemed stiffer, more unyielding to the day.

"I only meant . . ." Meena let her words drift. She hardly knew how to face an angry Muttacchi.

"Yes, it is sudden, but Konan says today is auspicious, so today it is." Muttacchi pushed her plate away, climbed out of her chair, and walked over to a spigot attached to a post, where she washed her hands.

"But it is difficult, is it not?" Meena stared at the food on her plate.

Breakfast had been a quiet affair until Muttacchi announced the plans for the day. A messenger from the astrologer had appeared at 6:30 with the news that a priest was willing to conduct the rite this afternoon. In the morning a puja was being performed to Shiva on behalf of a nearby family, and this afternoon the priest would be available to deal with Gauri.

"You don't look very happy about this, Muttacchi," Anita said. She had noted at once the old woman's doleful expression when making the announcement. For all her talk of curing Gauri of this new affliction, Muttacchi seemed worried about the path she had chosen for her maidservant. Anita didn't blame her. She was still stuck on the idea of leaving Gauri as she was — the maidservant certainly didn't seem worried about her condition.

"Who can be happy to have a longtime maidservant in such a state? But who can want her to undergo such a treatment? But Konan has made the arrangements. It is what I asked him to do. He is very reliable." The old woman's voice fell, swallowing her last few words.

"We can always change our minds," Meena said, leaning forward.

"If you're not ready, then we can wait. Gauri can wait. It's not as though she's causing any trouble," Anita said, watching Muttacchi weigh Anita's words. "I spoke with her this morning, and she seems fine, quite cheerful actually. She's willing to go forward, to wait, to do whatever you want. She's quite devoted to you, Muttacchi. These trances don't seem to have harmed her at all." For a moment Anita thought she had been convincing, but then the old woman blinked, and Anita knew the moment of advantage was gone. Damn, she thought, I really don't want to see Gauri go through something like this.

"I have put myself in Konan's hands." Muttacchi delivered the last with an unmistakable gloom, then paused and stared at her hands. She had grown heavy and thick over the years, and fingers that had once ground spices and tested their fineness, judged gold filigree and weighed earrings on her fingertips, had grown stiff and pudgy. "It must be done and I must not be foolish about this. It is time to go forward. I will send Gauri home, to prepare herself. We shall collect her later." Muttacchi rose from the table and wandered off, balancing herself with an outstretched hand against the trees and walls as she passed.

"Remarkable old woman," Meena said absently. "She must be nearing ninety."

"I hope this exorcism business isn't taking a toll on her," Anita said. "I don't think she wants to do this."

"Of course, she does, Anita. It is her duty, and she will always do her duty."

"Will you be staying to help with the exorcism?" Anita asked.

"Oh, no, Anita, I am relying on you." Meena sat up straight, the discomfort obvious now.

"Me?"

"Yes, you." Meena lowered her head and sighed. "I am flustered. This is terrible, this thing with Gauri. Yes, it happens all the time — someone or another going into possession. It is not bad, but it is the worry for Muttacchi." She lifted her head and stared hard into Anita's eyes. "I would be no good at the temple. But you," she said, clucking disapprovingly but with a smile sneaking across her face, "you will see it all with great skepticism. You are not in any danger of being deterred." Not for the first time Anita wondered about the woman hidden beneath the proper Nayar widow that was her Auntie Meena.

"Muttacchi will be hurt if you are not here," Anita said.

"She will understand." Meena paused and gave a harsh laugh. "She will understand, yes. I will tell her that Australian tour is coming in today — the tour guide is very hard to please. I must be there. If they are not happy, she has threatened every time to drive them off to another hotel."

"What other hotel?" Anita said, spooning more *sambar* over the *idlies.* The vegetable tomato stew buried the steamed rice and dhal cake. "This is the height of the season. She'd have to drive to the other side of Trivandrum, pay a fortune, and probably scatter her flock over two or three hotels. No, Auntie, she's not going to whisk them away from you. She's just being unpleasant."

"She is always being unpleasant, as you put it."

"If you put her in the little cottage across the street, she will calm down. Take her there first, as soon as you have handed out keys, and she will be happy." Anita added coconut chutney to her plate. "What she is really driving away from are all those people asking questions and wanting her to do something for them. But flight is no good in her line of work."

Meena laughed the laugh of weariness. "Could my dear sweet husband have known it would be like this?" She sighed. "Such a dear man."

"Last week he was feckless and oblivious to your needs."

"Last week I had unusual expenses."

Meena smiled without an ounce of guilt or embarrassment. "This week I am only annoyed."

"Tell me the truth, Auntie Meena," Anita said, reaching her hand across the table. "Why are you really going back to Trivandrum?"

"You don't think I'm going because of the Australian tour guide?" Meena said.

"No, I do not."

"No, you wouldn't." Meena, for all her apparent flightiness, had quiet depths. Anita recalled the woman who had stepped into the hotel business with the unexpected death of her pilot husband — an investment she had to claim or face losing most of the family assets. With barely a week's notice, Meena moved to Hotel Delite and took over, facing irate guests, worried vendors, difficult servants, and she had survived handily. "It is Surya. I want to find her and let her know how pained Muttacchi is at her thoughtlessness. She could at least have called. Does no one your age understand what is happening here?" She gazed out over the grounds. "I used to help her, Muttacchi, with so much of the family business when our family visited, even when your mother and I came alone. Her husband was away on business often, so we could do many things, your mother and I."

"Amma used to tell me about the kavus when we came here for visits. She said it was the real reason my father proposed — he wanted to own a pristine forest some day."

Meena laughed. "He used to prowl around them when he was here." The memory faded, and she grew serious again. "Muttacchi was never so worried then." Meena was still gazing at the kavu and missed Anita's sudden intense look. "I don't remember her looking like this before — worried and cold." Meena seemed to recall where she was and gave a nervous laugh. "Oh, listen to me. Such impertinence! Pay no attention."

"Absolutely none."

"You are a bad girl."

If she was staying, Anita decided, she'd better get things sorted out. She grabbed a small pile of laundry and went in search of Veej, the dhobi. The estate had its own small pond, or tank for laundry and bathing, for those disinclined to use the river. The pond waters rose and fell with the seasons, overflowing with the monsoon, and shrinking to a shallow puddle during the dry season just before the rains began. Not hearing the telltale sound of wet cloth slapping hard against the stones set in like steps down to the low-water mark, Anita wandered around to the back of the kitchen rooms. There she found Veej sorting through a pile of sheets and other items spread across the back veranda.

"May I add a few more?" Anita said, holding out her very modest pile. Veej waggled his head and pointed to a spot on the ground, where Anita dropped them. "Is this a normal amount?" Anita asked, surveying the growing piles as Veej sorted and tossed.

Veej shrugged while he continued working. He was a tall, lanky man with dark, wrinkled skin over thick muscles and veins. Anita knew that he had only recently had his first child, rather late in life for a long-married man, but gratefully welcomed nonetheless. She recalled him often with a bald head in past years, a sign that he and his wife had traveled to the temple in Tirupati, in Andhra Pradesh, to donate their hair to God in the hopes of conceiving a child. Apparently it had worked, and Veej's hair grew thick after his receding hairline, and was neatly trimmed above his shirt collar.

"Didn't Gauri help you with the laundry?" Anita asked.

Veej paused, then continued tugging a

particularly heavy khadi cloth sheet out of the pile. "Sometimes. She helps everywhere."

"I saw her yesterday, going through that trance." Anita stepped back just as a towel landed near her feet. "It seemed more intense than most of the times I've seen them in Trivandrum or in temples during festivals. I can't imagine her going through that a few times a week."

Veej grunted.

"They seem to be coming more and more often." A neighbor's cat, scrawny body and long thin legs, with large tented ears rigidly upright, skittered out of the trees and deftly skirted the piles of laundry, then headed off in the opposite direction. "Does her problem affect your work?"

Veej straightened up for a moment, again shook his head, his mouth turned down, then grabbed a large pile of towels and tied a small one around it, tossing the bundle close to the tank. "She is Amma's favorite. Amma will let her choose her work if it helps her at this time. It has no effect on me."

Veej's tone was so neutral and matter-of-fact that Anita couldn't tell if his observation concealed unseemly compassion for Gauri, or repressed resentment at what could be regarded as special treatment. It didn't matter that Gauri worked hard if she received special treatment no matter what she did.

"It's too bad it has come at this time, when Muttacchi is dealing with her disappointment over Surya, her failure to arrive for such a long-planned visit." Anita followed Veej to the tank with a small bundle of saris — all pure white, with no colored borders, and therefore, Anita assumed, a widow's wardrobe, all belonging to Muttacchi. "At least your work load won't increase right now."

"Ah." Veej pulled out a mundu and walked down to the water. He soaked the cloth in the pond, laid it on a flat rock, and began soaping it, turning it over again and again as he rubbed it thoroughly with a bar of soap.

"I'm disappointed, too," Anita said, settling herself on the lip of the tank and stretching out her legs. "It feels like I haven't seen Surya in ages, but I don't want to harp on that with Muttacchi. I just wish my cousin would call. No one knows where she is."

"Ach," Veej said as he soaked the mundu again. "She has gone to Chennai or Mumbai or Goa to see friends. Don't the young ones have friends everywhere now? Don't you travel on a whim?" He flashed her a quick smile, and Anita was again left wondering if his even-tempered words concealed resentment or affection. Did he compare his own difficulties in traveling to Tirupati with the ease with which Surya could stop off in Chennai or take a side trip to Delhi? How many years had he saved for a train ticket to Tirupati, while Surya, on the spur of the moment, hopped a plane to Singapore, or chatted on her mobile with friends in London about a trip to Paris.

"We are hoping nothing has happened to her," Anita said.

Veej paused in his soaking, then wrung out the cloth and began to swing it down onto the stone slab, slapping it again and again. He soaked and wrung it out again, then stood upright and studied Anita for a moment, looking away before his boldness became obvious. "She has many friends. She could be anywhere." Again he paused. "She is like you, isn't she? She has a mobile phone. Why do you not call her?" With that, he swung his arm out and brought down the cloth on the rock, working out any dirt still in the fabric.

"She doesn't answer," Anita said.

Six

The black Morris Minor bumped to a halt on the road and the driver pushed the gear into park. Then he sat, staring straight ahead. Muttacchi flopped around in the center of the back seat, pushing herself away from the door, rearranging her sari, brushing the hair from her face — at last her dignity was restored. The driver, an old man who could barely see over the steering wheel, leaned out the open window and spat onto the road.

Bindu turned around in the front seat, as though expecting someone to speak to her. Anita, squashed against the side door also in the front, waited. When they had first loaded up the car, it hadn't occurred to anyone that Muttacchi should break with tradition and share the back seat. As a result, Anita, Bindu, and the driver were packed into the front, and the old woman was bounced around in the back like a loose basketball.

"Ah, perhaps someone should go and get her." Anita wasn't sure if she should address the driver, Bindu, or Muttacchi.

"She knows we are here." The old woman spoke without looking at anyone.

Anita opened the door and all but fell onto the road. "I'm just going to stretch at bit while we wait." She slammed the door, but Muttacchi rolled down the window.

"We have gone less than a mile."

"The seat springs are bad."

"Ah, that is so." Muttacchi rolled the window back up, despite the stifling heat, and Anita wandered off toward the small house set back from the road.

Gauri's family home sat behind a sapling fence grown thick with shoots and leaves that encircled not only the house but also a small temple and a number of coconut palms and other trees. Anita counted jackfruit, banana, papaya, mango, and pepper trees scattered throughout the yard as she approached the gateway, marked by a row of sticks barely a foot high, to keep the chickens from wandering. It was a tidy little home, and Anita wished she were coming for a leisurely visit. She leaned in and called.

"*Teeee.*" Gauri came out from behind the house, fixing the nerid over her mundu and tucking the end into her waist. Around her neck she wore an old Shaiva rosary of wood and silver, and a plain brass stud adorned her nose. "Coming, Chechi, coming."

She seemed perfectly happy, to Anita, as though she were going on an afternoon outing. Her two-piece sari was freshly washed and pressed, she was scrubbed and shiny, her hair was tidily knotted at the nape of her neck, her expression cheerful and expectant. It left Anita wondering if Gauri understood what was going to happen — or perhaps Anita didn't understand what was going to happen. Perhaps she had misunderstood Muttacchi. Anita couldn't believe she'd be able to approach the same ritual with such cheerful equanimity.

Gauri headed straight for the front passenger seat, hopping in right on top of Bindu, and slamming the door. The two women seemed used to sharing the space and arranged themselves without any harsh words, though they couldn't have been comfortable. After a moment's hesitation, Anita climbed into the back, pressing herself hard against the door, to give Muttacchi the room she was used to. The driver released the brake and the car lurched forward. They rode in silence, with the barest of sounds from Muttacchi, when she told Gauri and

Bindu not to chatter.

The car turned off the road onto a dirt track and bumped along for over a mile before drawing up before a small temple. The passengers piled out of the car, and Muttacchi sent the driver off to wait in the shade.

The wooden entrance, with deep benches on either side for devotees who might want to sit and meditate or wait for others, was empty, and Muttacchi led them through this into the temple proper, a small shrine in the center of an open courtyard with a series of smaller shrines set around the stone perimeter. It had the feel of an organic structure, one that had developed from a small shrine on a raised stone plinth, around which was built a larger structure enclosing the image, and around this a larger structure still, until the original altar was lost in centuries of incremental additions.

"Ah, yes, you have come." An elderly priest appeared from around the back of the shrine and came toward them, nodding and looking warily at each of them in turn. He greeted Muttacchi with due respect, nodded to Anita after looking her up and down, and turned to Bindu, declaring her a servant of Bhagavati.

"No, no, not her." Muttacchi waved an

impatient hand at him, and pointed to Gauri. "That's the one."

Gauri stepped forward, a sheepish look on her face. The priest scowled at Bindu and turned to Gauri, looking her over carefully, before waving at her to follow him. Whatever speech he had been prepared to give Bindu he abandoned once he sized up Gauri. Gauri immediately trotted after him, and Anita, Bindu, and Muttacchi followed, hovering a few feet behind.

Only Gauri and the priest participated in the puja at the main shrine. A second, younger, priest joined them, standing back a few feet and fussing with the materials needed but not taking an active role in the worship. He arranged coconuts and bananas on a tray, searched for incense among the garlands, and generally helped prepare the tray of offerings while the priest chanted and Gauri prostrated herself in prayer.

Next the older priest led Gauri to a stone pillar, which she embraced. He tied a cord of some sort around her wrists while he chatted with the other priest, who had disappeared and then returned with a whip of grass. Anita and the other two women continued to hover, following Gauri and the priest from point to point like goats waiting to be milked, or tourists afraid they'd get lost in this strange land. Every few minutes Anita reminded herself to keep her mouth shut, not quiz the priest on what he was doing or why he thought any of this might be useful, and not, definitely not, tell Muttacchi that she had been taken in by a bunch of hangers-on. That became harder and harder every time the priest waved them back. Anita took one step back and one step forward, and whatever she did, her aunt and Bindu did. They might have been tied together as one.

A pair of young men dressed in dhotis, like the other two priests, appeared and, following the senior priest's direction, sat on the ground, legs crossed; once settled they placed small books on the stone floor in front of them and riffled through the pages. When they found the passages they were looking for, they signaled the priest. After some more fussing and consulting with the other priest, the old priest nodded to the seated pair, and they began to chant.

From what Anita could see, Gauri remained in her cheerful frame of mind, and Anita wondered if the woman knew what was coming and had drugged herself in preparation. Could anyone enter into such a rite with such poise, such composure and serenity? The younger priest drew closer and waited for a signal from the older man.

When the first lash fell, its threads of long thin grass loosely woven at the handle, Anita cringed and gasped. She had to force herself not to jump forward, putting herself between the priest and Gauri, but not a sound came from Gauri. Anita tried to reassure herself that this had been done before, Gauri understood the ritual, and Muttacchi wouldn't allow anything untoward to happen. But Anita winced and cringed at every fall of the lash. The chanting grew louder, more insistent. The young priest raised the lash again and again. Anita kept her eyes on Gauri, but she remained serene, almost happy looking.

After several strokes an old man came forward and threw a bucket of water over Gauri, drenching her and the ground around her. This seemed to be a time for the two priests to confer, and the three women inched closer. With a sigh that seemed more resigned than resolute, the senior priest stepped back and gave Gauri a thorough visual examination. When she turned her face up to him with a sweet, almost stupid smile, he sighed again and turned to the younger priest, giving him a curt nod. The chanting began again, and the priest took up the lash. The long threads of the lash may not have had much bite, but they could not have been without stinging, as Anita watched and counted. Nearby Muttacchi stood stock still, her posture rigid, ready to order a halt if necessary. Anita edged closer and closer, pulled by the lash and barely controlling the urge to rip it from the man's hands, cringing with each fall. Again a man threw water on Gauri, again she grinned. She couldn't tolerate this without being drugged, could she? Again the whispering between the priests. Again the lashes fell.

In an instant between lashes, when the priests were conferring and the younger ones were chanting, and no one was paying any particular attention to her, Gauri began to babble. The older priest held up his hand, staying the other with the lash and listened, while Gauri babbled on and on. Muttacchi leaned forward, took several steps closer, as though about to run to her maidservant, but again the priest held up his hand and said something to her, something Anita didn't hear.

Gauri muttered on and on, but Anita could only catch a word here and there, though the whole seemed strange, almost gibberish. Muttacchi shook her head, her face a mask of painful concern. After a minute Gauri stopped speaking and slumped to the ground. At a signal from Muttacchi, Bindu hurried to the other maidservant just as the old man threw another bucket of water, drowning both Bindu and Gauri. Anita jumped back, then rushed to the two on the ground. "Gauri? Gauri! Are you all right?"

The two maidservants sat on a bench beneath the tulip tree near the temple, the car sheltered nearby, the driver staring listlessly at them. Gauri was the picture of decorum and reserve, a quiet smile on her face, a startling reversal of her usual mischievous character, which stalled Anita from saying anything. Muttacchi sat in the back seat of the car, caught up in her own thoughts, every now and then glancing over at her maidservant. The old woman had given the priest a fat envelope at the end of an extensive blessing, and when Anita looked back as she and the others left the temple, she noted that he and his helpers wasted no time in disappearing.

Bindu and Gauri carried each other to the bench and sat with some relief. Bindu reached over and arranged the folds in Gauri's mundu, and Gauri smoothed Bindu's nerid. They gently patted, shifted, rearranged each other, letting the heat and sun dry their clothing. Bindu brushed back Gauri's hair, and Gauri tucked in Bindu's stray curls. They could have been sisters sharing secrets, taking a special pleasure in their friendship. When their hands fell still, each whispered encouragement to the other, and they exchanged reassurances in softer and softer voices until each fell silent, their arms wrapped around each other. They remained oblivious to their companions, Muttacchi, the driver, Anita, the few men hanging around the outer courtyard waiting for something to lighten the heavy heat of the day. It was an incongruous end to a frightening ritual, but perhaps, Anita thought, just perhaps this was the intent.

Muttacchi noticed almost none of this; she went straight to the car, sliding into the back seat, and settling deep into her own thoughts. When the two servants climbed into the front seat, gently arranging their limbs in the cramped space, it seemed to Anita they did so with less energy, but greater care for each other. The old woman watched them with an expression Anita couldn't quite make out. Was she worried about Gauri? Did she think the rite a success or a failure? Did she regret what she had done?

With the exception of soft murmurs of concern from the two women in the front seat, the ride home was one of uneasy silence, each caught in his or her own thoughts, turning away from the others, letting the scene in the temple revolve again and again in the mind's eye. Every now and then, the driver glanced to his left at the passengers, sometimes in the rearview mirror at Muttacchi, then braked hard to avoid a mishap — but no one reproached him, and he sped on. At Gauri's home, she climbed out and walked lazily to her house as the car sped away, neither turning to wave nor calling out. It was the eeriest and most unexpected ending Anita could imagine. She would nap well this afternoon, from relief as much as weariness.

At five o'clock, to the surprise of Anita and everyone else, Gauri was back, a tea tray in her hand and a broad smile on her face. She dropped the tray with a little bump on the table in the pergola and pushed it closer to Muttacchi.

"Tee." Gauri waggled her head before going off with a happy grin. The serene reserve that came over her after the exorcism rite had faded with the afternoon, evaporating like the damp in her clothing, or the morning mist on the river. She was back to her usual self, slightly impish, good-natured, ready for a little excitement if any should come along, though perhaps a little tired.

Muttacchi stared after her, a longing too deep for words flashing across her face beneath a mask of concern. It struck Anita that here was this old woman, the head of a large and prosperous clan, still in control of the family estate, whose relatives have grown and scattered and have no idea that now, to Muttacchi, the great matriarch, the servants are her children. She has grown closer to them than to her own relatives who call in the middle of the night and visit once a year if that.

"Are you all right?" Anita asked, leaning forward. She had called Auntie Meena to tell her the exorcism, as it were, had apparently gone as planned, that Gauri seemed contented and calm, and Muttacchi was subsiding into thoughtfulness if not satisfaction. Anita had decided to stay on, at the old woman's request, ostensibly to help her with the accounts and some paperwork, but mostly to ease her mind after such a difficult time. The entire process had been unsettling — the trances, negotiating with Konan, traveling to the temple and dealing with the priests, watching the ritual. But now, Anita began to wonder if she had spoken too soon, if the exorcism had not gone as Muttacchi had hoped, or if something else was bothering the old woman.

Muttacchi turned to her, her eyes sprinkled with pain. "You did see a difference in her afterward, didn't you?"

"Definitely, Muttacchi. She seemed very different. I think we all noticed it." Anita drew a full cup of tea toward her. "I have to admit, Muttacchi, that I was surprised. She seemed so different."

"Yes, she did." The old woman rested her hand on the tea tray, turning a teacup handle away from her. "And does she still seem different?"

Anita looked past the pergola to where Gauri had disappeared around the side of the house, perhaps to enter the kitchen through a back door. Muttacchi's question was disturbing, because it articulated a question Anita had not wanted to ask. She was so often accused of being a spoilsport, finding trouble where there was none, but now the old woman had done it for her, asking the very question Anita had set aside for her own private thoughts.

"No, she doesn't seem the same as when she came out of the temple. Now she seems the way she was when I first got here, just the same, and just the same as when we picked her up this afternoon for the ride to the temple."

Muttacchi nodded, her hand still turning the teacup back and forth. "Yes, I too think this."

"You're worried about it." Anita lowered her voice, aware of the servants going about their tasks, passing by the table to a plant that needed watering, bringing in the last of the laundry, searching for an errant chicken.

"She has been with me since she was a small child." Muttacchi's eyes unfocused, and she drifted deep into her own memories. "I hated to see her injured."

"It made me squirm." Anita looked back on the event and wondered how she'd managed to control her impulse to rush up and snatch the lash from the priest's hands. "Have you ever known this to work on anyone?"

The old woman glanced over at her. The question seemed to have reawakened something inside her. "What? Of course. Really, Anita. You act very peculiar sometimes." The old woman sighed. "What is it you doubt?"

That was the question, wasn't it? Anita thought. She listened for the sounds of the household, of normality and security, of a safe world that was hundreds of years old and would last for hundreds more. "She is not unhappy that Bhagavati has chosen her, Auntie. Should we really be trying to change her?"

The old woman sat up and pulled the tray toward her. "Of course we should. It is our duty. This is a practice we have great experience with. Many times I have seen this bring a troubled soul back to her own good nature. But Bhagavati is powerful. She made a choice among many and may not want to leave. So, we can only wait to see what all this has achieved." She picked up a *vadai,* a small round savory doughnut.

"You looked worried throughout the whole thing." Anita added more sugar to her cup. The old woman was studying her tea, tipping the cup one way, then another.

"Gauri surprised me."

Anita leaned forward. "What do you mean, surprised you?"

"Gauri surprised me. That's all, she surprised me."

Just then, Gauri reappeared with her broom and began her sweeping, moving across the courtyard, step by step, like a young girl lost in her own thoughts. Muttacchi turned to watch her. "I am not satisfied."

116

"Do you think the exorcism failed?"

"I am not satisfied. That's all."

"What are you going to do?" Anita paused. "You're not going to try again, are you?"

"No. Not that." The old woman looked Anita in the eye. "I intend to send her home, for her sake. You will take her."

The small whitewashed house sparkled in the light of the setting sun as Gauri led the way around to the front. She was calm now — none of the tears she'd given way to earlier when Muttacchi told her she would have to stay at home for a while. Perhaps Gauri was just resigned, confident that the time would come when she could return to the estate.

"Here." Gauri pointed, unnecessarily, to the front gate and stepped inside the fence. Anita followed her.

"Your parents' home?" Anita asked, and soon wished she hadn't. Gauri launched into a tale of family woe that would have sunk anyone else, and all the while a cheerful smile was on her face, as if everyone had such woes and why would anyone cry about it?

"I guess that's why this business with Bhagavati doesn't really bother you," Anita said, when Gauri paused for breath.

Gauri laughed, a light tinkling sound that made Anita feel she was being tickled. "Bhagavati is Bhagavati." She shrugged.

"Do you think she will come again?"

Gauri threw up her hands. Who knew?

"The priest was confident," Anita pointed out.

"Ah. He is a priest." She went back to her mildly stupid smile.

"Do you know him by reputation? Is he known for this sort of work?"

Gauri shook her head. "I don't know this man. He is new to me." She frowned, then the smile reappeared, and she pointed Anita to a chair near the house. Anita declined any more tea — she had begun to feel she'd float away.

"I thought perhaps he was known in this area for this kind of ritual," Anita said. "Konan suggested that."

"Ah, Konan." She turned away, pulling out the key for the padlock on her door. It was impossible to miss her change in expression.

"You don't like Konan, do you?"

"Yes, yes, I am liking. Very good man. Amma is very trusting of this man."

"But not you."

"Banana fry? You eat!" She slipped off the padlock, pushed open the doors, and escaped inside. There was nothing Anita could do but accept a plate of fried bananas when they appeared a few minutes later. Anita thanked her, tore off a piece, and ate.

"You're staying weeks with Amma?" Gauri asked.

"No, not me. Just for a few days. Meena Elayamma is trying to find out when Surya is coming."

"Not coming." Gauri was matter of fact, and sat down on the doorsill, wrapping her arms around her legs. "Surya will not visit Amma again."

"How do you know that?" Anita asked, recalling Muttacchi's distress when she first reported Gauri's predictions.

Gauri shrugged. "Don't know, but not coming. No more visiting."

"You have to have a reason for saying that," Anita said. She didn't exactly doubt Gauri. After all, Gauri was known as a woman of intuition, and to be chosen by Bhagavati meant the person had special qualities. But there had to be something that made her so confident. Anita probed, but Gauri was adamant. She just knew.

"What were you saying during the ritual?" Anita asked, changing the subject. "You were speaking in a language I didn't recognize. At least I thought it might have been a

119

language. Was it just gibberish? I couldn't tell. I caught some words, I thought, but not the whole thing. Do you remember?"

Gauri threw up her hands and laughed. "That is not me. That is Bhagavati." She stared back at Anita, then seemed to understand the questions had been serious. "There is so much trouble, Chechi. Bhagavati is not coming if there is no trouble."

Seven

Anita heard the rooster crow at two in the morning, then at three, and again at four, and wondered not for the first time how anyone got the idea those tormentors began their work at dawn. How on earth, she wondered sleepily, did anyone get any rest out here? She missed the thunderous breaking of waves punctuating a deep silence. Once again Anita rolled over, pulled the pillow over her head, and snuggled under the sheet. But each time, as she tried to force herself back to sleep, she knew the rooster was not the problem. Gauri's words echoed through her dreams, her hazy wakefulness, and Anita rolled onto her back and stared up at the netting in resignation. Gauri was a woman who knew things — either because Bhagavati inhabited her and graced her with sight, or because she knew other things about the family she was not revealing, things even Muttacchi would not admit to.

But why have these thoughts now?

The late night breeze brought a welcome cooling and a mild distraction, but still Anita didn't sleep. She tried to drug herself into sleep with a detailed meditation on the features of Muttacchi's Ganapati, his jeweled headdress, gently curving trunk, rotund torso, his oddly configured limbs in a semblance of a meditation asana. But there was something troubling about this image — she saw the rotund, adored elephant-headed god, and instead of feeling a river of warmth rise within her, she felt uneasy. What was gnawing at her?

When she again found herself awake, she looked up at the slatted wall for some sign of early morning, adrift from her earlier obsessive worries. The inchoate sounds of night coalesced into frantic voices and a wail of anguish that sounded like Muttacchi. Anita bolted from the bed, grabbing a robe as she struggled with the door.

Sett hurried past her awkwardly, his bowlegs making him sway along with the lantern held high in his right hand. Behind him came Muttacchi, her long white hair flying out about her head. Anita called out to her.

"Bindu. Something has happened to Bindu." Anita grabbed a flashlight, and hurried after them, joining the servants crushing together in the weak lamplight. The old man led them along the path, across the scrub toward the water. But before they could reach the river, he stopped and jumped lightly to the side of the path, holding his lamp high.

Muttacchi gasped and fell to her knees, her hands reaching out but stopping short of touching. Bindu lay flat across the path, her thick black hair splayed across her back and over the sand, its strands matted with darkening blood that had spread onto the side of her face and dried there.

The old woman began to cry softly. "Child, child, child. What has happened?"

Bindu lay face down, one hand stretched out in front of her, the other partly to her side, entangled with the clothing she had been carrying. Her mundu was wrapped around her chest, falling to her knees, her choli and nerid bundled beside her. A cloth bag with soap and a toothbrush lay nearby. Veej, the dhobi, leaned down, and grasping Bindu's shoulder, turned her over.

Anita gasped.

Bindu's face was contorted in an expression of terror — then her eyes fluttered and a soft moan escaped her. The quiet of her body as it lay face down was shattered by the damage to her face. The crowd of servants fell back, babbling among themselves about what they should do. Then as one they surged forward, ready to lift up the nearly lifeless body and drive it to the nearest hospital.

"No!" Anita said, holding up her hands. "Call an ambulance at once."

Lata, the cook, leaned down and wrapped her arms around Muttacchi and lifted her to her feet. As a single entity the two turned and stumbled back to the house — horrified, shocked, fearful, heartbroken. Sett ran ahead, and Anita could hear him shouting into the telephone.

Anita knelt down and called Bindu's name, sending warm breath across the maidservant's cheek, trying to ease the wandering Anita could see in her confused and pained eyes just as they rolled back and the color flashed in and out of her face.

"It's all right, Bindu. We're taking you to hospital." The pain and fear that seemed to flash across Bindu's face pierced Anita, and she prayed Bindu would hear and believe her promises.

She felt a rush of anger and also of frustration. She wanted to reach out and grab whoever did this to a sweet, innocent young woman, a harmless servant, but there was no one there. Instead, she felt her brain spinning, her mind calculating, and she put everything else from her thoughts but finding Bindu's attacker. "I have to be calm," she said to no one in particular. "I have to see the messages left behind."

When Lata returned, Anita told her to hold Bindu's hand and call her name while Anita tried to retrace what had happened. Anita shone her flashlight onto the path, following it down to the river and back. It seemed whoever had struck Bindu on the head, hitting her hard enough to nearly kill her, had simply appeared on the ground beside her. There was no sign of footsteps anywhere from where Bindu lay to the river, nor footsteps up to the house, unless they were mixed in with those made by the servants and Muttacchi as they hurried to Bindu's side. Only at Bindu's feet was there any sign of disturbance in the sand, something more than a single footstep marking Bindu's passage. Otherwise, there was nothing — no sand disturbed, no broken shrubbery, no grass torn up. But whoever had done this had to have come from somewhere.

Anita turned around full circle. To the north lay the path leading to the Karamana River, a long, winding muddy green body of water that carried both working and touring boats. Though never producing anything of the size or history of the river culture of central Kerala around Ernakulam and Kochi, the Karamana River had nevertheless been an important waterway for Travancore in southern Kerala. Even now Anita sometimes found herself watching coir- or sand-filled vellums plying the river beneath the bridge while crossing the bridge near the Parasurama Temple. More of the boats were for tourists, but a few vellums with a pole across their bow or stuck in the mud to keep the boat pressed into shore were still to be seen, a silent reminder of a more ancient way of life in Kerala, beneath the high rises, mobile phones, and other accoutrements of modern life.

To the west was the path leading downriver, to houses and hamlets of greater density the closer they came to the new highway. To the east was the kavu, the sacred grove that the path skirted on its way to the river. To the south lay Muttacchi's estate, three separate buildings with over eight people on any given night sleeping, wandering around, relaxing, talking. It never ceased to amaze Anita how awake people were in India throughout the night — cowmen, workers, tradespeople. It was the country that never slept. But this was the exception — this night no one had heard or seen anything, it seemed.

Anita scanned the ground looking for some sign of another person approaching Bindu. The attacker had to come from somewhere — the blow to the back of her head was no accident. Subconsciously Anita looked up, half expecting to see a coconut palm with heavy ripe coconuts ready to fall, then she looked around the ground, once again half-expecting to find a coconut rolled into the brush with blood caked on its rough surface. It was an absurd idea, a desperate idea. But she looked anyway, and found nothing.

Glancing around her once more, she followed the path, walking parallel to the edge, down to the river. The path was less than a city block from house to river but distances in the countryside thick with brush and overgrown trees were deceptive, and paths narrow and smooth through uneven terrain were slow. At the river she looked for signs that a boat might have come to the bank. The river was quiet, and even in the heavy darkness she felt safe taking the stone steps down into the water, the nearest set of many cut into the riverbank over the centuries: she saw no sign of a recent mooring or landing. She peered at the nearby shrubbery, but that showed no sign of a landing or docking — no broken twigs, no scattered leaves, no soaked branches.

Anita turned back toward the house and the lights shining in the distance. The path leading to Bindu was the only one showing signs of traffic. But we all came together, thought Anita, and all of us left footsteps. One of us came twice, Anita thought. One of us. Muttacchi, Lata, Sett, Veej, and Arun. And me. Who else could have come down here through the estate?

The sound of a car door slamming and voices calling out brought Anita out of her meditations. The ambulance, she thought. She walked through the scrub one more time, fixing Bindu's position on the ground in her memory. Yes, she'd been moved, turned onto her back, but here she lay a few feet from the river, no sign of anyone else having come near her, her bathing materials and clothing scattered nearby.

Aware of the little time she had left, Anita knelt down, whispered words of comfort, and studied Bindu's face one more time. The maidservant wore no earrings, no nose ring, no jewelry whatsoever. There appeared to be no marks on her limbs. A single bruise marred the base of her throat. Anita leaned closer, shining her small flashlight over the woman's features. At the hairline, almost hidden beneath a thick black curl, were two red marks, almost like insect bites. Anita lifted the lock of hair and studied the spot just above the left temple. Nothing in Bindu's appearance could explain the terror on her face.

"It's all right, Bindu. You're safe."

Anita felt her stomach seize as she let Bindu's expression invade her, imprint itself on her memory. Her body grew hot with an unexpected rage. She willed herself to be still, to let the experience of Bindu's silent plea seep into her, to open herself to knowing as much as possible from the body lying in front of her. "I'll have to talk to Gauri about this," Anita thought. "She'll understand what I'm feeling now."

The voices grew louder, and Anita looked up from Bindu to see the medics hurrying toward them, a constable following several steps behind.

"An innocent, a complete innocent." Muttacchi spoke with passion, but Anita recognized the pain beneath the words, the voice that caught as she grew more emotional.

"Yes, yes, your servants are known for their goodness." The medic nodded and knelt beside Bindu.

"Who would want to hurt Bindu?" The old woman and Anita stepped out of the way.

"God Yama does not listen to our reasoning," the man said.

Anita moved back, turning her attention to the household. Which one of these wouldn't mourn Bindu's death? Which one cared so little? Lata hovered near Muttacchi, Sett swung his lamp and seemed to sway along with it, Veej hung back, and Arun, poor young Arun, tried to creep closer and closer, but each time he was waved back and reluctantly obeyed.

One of us, Anita thought. Is it possible?

EIGHT

Anita unlocked the heavy wooden door to the old estate office and pushed it open. The windows faced the street, and she was confident that no member of the household staff could overhear her call to Auntie Meena. The servants were desperate for information and not a little afraid, as evidenced by their probing questions and appeals for reassurance. After all, Bindu was an inoffensive, unimportant maidservant who couldn't get into trouble if she tried. But even if someone like Lata got only a fragment of a sentence, Anita didn't want anyone repeating any of her conversation to others. Too much was at stake. Anita glanced back through the door before she pushed it shut, the squealing of the wood like someone in pain.

Anita walked over to the most comfortable-looking chair, pulled it away from the wall, and brushed dust and cobwebs from the seat. The stale air and general feel of neglect held her, and she looked around the office more carefully. She hadn't noticed it before, or if she had, hadn't thought much about it, but it was abundantly clear just how far the family had fallen — no clerk came in every day, no tradesmen lined up outside the door ready to provide goods, run errands, bid on jobs. In this room where villagers and tradespeople had come to meet with the head of the family or other members, conduct their business in comfort, a thick layer of dust covered just about everything. Whatever had been removed from the shelves, leaving little indentations now filled with thinner layers of dust, could not have been of importance — this was a place in decline.

The room looked the same as it had in Anita's childhood, but that was only outer appearance. The walls were lined halfway up with narrow shelves holding books printed in manuscript format, in the shape of old pencil boxes but twice as thick. Between the wooden covers were loose printed pages, the whole tied together with colored string. A desk sat low to the floor with a cushion nearby, for the clerk or family member to sit on cross-legged. A taller desk stood next to the front wall. Anita had that feeling of the world going on without them, leaving them locked in this misery of unexplained violence in a world that had long died elsewhere.

Bindu's attack left Anita feeling like she was teetering, as though something were pushing all of them out of their safe, familiar world. But what? Yes, of course, such violence itself wasn't right — it was ghastly and wrong — but there was something else about it that threw her off. Something she couldn't quite wrap her mind around.

There was no sense in the way these things were going on at once, Anita thought. First, Surya failed to show up. Yes, she had always been a bit flighty, but this time she was especially discourteous. That by itself put the household on edge. Then Gauri's possessions unsettled everyone and brought out how little the servants liked each other. And that exorcism, which was worse than any harm the trance might do, hadn't resolved anything. And now Bindu. Poor, innocent Bindu.

Anita had come in here to make a phone call and keep it private, but instead she was falling deeper and deeper into a morass of unproductive ruminations. Anita flipped open her mobile and called her aunt Meena. Anita broke the news as gently as possible, but was mostly surprised at how calmly Meena seemed to take it. Perhaps she was stunned.

"Auntie? Are you all right?"

"I am sitting, Anita, sitting." Meena breathed softly, just loud enough for Anita to hear. "You are quite certain it is Bindu?"

"Yes, of course we are. Is there a reason for asking?" Anita was used to her aunt's odd reactions to the various violent experiences Anita encountered, but this was among the oddest.

"It's just that, she is so — unremarkable." Meena sighed, a ragged, breathless sound. "And it is very sad, a sweet thing she is. I suppose she will recover?"

"She's been taken to hospital."

"And the police? What are they doing? Are they confident of an arrest?"

"They are waiting until they can interview Bindu," Anita explained. "The constable suggested she hit her head on the stone bathing steps at the river, and he wants to be certain before he does anything." Anita didn't bother telling Auntie Meena what she thought of this explanation.

Once adjusted to the news, Meena went on to offer her version of assistance — clean clothes, the car with Joseph, the driver, a place for Muttacchi to stay? Anita declined them all, though she wasn't sure about the offer to Muttacchi.

A moment later Anita flipped shut her mobile and tried to think. The teak chair creaked as she stretched. She just wanted to know who had attacked Bindu — and why.

Anita pushed herself out of the chair and pulled open the door. Outside, the sun was high in the sky, beating down as though to punish those who had the temerity to go on living after such violence to Bindu. Anita pushed her hair away from her face, closed up the room, and headed to the river path. Somewhere down there was the answer to Bindu's attack, and Anita was going to find it.

Anita gave a wide berth to the section of the dirt path where the maidservant had been found, unconscious and bleeding. She kept walking until she came to the intersecting river path, then crossed it to the stone steps leading down into the water. At some locations along the bank, stone steps, maybe two hundred years old or more, led down into the water, to make work easier for the dhobi or boatmen or anyone taking a bath. The steps were rough hewn and wide, set within walls. Anita could hear laughter and splashing farther down the river, and she took the first step, leaning out to get a better look. Then another. The water was tepid, pleasantly so, and she was soon knee-deep in the river wondering just how many steps there were.

Once again Anita scanned the water, but other than a wooden vellum piled high with sand floating slowly toward her, no one else was in sight. She climbed the steps and at the top pulled her soaking pants away from her legs. She held them there and gave a shake, then wrung out as much water as possible.

The path sloped up a bit, and Anita walked back along the scrub. It didn't make sense that Bindu had been struck from behind and that someone would wipe the path clean. How could he or she leave no mark of their own passing? So many people came down to the river for any number of reasons that not having footprints was far stranger than an abundance of them.

Anita knelt at the spot where Bindu had been found. Patches of scrub grass were stiff and black now with the dried blood, contaminating the entire area. Anita closed her eyes and conjured from her memory the image of Bindu lying sprawled on the path, one arm out, laundry scattered around her.

She opened her eyes and looked down at

her own pants, now almost dry in the intensifying heat. She had once spilled a bottle of water on her outfit sitting in traffic outside Secretariat in Trivandrum, and she was dry before she got to East Fort, a distance of barely a mile. The only sign that anything had happened was a certain softness in the fabric. Her pants were drying now, the same softness spreading from knee to ankle. She hadn't been surprised that Bindu's outfit was dry after lying in the heat, but now as she recalled the figure lying there, she remembered what struck her about her mundu tied around her chest. It was still without wrinkles, still neatly pressed. There was none of the softness and roughness that would have appeared after a dip in the river.

"Of course!" Anita jumped up. "How stupid of me." She looked at where Bindu's feet had lain, where the woman's footsteps seemed confused with another's. But no. Those had all been Bindu's. Bindu hadn't been returning from the river — she had been still on her way there. She had been confronted and terrified and tried to turn and run — but it was too late. Whoever it was hit her from behind as she tried to flee.

Anita stepped onto the path, looking back toward the river. Bindu had met someone, turned, tried to run, and been struck down at once. Something had frightened her beyond belief. But what? Whom had she met? And where had they come from? There was no sign of a recent boat docking, no sign of footsteps in the scrub.

If not from the river, the murderer had to have come from the land — down from the house. Was that possible? It didn't seem possible that such a modest, tranquil place could be the scene of such violence, for surely the intent was to kill Bindu. The force of the attack said so. But could Muttacchi's home really harbor a murderer? Who would want to kill a maidservant? Who would want to kill Bindu?

Muttacchi pushed herself up from the floor and fell heavily onto the bed. "I know you're there, Anita." The old woman spoke without turning around, her white nerid lying on the bed, her choli and the rest of her upper torso uncovered. "Come. You have been lingering for some time."

"Only a few minutes." Anita stepped over the high wooden threshold into the room.

"I was doing some exercises. I have a doctor who insists on exercising after a nap. Odious man." Muttacchi snorted in derision.

Anita chuckled as she gathered up the mosquito netting, swept it into a single stream and bundled it into a knot hanging high above the bed. "I was down at the river and the path, where it happened." Anita leaned over the old woman, to be sure she had heard.

The old woman looked wretched, as though she had lost one of her own children. And I suppose she almost has, Anita thought. She was never one to neglect her servants, no matter how hard she worked them.

"Do you feel up to talking about Bindu?" Anita pulled up a stool and sat in front of the old woman, who lifted her eyes to Anita's and gave her a sad, resigned smile.

"She was a sweet, innocent child. She should have been married, but she was not going to do that. No, she was no more than a child herself, and never would be more." Muttacchi sighed heavily. "Did you notice that? She was girlish in a real way — she was not going to grow old like the rest of us."

"No, I hadn't known that." Anita frowned. She had somehow missed that about Bindu. The maidservant seemed perfectly normal, a little light-hearted and silly sometimes, but otherwise perfectly normal in her behavior and interactions.

"It is not the kind of thing that is notice-able in a large household." Muttacchi straightened herself, and Anita could see the old steel returning to her. The brief capitulation to distress and anxiety was over. "She has a father — he works on the river. He brought her snacks if he was passing on the water and saw her there. Someone must go to him — he will need money for her medical care."

"I'll go. Don't worry about that."

"Thank you, Anita. So, what do you want to know?"

"What time did Bindu and the other servants normally go down to the river for their bath?"

"Early, perhaps five or five-thirty. Some-times earlier if it was a festival day and much needed to be done. And sometimes not till the end of the day, when work was done. Does it matter?" Her look was chal-lenging, as if to say, you had better have a good reason for disturbing me with such a mundane question.

"It could." Anita rested her chin on her hands. "When I first saw Bindu lying there, I thought she was returning from her bath and had been hit from behind. Something frightened her, that's for sure, but I thought she was headed back."

"And now?"

"Now I think she wasn't returning. I think she was on her way to the river. I think she saw something that frightened her, and she turned but couldn't get away."

"I see." Muttacchi leaned back on the bed, her hand searching for her nerid. "And why does this matter?"

"It means she was going down to the river much later than I thought, but it was still quite dark." Anita tapped her index finger against her lips. "It would have been hard for her to see anything until she was right on top of it. It's very dark then, and particularly in that part of the property."

"What could be there to see?"

"Or she could have been seen."

"Eh?"

"Someone might have been afraid she'd stumble on something."

"She did stumble on something, Child, if you recall the look on her face." Muttacchi shuddered.

"Yes." Anita was still absorbed in her thoughts. "Tell me," she said, suddenly standing up, "has anyone tried to buy your property lately?"

Muttacchi started, her nostrils flared, and she gave Anita a withering look. "Certainly not. Everyone knows I will never sell. This land goes to family."

"Okay, okay." Anita did her best to mollify her. "Well, has there been any trouble along the river?"

Again the old woman sneered, but this time she leaned away, staring out the open door. "What trouble could there be? The world has passed us by. We have nothing the world wants now."

"Muttacchi, someone attacked Bindu — it was vicious."

"We cannot understand karma." The old woman pulled the nerid around her like a shawl, though midday heat was growing intense, and muttered the homily roboti-cally.

Anita was ready to throw up her hands and abandon tact. Every time the concept of karma was trotted out to explain the most awful behavior, she wanted to scream. She shut her eyes, recited the first two verses of the Ramayana, and took a deep breath.

"Her father must be so unhappy — she is the only child, and his wife is dead. He wanted her to stay close or work in a big hotel, where she would make more money. He did not want her staying here. Only this week is she staying because I have sent Gauri home. It is Gauri who is going so early to the river to bathe every morning. It is Gauri who is on the path every morning in the dark while the others prepare the breakfast and bathe here at the spigot. Lata and the others bathe in the river in the afternoon, when work is done. Gauri bathes in the river in the morning — it is part of her puja. She is devoted to her morning worship."

Anita sat down on the bed beside her great aunt. "*Ayoo.* That changes everything."

"It changes nothing. Bindu is the one who lies dying in hospital — sweet, innocent child."

"But don't you see, Muttacchi?" Anita lowered her voice to a whisper and hunched over to speak to the old woman.

"What is wrong with you?" Muttacchi tugged at her nerid, trying to get it into place.

"That's the point. It was Gauri they were after, and Gauri is anything but a sweet, innocent child. She is a thorn in everyone's side when she feels like it, a woman possessed at the most inconvenient times, a servant who defies her employers and the other servants. Of course! It was Gauri they wanted."

Muttacchi turned to stare at Anita, understanding slowly coming to her, her mouth twitching in distress. "Gauri? Someone wants to hurt Gauri?"

"I'm afraid so."

"But who?"

"That, Muttacchi, is the question. But at least the question makes sense."

"I don't see how."

"Tell me about Gauri." Anita took the old woman's hands. "Somewhere in Gauri's recent life something has happened that's made her dangerous to others, or hated by someone. That's what I have to figure out."

"Oh, no, not Gauri too." The old woman squeezed Anita's hands so tight that the younger woman almost cried out. "Not my little Gauri."

"Yes, unless we find them and stop them, whoever it is." Anita leaned closer. "You have to tell me all about Gauri. Her possessions, how the others feel about her, her place in the village, her family."

The old woman seemed a little stunned by all this and pulled her hands away. Perhaps it was too much for an old woman all at once, Anita thought, as she waited.

"Everything. You want to know everything." The old woman rubbed her mouth, then, once again, seemed to gain strength.

"Whatever you know."

"All right, let me think." She lowered her

144

hand slowly to her lap. "Gauri. Gauri has been with me since she was a child. I told you that. Her family has a house near here — you have seen it. Her mother died some years ago — Gauri was little more than a child then, perhaps eight years old." Muttacchi's face softened. "She will always be one of us." Then she sighed, and looked annoyed. "And Gauri, ah, Gauri. She is troubling but still she is a good girl. Very honest and very clean."

"What about the trances?"

"The trances started some time ago, out of the blue. One morning she is sweeping and humming to herself, and next that we know she is suddenly taken possession of and we can do nothing. We give her water to revive her, but nothing more."

"Where did these incidents happen?" Anita stood up. "Can you show me?"

"If you wish. Let me dress. But first I have a job for you."

Anita sat on the edge of the veranda as she counted the stack of hundred-rupee notes a second time. Muttacchi had handed them to her, telling her to take them to Bindu's father for her medical care. He was poor, she said, too poor to manage without hardship. Anita and Muttacchi had avoided each

145

other's eye as the crisp new bills changed hands.

Anita walked to the road and waved down an autorickshaw. In a few minutes the auto reached the main highway, crossed over, and headed down the hill on a dirt road leading to the dock at the other side of a new boat club. Tied side to side as they spread out into the center of the broadest part of the river were a series of brightly painted vellums recalled from carrying sand or coir to carrying tourists, traveling leisurely from dock to lagoon and back to the dock. The road narrowed past the club and ended in a small patch of sandy ground.

"I suppose the police have already come to tell him," Anita said to herself, "but still, I hate to be the one to have to look him in the eye."

The auto driver pulled up under a tree and turned off the engine. "Waiting?" Anita nodded and climbed out. Half a dozen laborers stopped working and watched her approach.

The sight of the stranger acted like a magnet, pulling the men from their work, out of the boats, away from the loading dock and piles of sand. One man put down his shovel, straightened up, and stared hard at her, and three men clambered off a boat, dropping their tools, and drew close together, moving forward like a single organism.

"Bindu's father?" the head man asked. "We are learning the news from the constable. It is a great shock to him — this is his only child, and his only close family. If she dies, he will be poor indeed."

The men crowded closer and closer as the head man delivered this report, his words coming slowly as though he had to think through each one before letting it go into the sentence. He swung his head from side to side as the sentence took shape, as the laborers moved closer, until at the end Anita felt the sadness they must have all felt when they first heard the news. The men didn't show any emotion on their faces, but their intense looks and serious miens seemed a cloak around all of them — three men, tall, short, all muscular and thin, wearing plaid lungis with dusty feet and hands, as though they were wearing beige socks and gloves.

The head man glanced in the direction of the other workers. "These are his friends. We weep for him." Three men nodded as one.

"Can you tell me where I can reach him?" Anita said. "Punnu Chellamma wants to contribute to Bindu's care. She is very fond of Bindu." Again the men nodded their approval. Only one had gone on working, keeping the boats from drifting away, his bright green lungi shimmering in the sunlight.

The headman motioned her to stand near a hut while he disappeared inside. After barely half a minute, he leaned out and waved Anita to enter. Bindu's father was sitting at a table working a mobile phone, probably the owner's, and he looked up at her with a confused and achingly painful look in his eyes.

"I have something from Punnu Chellamma for Bindu's medical care." Anita reached inside her purse and pulled out the envelope, wondering partly if she dared just hand him so much money all at once. She had what she tried to tell herself was an unreasonable fear of carrying large sums of money on her person — or seeing anyone else do so — but she knew millions of Indians carried their modest pay in their shirt pockets — one of the reasons for so many successful pickpockets in the country. She shut her mind to the anxiety and handed over the envelope.

"I have not seen her in days," the man said. "We were planning a festival trip soon."

The headman clapped his hand on the

worker's shoulder and squeezed hard. "She is a good girl, a sturdy girl, and you are a good father to her, a good *acchan*. She will recover." A shout from outside took the headman to the door, and a moment later he was shouting and cursing and racing toward the dock.

Anita waited for the father to open the envelope and count the money, but he squeezed the envelope tight in his hands, as though doing so would keep him from any more pain. She wanted to encourage him, but every thought sounded false in her head. Bindu was viciously attacked and had barely survived; it would still be a while before anyone knew for sure if she would live or die.

"We are very concerned — she is so sweet and kind and fun," Anita said. He nodded. "We want her to have the best care."

"She loves everyone in that house, all of them out there, even that crazy one." He twisted the envelope so hard Anita thought it must tear.

"Gauri? She told you she loved Gauri also?" Anita paused, then sat down opposite him. "Did she say anything else about Gauri? I'm sorry to ask, but I need to know."

He turned his attention to Anita's question, his hands loosening their grip on the envelope of cash, probably as much as Bindu earned in several years. "I call her the crazy one, but Bindu, my little Bindu, she is saying, no, she is not crazy. She knows things, many things."

"Did she say what things?"

"Who is good, who is not good. Who will become rich, who will die in pain." He sighed. "She told me once, that Gauri, when she came here to take Bindu to the Parasurama Temple across the way, that Bindu is good. She is good." A great sigh escaped him. "She meant Bindu's karma is good. There is so little in her to bring down evil upon her."

"What do you think she meant by that?"

"She loves my Bindu, but I think she sensed a bad end — good life, but a flash of karma at the end, the residue of some long-past evil deed." He leaned back in his chair, frowning over the recollection. "Gauri came to collect her one day, a few months past, and she had only begun to have these trances. One man asked if he could bring his son, a troubled boy, to her for cure, and she said no, not yet, perhaps another time. They talked, all of the men thought she could help in some way and urged her to reconsider. Except one. He didn't like such cures. She wouldn't talk to him, and he wouldn't look at her after that. A surly fellow, but a good worker, a good boatman."

"Is he here now?"

The father nodded, and pointed through the open door. "There he is, Gokul, tying up that boat." Anita followed his outstretched hand, to the wiry man in the solid green lungi working on the dock.

NINE

Anita pulled another chair up to the table beneath the pergola and brushed away leaves fallen from the vines above. She felt a change in the air around her as she worked at rearranging chairs, pulling the table this way or that to avoid the sun, and wondered if now was the time to confront Muttacchi. The old woman continued to page through the accounts book, and Anita took longer than necessary cleaning off one chair as she decided to wait until another time, when she was confident of holding the old woman's attention without interruption.

The sound of a car drawing up to the house broke the midday quiet and was a welcome relief for Anita. The driver cut the engine, and after a moment of silence a car door slammed.

"That will be Joseph," Anita told Muttacchi. "I asked Meena Elayamma to send me a few things." Anita went down the pathway to the entry gate and stopped in surprise when she saw the car and driver. Oops!

Anand slammed the boot shut. "Your requirements, madam," he said with a broad smile as he motioned toward a suitcase and an embroidered cloth tote sitting on the ground. "I believe you requested this?" He walked toward her and handed her a pair of binoculars.

"Anand, you're totally unexpected." Anita quickly took the binoculars in an effort to hide her confusion. She could feel herself blushing as she looked them over, gripping them with both hands. Somewhere in the past few weeks Anand had gone from being a casual friend to something more — she knew it, and he did too — but she was not ready to have her family know it, since she was still struggling with the implications for her freedom. And this made her feel awkward and stupid when he and her family came together. But there was nothing she could do about it now. She held up the binoculars and thanked him. "I had no idea you were coming."

"I can see that." He smiled as he drew up the strap and draped it over the binoculars. "Shall I get back onto the road?"

"No, no." She let her eyes linger on his, then blushed. "Let me introduce you to

Muttacchi. She's standing at the gate, isn't she?" Anita said, lowering her voice. "She'll be delighted to meet you." Anita tried not to think how badly all this could go.

"As much as Auntie Meena?" Anand winked as he turned to the entryway. Anita led him to the gate and made the introductions.

"Nambudiri?" Muttacchi said. She repeated the name of the highest caste of Brahmans in Kerala as though it were a new word worth trying out, enunciating each syllable as though to herself, to help her remember it, unlike her usual method of running every sound into another and eliding as many as possible. "Nambudiri?"

Anand allowed as this was so, then picked up the bags and carried them through the entry and onto the path before the dhobi, Veej, came hurrying along and grabbed them. Anita wished she could get a photograph of the old woman's expression when she saw the son of a high-caste Brahman carrying a suitcase. She probably hadn't seen a Nambudiri carrying anything, let alone a suitcase, in her entire life. Mixed in with the old woman's amazement was a shrewd examination of Anand's every inch and limb, his hands, his head, his carriage, his feet (he left his shoes at the entry). But

154

when he turned around to face her, she gave him a sweet, modest smile, the look any grandmother would give a visiting grandson. Anita held back, afraid she'd burst out laughing.

"You will take a meal. But I insist." Muttacchi raised a hand to forestall his objections, then called out her orders. In a moment Sett appeared with a small table, placed it in the courtyard, and covered it with a brightly printed cotton shawl. Arun appeared next with a water bottle, glass, and plate. Sett pulled up a chair for Muttacchi and another for Anita, and the two women sat to the side. Anita was torn between acute embarrassment and mischievous amusement at Anand's predicament as she watched him tumble to what was about to happen. She would owe him big-time for not preventing this.

Lata emerged from the kitchen to supervise the delivery and arrangement of the seven dishes along with rice that constituted lunch, ordering Arun to push the sautéed okra closer when she noticed Anand's interest it.

"Eat, eat," Muttacchi commanded once the table was fully laid, and Anand ate. Sett served rice and vegetables as needed, then retired to a perch under the pergola; Lata stood at the edge of the veranda in front of the kitchen, waiting for word on what bowls to replenish.

Really, thought Anita, this gorgeous man is so accommodating. How many gentlemen friends could stand to suddenly be presented with a meal and be forced to eat with an audience? And he's so complimentary about it all. Anita couldn't help noticing how pleased both Lata and Muttacchi were every time Anand praised a certain dish, the use of a certain spice or manner of preparation. And he backed up every compliment with another mouthful.

"Why did you come alone?" Muttacchi said when it looked like Anand would actually stop eating.

"Ah," Anand said, returning from the spigot after washing his hands. "I stopped in at Hotel Delite to see Anita, but she was not there."

"No, she is here."

"Yes, so Auntie Meena explained. She also explained that she was in some difficulty." Anand turned to Anita. "You asked for some things, and Auntie Meena is unable to get away to bring them here, so she asked me to bring them over."

And that must have taken ten years off her life and turned her hair into gray wire,

Anita thought. Auntie Meena got chills when she thought of the friendship that might develop between her and Anand. She smiled and said, "How nice of you to help her out."

Anand grinned. "It seems she has a tour there and the tour operator is rather unhappy and is requiring a lot of attention. I believe the woman was in the office while I was there, and your aunt didn't dare leave her a moment longer than necessary. So I was pleased to help out."

"Is this the infamous Sophie?" Anita asked.

"I think so."

"Auntie Meena can handle her," Anita said with complete confidence.

"I hope so," Anand said, "because when I left your aunt was explaining that you weren't around to lead her tour group as you did last year. It seems she remembers you from some excursion you organized."

"Me?" Anita squinted at him. How could she possibly remember all the little trips she arranged for hundreds of foreigners? Most of them didn't remember any of what they saw, except the old woman carrying bundled sticks on her head or the cow wandering along the edge of the road. "Ravi can do a much better job."

Muttacchi shook her head and sighed. "These foreigners require so much attention. But you are here now. *Payasam,* yes?" The old woman called out another order to Lata, but the cook was ready for her and hurried forward with a small tray holding a bowl of payasam, the sweet rice pudding made with raisins and cashews. Behind her stood Arun holding a tray with a glass of pink-tinged water, the glass of *patimukham* that concludes the meal. Anand lavished his praise on the payasam.

Muttacchi relaxed in her chair as the payasam disappeared, and Anand complimented her on the flowering trees and plants all around them. She seemed to relish the attentions of a handsome young man, and she smiled and laughed and slipped in her questions about his family between the answers to his questions about the names of flowering shrubs, the architect who bought a piece of land across the road, the new boat club farther up the river.

"Ah," she said at one point, after receiving what must have been a very satisfactory answer to one of her probing questions, and let a warm, somewhat stupid smile settle on her face. "Why has Meena not told me about you?" This rhetorical question was Muttacchi's one comment after exploring the extent of Anand's family tree, his occupation, education, plans for his future, and various other matters of interest only to an elderly relative used to arranging marriages.

"Since I came unannounced, I have probably interrupted your plans. But I haven't been in this area before, so perhaps I can walk around a bit before we talk, eh?" Anand rose as the dishes were cleared away. He thanked Muttacchi profusely for her hospitality, nodded to Anita, and went back out to the lane.

Muttacchi was silent for some minutes after he disappeared, while Sett and Arun removed the tablecloth and table, and repositioned the chairs. When Anita heard them setting the table under the pergola for their meal, she turned to the old woman. "Our turn now?"

"I have heard about his father," the old woman said, rising from her chair. "The high-caste Brahman who married the orphan of no-caste." The girlish warmth that had crept into her face faded, and once again she was the hardnosed and shrewd matriarch of a once powerful family. "They are quite active in certain circles."

"So I've been told," Anita said, following her relative to the dining table.

"His father and mother have been arrested, I believe — many times. The father argues a great deal with his relations in government." She shuffled over to the table. "They always let him out after a suitable stay."

"So I've heard."

"Good-looking, he is."

Anita smiled but said nothing.

"Meena does not like him, does she?"

Anita started. "Now, how did you know that?"

Muttacchi paused with her hand on the back of a chair. "She absorbs all the old family stories and believes they predict the future. A love match never works, least of all between a Nayar and a Nambudiri." She lowered herself into a chair. "She is right sometimes."

Anita sat opposite her, waiting for the rest of it. It annoyed her the way her family studied, judged, and dismissed everyone so easily, when she and Anand were still just enjoying each other. She was in no rush to pass through this stage in their relationship — the discovery that something moved between them — she wasn't ready to acknowledge the possibility of a future with Anand.

"They have produced a fine son." Muttacchi pulled a plate toward her. New bowls were freshly filled with vegetables, chutneys, two different kinds of rice, as much as Anand had been served and more. "Meena will never approve of him." She gave Anita a nod and set to her meal. "Now tell me what the binoculars are for."

While Anand explored the neighborhood, Anita followed Muttacchi around the estate. For an old woman, Muttacchi moved with surprising ease and grace through her property, going from one tree to the next, pointing out its special qualities — particularly fragrant blossoms, medicinally useful seeds or bark or roots, rare plants flowering every few years, a now-dead relative's favored tree — going on and on as she halted, looked around her at the grounds, and pointed to a spot, saying only, "There. Right there." Anita followed along, fascinated by this new, energetic view of the old woman.

At first Anita had begun the mini-trek by writing down these sites of Gauri's unexpected but stunningly magnetic trances, but as the list grew it was obvious that Gauri's trances took hold in the outdoors, near a tree, a shrub, a potted plant, but always away from the built properties. But also at each site, Anita noticed, Muttacchi became warmer and warmer as she spoke of Gauri.

"Where was the first trance?" Anita asked.

The old woman turned slowly and let her attention move across the scrub to a far corner of the kavu. She stared at it for a long moment before saying, "There. Just there."

"Is there anything special about that spot?"

"Nothing." Muttacchi shook her head, still staring. "It is just dirt and brush."

"What did she say after her first trance? Was she surprised or worried or sad or happy?"

Again the old woman shook her head, slowly, heavily. "She came to with water splashed on her, looked around, and walked away. But she was very quiet for the rest of the day."

"Did you ask her why this trance might have happened?"

"She said she thought her puja was not acceptable to Bhairava."

Anita turned quickly to face the opening into the kavu, perhaps twenty feet from the spot the old woman had indicated for the first trance. "When was the first trance? What was she doing?"

"Early morning, just after a puja. She

often undertook a small puja, her private worship, in the morning, very early. Not every day, but two or three times a week in the morning. Nothing big. She is poor, you know." Muttacchi turned away and went on with her tour, pointing to one site after another, there and there and there and there.

"You are not inclined to discipline her, are you?" Anita said when the spaces between locations became greater and greater, leading to long periods of silence as the old woman crossed the yard to the next spot.

"Discipline Gauri?" Muttacchi looked amused. "Why would I do that? If Bhagavati loves her, who am I to interfere?"

"But you did take her to an exorcist?" Anita pointed out.

Muttacchi winced and pulled down the branch of a nearby tree. "Look at this leaf — how beautiful. When this tree blossoms, such a fragrance." She moved closer to the tree to rub her hand along the trunk, fingering the loose bark. "Yes, I did. Konan advised it, and he is wise. You heard him. He has not failed me over many years."

"Was that the only reason?"

Muttacchi shrugged. Who knows why we do things, she seemed to be saying.

"Do you think it worked?"

"How am I to know until the time passes and she no longer is possessed?"

Anita nodded. Muttacchi was sensible, for sure. "How long will it take, for you to be satisfied of the cure, I mean?"

Muttacchi rubbed the tree trunk again and looked up among the thick branches. "Two or three months perhaps. When it started, it happened once, then not again for a month or so, and then again, once a fortnight, then soon once a week it seemed. And then more often. The trances have increased to twice a week or more." Muttacchi moved away to pick up fallen twigs.

"So we'd have to wait over a month or more." Anita leaned against the tree and wrapped her arm around the trunk. The old woman straightened up and instantly a smile spread across her shiny wrinkled face.

"You stand before me like a *yakshi*. Did you know that *yakshis* can take the form of a beautiful woman?" The old woman stared hard at Anita. "Some cause insanity, and they must be worshipped to cure the victim."

Anita leaned her head against the tree trunk. "And some are benevolent forest spirits that watch over the villagers."

The old woman shook her head. "Perhaps I am too worried." She patted Anita's cheek.

Anita laughed and moved away from the tree. "How about outside the estate? Did Gauri ever fall into a trance in the village or at a temple or at her own home?"

Muttacchi shook her head. "Only here as far as I know." She turned back toward the buildings. "She said here Bhagavati is angry."

Anita repeated the simple statement. "What do you think she meant by that?"

Again, Muttacchi shrugged.

"Was that her only explanation?"

Muttacchi rested her arm on Anita's shoulder and leaned into the younger woman. "It was not an explanation. It was information she shared with me. She told me one morning before she went for her bath that Bhagavati was angry here, not at me, but here on this land Bhagavati was angry." The idea of the deity being angry seemed to burden the old woman, and Anita felt the full weight not only of the old woman's body but of her emotions. Anita slipped her arm around the older woman and led her back to the house.

"Did it frighten you?" Anita asked.

"It worried me, of course." Muttacchi paused, kicking some leaves out of her path. "I cannot be frightened of the signs that the world is off kilter — I too think it is off kilter. But I was concerned — to be chosen to carry a message such as that means more than someone like Gauri understands at first."

Anita thought about this — Muttacchi was obviously seeing this as more about Gauri than about the estate. "What else did she say? Did she ever become more specific?"

"That was specific, for me." She started walking independently again.

"When was this, when she told you about Bhagavati being angry? Was it right after a trance?"

"She had not had a trance for days — it was early on in this business. She came to me, so calm, reserved. It is not her usual way. She is more often mischievous, but her demeanor, her words — I knew they came from Bhagavati. I went to the temple at once and arranged for a puja for harmony in the home. It was quiet for two or three weeks."

"And Gauri?"

"She has said nothing more about it. She does not consider it something to talk about. It is just something that has happened." Muttacchi moved to a chair near the veranda and lowered herself into it. "I am thirsty."

"She seemed to have a lot to say during

the exorcism," Anita said after motioning an order to Arun.

"Ah, yes, that."

"What did she say then?" Anita pulled up a chair and sat down. "I listened to Gauri's rantings during the ritual but didn't understood more than a word here and there. I took it as gibberish." Of course, she added to herself, I was watching what was happening to Gauri physically, more worried about her apparent pain and anguish than her incoherent babbling.

"Even though you spent much of your childhood in India, your mother neglected parts of your education," Muttacchi said. "That was Sanskrit."

"She knows Sanskrit? What did she say?"

"You know she doesn't, but when Bhagavati speaks, we repeat, and the language is kept pure."

"You understood it all, then? What did she say, or, rather, Bhagavati?"

"Things, unexpected things, strange things."

"Is this what Konan was warning you about? That Gauri might say things, offensive things?"

Muttacchi frowned and stared into the distance, as though recalling the moments in the temple. "Perhaps. But it was not so awful." Anita leaned forward, urging the old woman to continue. "Gauri used to be quite committed to the study of Shiva," she said. "She read her Shiva Purana nightly, but it was in a Malayalam translation. She recited bits of *slokas,* sacred verses, about Yama and the wrath of Shiva when his home is invaded — the Malayalam is very close to the Sanskrit in a case like this. Do you remember the story about how Ganapati got his elephant head?"

"Sure, every child knows that story." Anita leaned back in her chair and smiled. "Shiva and Parvati's son interrupted them while they were making love, and Shiva cut off his head in anger. Parvati was so distraught that Shiva promised he would give their son the first head that came along, and an elephant was the next creature to come along." Anita laughed quietly at the story. "It's a great story."

"It tells us something humorous about Ganapati, but also something about Shiva — how wrathful he can be even against his own family. It's true. Shiva is not to be trifled with."

Anita looked across the grounds toward the shrine to Bhairava, the most terrifying and wrathful aspect of Shiva, the form most feared by his devotees, with his necklace of skulls, snakes entwining his neck and hair, and the bloody fifth head of Brahma dangling from his hand. Secretly, Anita thought Gauri was brave to be willing to hear the call of Bhagavati, a female form of Shiva.

Later in the afternoon Anita led Anand around the property, repeating Muttacchi's list of sites where Gauri had fallen into a trance, telling him about the nature of her possessions and about the puja at the temple to exorcise the spirit taking her over and return Gauri to her usual state. When she was finished, it seemed to Anita that the land was permeated with the spirit of Bhagavati and her anger, as well as efforts to placate her.

"Right now I've about had my fill of pujas," Anita said as they turned down the path to the river. "We've had Gauri's puja at the temple, Gauri's daily puja at the kavu, the family priest's puja to purify the grounds after Bindu's attack, a puja for harmony, a puja for Bindu's recovery and another for Gauri, and I don't know how many others. The priests and flower sellers are doing well this month."

Anand laughed and followed her along the path.

"That's it, right there." Anita nodded to a

stick stuck in the ground. Even though she tried to be rational and matter-of-fact about the investigation, coming once again to the site of Bindu's assault sent a wave of anger and sorrow through her, as though the evil that had befallen the maidservant had settled onto the sandy spot, poisoning it for all time. "We call the hospital every hour asking about her. But there is no change. She is not dead and she is not alive. Only a coma."

Anand listened, then stood aside and studied the spot. He took a few steps, then looked toward the river and back toward the house.

"I had to mark the spot, just to keep myself oriented — I didn't want to think later that I had walked over it. It's so easy to forget where things happened, or who said what. I didn't want to start wondering and doubting myself. So there it is." Unconsciously perhaps, Anita moved away from the area and walked through the scrubland as she spoke.

"From your description of Bindu she hardly seems like someone who would be the object of an attack — she's rather innocuous." Anand rested his hands on his hips, perplexed, quiet. "Simple, innocent, as

Muttacchi said, inoffensive from the sounds of it."

"Sweet, really sweet." Anita sighed and felt the sorrow rise in her chest. "Muttacchi and I were talking earlier, and, well, I don't think whoever it was meant to attack Bindu. I think they were after Gauri."

"You think it was an accident?" Anand stood up, dusting off his pants from kneeling in the dirt. "From what you told me, it doesn't seem possible."

"Bindu doesn't usually spend the night here and work so early in the morning, but Muttacchi thought Gauri should stay home for a while, to recover."

"And Bindu didn't mind?"

"No, they're very close." Anita shook her head, remembering the two women together after the puja. "You should have seen them together — Gauri and Bindu — at the temple. They were so loving and caring toward each other. Like sisters. Each one holding up the other, brushing down each other's sari skirt, arranging the folds in the sun to get them to dry. Just sitting there with their arms around each other."

"What happened to them?"

Anita explained the way the assisting priest threw water on them at the end of the puja. "They both got drenched." Anita

171

started toward the river.

"In the temple?"

Anita paused, trying to catch the expression on his face. She nodded.

"Who else was there?"

"There were the two priests who did the puja, two students reading hymns, the old man in charge of bringing the water, me and Muttacchi, and Bindu and Gauri." Everyone else had left, she realized, as they arrived.

"Konan wasn't there?" Anand frowned, apparently intrigued by this absence.

"No, he wasn't. I thought it was odd, but no one else did." Anita shrugged. "I was still feeling rushed through the whole thing. He pushed for the ritual to be done soon — he was not recommending waiting, and Muttacchi is not a hurrying sort of person." Anita smiled at the thought of Muttacchi hustling off for business.

"What about afterwards, when you were leaving? Was anyone around — anyone who stood out?"

Anita frowned, surprised at the question, but thought back to that morning. "Not really, just the usual hangers-on outside, you know — the men hanging around hoping for work, or a meal, or just hanging."

"I think you're right about Bindu being

mistaken for Gauri, but not because they ran into her early in the morning on the path. They didn't know the difference between Bindu and Gauri."

"But —" Anita paused, thinking. "Of course, you're right. It makes perfect sense. Someone was after Gauri for something she had already seen, not something she might have seen right then. Gauri and Bindu looked the same when they came out of the temple — both were drenched after the puja. They stayed together like Siamese twins. And the next morning, instead of Gauri going to the river at her usual time, it was Bindu."

"Who wasn't supposed to be there. No one was supposed to be there, in fact. Gauri was supposed to be home recovering, but instead a maidservant was back at work, wandering around the estate as usual." Anand spoke directly to Anita.

"Muttacchi said Gauri was quoting the Shiva Purana during the exorcism, about Yama coming for her and Bhagavati being angry here, on the property. But she was speaking in Sanskrit." Anita moved slowly in a circle, taking in the buildings, the grounds, the kavu, the river, the land behind Anand, who was standing on the opposite side of the path. "After her very first trance

173

she told Muttacchi that she was afraid Bhairava didn't like her puja."

"Was she doing the puja for the kavu deity?"

"She was. She apparently adopted Bhairava, at least some of the time, and did the morning puja a few times a week."

"Whatever is behind Bindu's attack it's right here, and Gauri is the key."

Their eyes met, and Anita saw an intensity of thought in his eyes. Behind Anand was the family estate, a place she once loved for its tradition and privacy but that now seemed contaminated by evil and secrets she could barely imagine.

Anand pointed to the binoculars hung around Anita's neck. "What about those? You must have had some reason for wanting them."

She let her hands rest on the binoculars. "I just have this feeling that the answer is right under my nose, and I thought these might help me get a better sense of the area. I can't see much of the river, and I can't tell if anyone docked along here."

"Let's take a look," Anand said, heading toward the river. "Has Gauri been back since Bindu's attack?"

Anita shook her head. "Muttacchi won't let her come here — she's terrified something will happen to her. Gauri came to work here as a child, so Muttacchi feels responsible." At the top of the stone steps going down into the water Anita paused, looking up and down the river, before starting down. The warm water lapped at her ankles, then her calves. When she was up to her thighs, she put the binoculars to her eyes and scanned the riverbank east, along the edge of the kavu, up to a bend where the river widened and the bank grew steep.

"Anything?" Anand asked standing on the top step.

Anita shook her head and swung the binoculars to the opposite shore.

"That looks much more promising if only because there's more building going on over there." Anand followed the sound of a honking lorry moving along a road on the opposite shore, the shrieks of children playing, a dog whining. Anita lowered the glasses.

"But why would anyone want to attack someone here?" She glanced at him, over her shoulder. "The way Bindu looked, Anand, that assault was vicious — I'll never forget it." Anita felt a little chill run through her as her mind went back to the moment of discovery.

"Anita." Anand called softly, then rested his hand on her shoulder, bent over and gently placed his hand beneath her elbow. "Come on. Let's look around some more." Immediately she relaxed.

"Thanks," she whispered as he drew her back up the steps.

They walked back toward the buildings, then turned to pass in front of the kavu, where Anita stopped to replace some blossoms on the small stone altar at the entry.

Anand peered in, but was careful not to pass beyond the altar. "Is that Bhairava?"

Anita nodded.

"May I?" Anand stretched out his hand for the binoculars, held them up to his eyes. For a full ten minutes he walked along the edge of the sacred grove, studying the interior of the kavu, its wild unkempt mass of trees and lianas and shrubs and ground cover all tangled together, the birds flying in and out almost unseen, the lizards and snakes and rodents stalking through the leaves and branches, safe in their own world, safer than they could ever be anywhere else.

"What is it?" Anita asked, drawing closer.

"I'm not sure — maybe nothing." He handed the glasses back to her.

"I used to crawl around the border when I was a child, fascinated by the life inside." Anita named some of the plants, catching sight of a gorgeous butterfly, its royal blue

176

wings tipped with black. A male paradise-flycatcher rose up above the trees, his long tail fathers twisting like lace in the soft air while he snapped at flies. "It's our duty, keeping this kavu."

"The attack won't affect it," Anand said.

Anita felt enormously relieved — she hadn't realized how much this fear had been gnawing at her. "Good," she whispered. "I think of Gauri as a generous person even if she is difficult sometimes," Anita continued. "Actually, I thought everything she did was good for the family, but no one else seemed to see it that way. Konan didn't seem very warm towards her either."

"Is there some disagreement between them?" Anand asked.

"I don't know. I asked her something about Konan, before the puja," Anita said, "and she wasn't enthusiastic about him. She was diplomatic — after all, he's Muttacchi's astrologer — but she cooled at the mention of him." They started walking across the scrubland.

"Maybe that's why he didn't go," Anand said.

"What do you mean? If Konan were present during the exorcism, Gauri might say something that would embarrass him?"

"I think you have another question within

this one." Anand took the binoculars from her again and studied the upper branches in the kavu.

"You mean, why wasn't Konan present? Yes, I see your point. Perhaps it was safer for Konan not to be there," Anita said. "Perhaps Konan has done something to displease Bhagavati, and Gauri senses it. He would not want anyone to hear what might be said."

"And that's a good reason not to be present." Anand's lower lip turned down as he mulled this over.

"I want to know why Konan was not present, and why he was in such a hurry for this exorcism to take place," Anita said.

"Perhaps that is him?" Anand said, nodding toward the edge of the parking area.

"No, no. That's Kedar. He's the businessman for the estate — he determines the harvesting, who buys, and the rest of it. I'm surprised to see him here today."

At the edge of the parking area Kedar was listening to Sett, who spoke with his hands flapping in front of his bony, hunched-over chest.

Kedar nodded and slipped a pencil into a tiny cloth bag hanging on a string around his neck. As Anita approached, Sett turned away and walked back to the house.

"I have heard the news from Sett," Kedar said, unconsciously taking a few steps backward toward the road. "It is unclean, that spot." Kedar eyed Anand, who stood apart, walking among the trees.

"You mean where Bindu was attacked?" Anita said.

"The very same." He lowered his eyes as he spoke. "There. You can go around there, in the trees on the other path." Anita looked in the direction he pointed, west, away from the kavu and the path. "It is safe and available."

"That's not part of another property, then?"

"No, no. The land goes quite far in odd configurations." He nodded to the land behind her as he turned to walk to the parking area. "Sett has told me the news. Amma does not want to review business decisions today; now I understand why."

"Before you go I want to ask about the kavu. I'm confused about some things." She drew him away from the house.

"What are they, these confusions?"

"What can you tell me about the trees in there?" Anita asked, pointing to the kavu.

Kedar studied her, lowered his eyes, and turned to look at the kavu. "It is kavu, you know. Sacred grove."

"Yes, I know, but I was wondering about what was in there. You manage all the harvesting on the estate, and I've noticed that both kavus seem smaller than what I remember from when I was a child."

"You were smaller when you were a child and the forest would seem larger. It is only natural." He studied her as he spoke.

"I was just wondering if you have been doing harvesting, that's all."

Kedar tensed, but he shut his eyes, and seemed to force himself to relax. "Amma would never allow such a thing. The kavu is never to be touched. You are aware of this." He coughed, as though warning her he would continue to speak. "Even if Amma gave permission for one to do such, I would never be the one to do it. First, I object to the violation. Second, I am not of this community. The kavu is sacred for this family. It is for others to enter and make such changes." He turned an accusing eye on her, and Anita felt scalded by his expression.

"I see." She softened her voice, worried if she offended him she'd lose any chance of getting any real information. "So even if you saw a plant in there that might be important for the ayurveda doctor around here, you wouldn't get it for Muttacchi?"

Kedar turned slightly away, his head back, his chin up. "Certainly not." He blinked once, and relaxed. "But such a thing is not necessary. The kavus hold many old and rare plants, but the birds also serve us. They are collecting seeds and spreading them, and we are finding throughout the estate evidence of their work."

"I didn't consider that. Do you gather these?"

"Even so." He flashed a smile, more to himself than Anita, before composing himself. "I am finding and locating and transplanting. Some are kept, and some are sold. The kavu repays us."

"I should have thought of that." Anita paused.

"You do not live here, you do not observe. The most obvious is least seen." He settled into a satisfied smile, as though he might be an aspiring Buddha.

Anand coughed and approached. Anita completed the introductions before Anand also pointed to the kavu. "It is very dense here — denser than most, it seems. Does that affect the timing or quantity of blooming?"

The question seemed to confuse Kedar and he squinted at Anand, as if to bring him into focus. Then apparently deciding the question was not worthy of serious consideration, he arched a brow and shook his head. "All is as it should be."

"So, it doesn't mean anything that certain plants haven't produced any blooms this year," Anand said. The color drained from Kedar's thin face and he glanced quickly toward the kavu.

"The kavu is always untouched. If a plant does not bloom, it is the matter of Bhairava, not of us out here." Kedar began to back away again, then stopped. "I shall take this matter up with Amma when she pleases. This will be a matter for close attention." He pulled a pencil and notebook from the small bag hanging around his neck, made a note, and stowed both again in the pouch. "Going."

Anita knew he usually came by bus, and he would have to wait at least half an hour for another one, but he moved as though he heard one coming and didn't want to miss it.

TEN

"Did you really notice something wrong with plants in the kavu?" Anita asked Anand after Kedar had reached the road and turned toward the bus stop. They could see him moving through the trees, his white mundu flickering in and out of sight like a shy man stuttering when he would rather not speak at all.

"I expected to see certain vines in flower, and I didn't," Anand said, walking toward the car. "Sometimes the kavu is so dense that some plants don't flourish — they don't flower if they're deprived of light."

Anita followed him to the car and leaned against the bonnet. "He didn't offer that as a reason, did he?"

"He acted as though I were accusing him of plundering the kavu," Anand said.

"Interesting, isn't it?" Anita crossed her arms and frowned. "Everyone seems threatened over what's happened in the last few days. Lata and Sett argue all the time, bickering — they don't like each other at all, something I never noticed before. Veej is hostile, and I feel like he's watching me all the time. Muttacchi is withdrawn but I feel like she's waiting for something — for something to become known. And Bindu's father — he told me about a visit Gauri made to the boatyard." Anita repeated the conversation. "I didn't particularly like the looks of one of the boatmen, either, but I didn't sense anything more. He just looked surly."

"Do you think all this goes back to Gauri's trances?" Anand leaned against the car, his arm resting on the roof as he gazed around him. The afternoon had grown quiet; it was the time when most people took a nap, or read, or picked up a small project such as mending, before returning to work later in the afternoon.

"That's a good question. I wonder if Muttacchi asked Konan about more than just Gauri's trances." Anita turned to Anand, who nodded, and opened the door for her. "I think it's time to talk to the man who started all this."

Anita pointed to a dirt road, and Anand turned off. The car rocked around potholes and over ruts. She leaned forward, peering through the windshield reading house numbers and names. After passing through the new development the road widened, flattened, and ran alongside a marsh slowly thickening with rotting tree trunks, dead branches, and other debris. Beyond this appeared a second set of houses, but these were much more modest, without compound walls and second stories, the houses of laborers and small office workers. At the end was an old house with a new second story that consisted of only one room on a large flat roof, leaving the rest of the roof as open terrace.

"That's it," Anita said, pointing to the house. "Konan talked about putting on a new room. I thought he meant a second floor like a second floor, but he meant he was literally adding a room on the roof."

Anand drove onto the shoulder and let the car drift to a halt. "Why didn't you just call him?" he asked. "You could have asked him over the phone. He has a mobile, doesn't he?"

"Everyone has a mobile, even the guy selling coconut milk along the road with only a pile of coconuts and a bicycle to his name." She studied the house.

"It might have been more discreet," Anand

said. Anita gave him a long look.

"Violence is not discreet, Anand, and neither am I. Besides, I wanted to see where he lives — get a sense of who he is. Muttacchi has relied on him for years, but I wasn't comfortable with him when he came to the house to talk about Gauri. Everything he suggested seemed so extreme — sending Gauri away to the north for three months, the treatment, the exorcism and then rushing into it. It all seemed too hurried and unsettling."

"Yes, I see what you mean." Anand checked the parking brake, then leaned into the corner made by the seat and door. The neighborhood was quiet, every sound absorbed by the trees and brush.

"And then he wasn't at the exorcism either. I thought he'd be there, to make sure everything went well." Anita began to chew her lower lip.

"And Muttacchi didn't seem to mind?"

Anita shook her head. "You don't know her. She'd never criticize Konan — she's relied on him too long." She pushed open the door. "I'd better get on with it." She gave him a smile and climbed out of the car. "I won't be long."

The chickens scattered when Anita stepped over the short sticks stuck in the entry and approached the house. Even though it was newly whitewashed, with blue trim on the windows and door, the house was simple, with neat plaster patches dotting the lower half of the exterior walls. By the side of the house stood a new motor scooter, a helmet hanging from its handlebars. Anita tried to recall the ages of Konan's children — she vaguely recollected they were grown and out on their own — and wondered if this was a sign one was visiting.

A woman in her forties appeared in the doorway, called back over her shoulder, and stepped out onto the stoop to offer a welcome. She was quick to smile when she heard Muttacchi's name, and she drew Anita to a plastic chair, inviting her to sit. Then the woman went inside to call her husband.

"How welcome you are?" Konan emerged from the side of the house in a lungi and an undershirt. He took the stool placed there for him and sat on it cross-legged. Anita quickly reassured him that her family was well, the household was well, and she was just pursuing a minor question. "How long before we know if Gauri is cured?"

Konan pulled a face. "Gauri is a strange one. If she has been cured and returned to her usual state, then she will never have another trance. She will be amenable to Amma, and she will follow orders and not make trouble."

Anita stifled a laugh. "I don't think Gauri has ever been like that."

"Ah, this is so." Konan sighed, but it seemed to Anita he also winced, as though Gauri was a particularly touchy subject.

"So, if she has no trance for two or three months, she is cured. But if she has a trance after that, is it the same possession or another one?"

"Another one?" The question startled him and he peered at her, concerned and worried.

"Yes, another possession. Is it possible that she's now prone to calls from Bhagavati or from any other deity? Maybe she'll have trances all the time now, and the new ones won't be connected to the ones she just had." Anita thanked Konan's wife as she held out a cup of milky coffee. From inside the house Anita could hear voices on a television, rattling and bouncing through the air in a singsong movie speech.

"Gauri is a difficult person, so easily out of sorts with her better nature." Konan spoke robotically, his eye on Anita.

"I guess what I'm wondering is if this was

to be expected? Is my family in a period of problems and troubles? Did you foresee this happening?" Anita tipped her head to one side, to soften the barb of the question. Konan certainly couldn't like having his basic skill as an astrologer challenged. His eyes flashed at her, but then he lowered his head and began to speak.

"Of course, we are working closely together, Amma and I, on the matters of good periods and bad periods and the necessity of preparing for them and averting difficulties." He swung his head back and forth, which Anita now recognized as a sign he was not entirely telling the truth. "These things that happen do not happen to Amma, but around her. This is significant difference."

"Yes, I guess you're right." Anita finished her coffee, thanked him for explaining things to her, and stood up. "That's a lovely addition you've made. It must be especially valuable in the hot season, when you can sleep up there and get some breeze."

"Yes, yes, we are very pleased with it." Konan smiled, but Anita didn't miss the impatient look his wife gave him before she collected the coffee glasses and took them inside. "How do you like your motor scooter?"

Konan shrugged. "A man must reach his clients." The effort to be nonchalant failed — he couldn't conceal his delight when he looked at the shiny blue machine. Anita took a step closer to it, leaning over to read the sticker advertising the make and model. The scooter was shiny and new, not old and well cared for.

"I've been thinking of getting one. Are you satisfied with this brand?" Anita walked around the scooter, touching the shiny orange and black helmet, which was also clearly new, the pillion seat, and the handlebars. She leaned over and noted the mileage — barely three thousand kilometers — but more than it would have been if he'd purchased it a week ago.

"You have no need," Konan said like a stern parent. "You have a car and driver from Hotel Delite, isn't it? This is business, not frivolity."

Anita almost expected him to start telling her how important he was.

Anita slammed the car door, and Anand headed back down the road. He had turned the car around while he was waiting, taken a short walk down the road and back, and returned just as Anita was stepping over the short sticks at the entry.

"Well?" Anand asked without looking at her after they left the little house behind.

"He has a new room on the roof, probably less than he meant to build, a new motor scooter probably three or four months old, and a television." She slumped down in the seat thinking hard.

"And?" Anand said.

"And," Anita said. "He's deeply in debt, for one thing."

"Maybe he inherited some money."

Anita gave Anand a look that told him just what she thought of this idea. "His entire family is poor; he's always borrowing little sums from us. And he's a gambler who never wins. I don't believe he won big and didn't tell Muttacchi about it. No, these new things mean he's taken on a lot of debt, or he's doing something he shouldn't be doing." She glanced over at Anand.

"And for another thing?" Anand asked, swinging the car around a corner.

"Why would a man with a motor scooter hire an autorickshaw to visit his most lucrative client?" Anita turned to the countryside passing by. "That's what I've got to figure out."

ELEVEN

Anita prided herself on her observation skills, but right now she was racking her brain trying to recall every single detail she could of the man who had driven Konan in the autorickshaw to Muttacchi's house the day he came to discuss Gauri and ended up recommending an exorcism puja. Anand pulled over onto the shoulder when they reached the outskirts of the small village.

"I'd know him if I saw him. But that isn't much help, is it?" Anita rolled down the window and rested her arm on the door. "He has to be somewhere around here. I'll just have to start asking."

Anand walked around the side of the car and opened her door. "And while you do that, I think I'll make a few calls." He pulled a mobile from a case on his waistband and flipped it open.

"If you find out more than I do I'll be jealous." She watched him punch in a number, thought about how glad she was to have his friendship, and turned to the village shops.

Anita studied the village center before her — a row of shops on each of the four corners of the crossroads, all of them open though customers were scarce at the moment. She knew things would pick up as soon as villagers were ready for the evening shopping, and she decided that now was as good a time as any to question the shopkeepers. She walked over to a coffee wholesaler and climbed up the three steep steps into the cool interior. The minute he saw her on the platform, the owner flipped a switch behind him. A ceiling fan began to turn and a row of lights flickered on. The owner greeted her politely but skeptically. Anita rummaged through the various packets of coffee and selected one with a medium price.

"Yes, this is good," he assured her as he began to wrap the plastic bag in day-old newspaper, which he then tied with thin string.

"I thought I'd take it back for my family. They especially like this brand, as I recall." She walked around the shop while the owner took her money to the cash register. "An autorickshaw driver mentioned this place to me first, some weeks ago. Perhaps you know him?" Anita described him, down to his oddly shaped leg. She was rewarded with a piercing look and a firm shake of the head. She thanked him and headed back to the street.

By the time she had visited almost a dozen shops, she had gained a large cloth bag, which contained her various purchases — coffee, cupcakes, a new spatula, a dozen brightly colored plastic bangles, a small envelope of fresh peppercorns, a chit for making a new choli in an especially vibrant pink (that she would never wear), and a spool of white thread. At the newsagent she examined a number of magazines and settled on a wall calendar for the current year. The salesman began to wrap the item in newspaper.

"That's all right," Anita said. "I can slip it in here. Someone mentioned to me that the Dipika calendar was one of the best."

"Yes, the auto driver." The owner slipped a rubber band around the calendar and handed it to her.

"Hmm. My fame precedes me." Anita managed to smile but let the smile fade when he continued to glare at her. "So you know who I'm looking for."

"You are looking for an auto driver."

"Do you know who he is?"

"Everyone knows who he is if he walks that way you described."

"I was wondering about that. I usually get a lot of discussion and fussing when I ask a shopkeeper something because they always want to help if they can — it means another happy customer." She slid the calendar in among her other parcels. "But not this time. Who is he?"

"If you need a service, you need only ask." He handed a newspaper to another customer and took the rupee notes.

"Such as?"

"But you do not need such a service." He began organizing his stacks of newspapers and magazines, calendars, and small Malayalam-language schoolbooks. "Why are you asking for him?"

"How do you know I don't need such a service?"

He looked along the road toward the white car and Anand leaning against the bonnet. "A very nice car."

"It's not mine."

"But it could be."

Anita studied the car, then turned back to the shopkeeper. She wasn't quite sure how he meant it — that she could marry Anand and then own the car, that she could buy one of her own, that she was the kind of person who might own such a car. She hated ambiguity — it left her off balance. "It could be, but it's not."

"But you do not deny you could buy it without trouble, yes?"

"No one buys anything without trouble," Anita said, and left it at that. Her finances were not his business. "Can you tell me his name?"

The newsagent made change for another customer and tidied up another stack of newspapers. "A strange woman comes into our village and visits someone and then comes here to ask questions. Why did you not ask the friend you visited?"

"How do you know I visited anyone?" Anita's mind was spinning; she didn't want to turn around to see if the road to Konan's house was visible from where she stood, but she was guessing it wasn't. She gambled. "Did you see me going to a house?"

"No." He spoke without looking at her, his attention on his cash box.

"Well, then. If you know the driver's name and won't share it, there must be a reason. Is there a reason?"

The newsagent's dark eyes grew darker and he glared down at her, then a sly smile broke over his face. "It can do no harm for you to know his name. It is Mootal."

"Where does he live?"

"He lives other side, but he is not there now."

"No? Where is he?"

"Away." The agent reached for a glass of coffee and surveyed the street from his small shop, which was really no more than a large wooden closet set onto the sandy shoulder of the road. When he was finished drinking, he set down the glass and again gave her his attention. "He is rarely at home — his business keeps him out and about. You should not go there anyway. If you are in need of funds, he will come to you. Shall I send him to you?"

"I'll think about it." Anita unconsciously took a step back. She had learned what she wanted, but it wasn't exactly what she was expecting.

"Perhaps a telephone call you are preferring?" The newsagent leaned over his papers, resting on his elbow; he smelled of garlic and coconut milk.

Anita shook her head. "I prefer to negotiate in person." She picked up her cloth bag and headed back to Anand and the car.

Half an hour later Anand pulled up in front of Muttacchi's house and parked the car. He shut off the ignition, rested his arm along the back of the seat, and turned to Anita.

"It gave me the creeps," she said.

"Aside from bruising your ego," Anand added.

"All right, so I'm not terribly discreet when I'm looking for someone."

Anand laughed.

"All the shopkeepers knew who I was looking for, but it sure took them long enough to decide whether or not to tell me." Anita pushed the cloth bag away from her and turned in her seat to face Anand, drawing up her knees.

"They were deciding whether or not to trust you," Anand said.

"Possibly," Anita said. "But usually if I ask someone about who can do this or that, I get a quick answer."

"You don't look like you need a loan from someone like Mootal." He leaned back against the car door.

"Or maybe they didn't know him. Maybe he's new to the area."

"That could be," Anand said. "But I wonder if Konan would go to a new money-lender, someone who hadn't established his bona fides. That would be risky."

"I guess you're right." Anita slouched lower in her seat. She felt like she was hitting a wall with every idea.

"Besides, if you did need a loan, would you go to someone like Mootal, an ordinary village moneylender?"

"Why not? Not that I've ever gone to any moneylender."

"The rates, for one thing. His clients are villagers who need cash, small amounts. He makes his money on the interest. He probably charges ten percent a month, just in interest. And then when you're flush, you pay off the principal all at once."

"I might not want my family and friends to know I need money," Anita countered. "I could be someone who gambles, and I'm ashamed, and I don't want anyone to know."

"Very possible," Anand said. "But why go so far from your home territory? Moneylenders can be discreet."

"I've tapped out the ones in my area?" She waited for him to reply to this.

"Reasonable. And you're willing to pay the rate to cover the trouble you're in."

"Ten percent." Anita shook her head. "No wonder everyone's so poor in this country."

"Not everyone," Anand said. "Men like Mootal are doing pretty well. They count on people like you — willing to pay a high interest rate over a long period to have these things. It's not about food and medicine anymore. No one's pawning a ration card these days for food."

"You mean I'm as likely a customer as anyone else?"

"Especially now."

"I wonder how much Konan owes him?" Anita pulled out a small notebook from her purse and opened to a blank page; she fished out a pen and began jotting down some figures. "Motor scooter. Television. How much do you think that room on the roof cost him?"

Anand suggested a few figures. "Add the new refrigerator."

"How'd you know about that?"

"While I was out walking I got a good look at the back of the place. They built a small extension just to house the refrigerator, I think. At least that's what it looks like."

"Oh, brother. So Konan is deep into debt to Mootal. That must be why Mootal drove him to Muttacchi's house — to make sure he collected whatever was paid him."

"Did she pay him?" Anand asked.

"No, actually, she didn't." Anita lowered the notebook and tapped the pen against her lips. "She didn't give him any money that day."

"Did he ask for any?"

Anita shook her head. "Not that I could

see. I don't know what the usual arrangement is, but no money changed hands. That's odd, isn't it? There is usually an envelope of money for anyone who comes — it's all very discreet, but it's there."

"And he wasn't at the temple, was he?" Anand leaned forward and took the notebook from Anita's hands, scanning the figures. "So he couldn't get the money directly from her then."

Anita tried to remember what she had seen. Yes, Muttacchi had given an envelope thick with bills to the priest. That had been all out in the open. But had she also left behind money to be given to Konan? Anita didn't think so. "I can see them all standing there, doing what they were doing, but at the end I only remember Muttacchi giving one envelope to the priest. I don't remember her leaving anything to be given to Konan."

"I wonder if she's paid him yet for his counsel." Anand pushed open the door and climbed out; Anita did the same.

"She must have paid him somehow," Anita said.

"If not in cash, then how was he paid?"

"You don't think he recommended the exorcism puja because he'd make much more money from it, but she didn't have enough money in hand to pay him, do you?"

Anita asked.

"Do you?"

Anita shook her head, recalling the astrologer's visit to the house. "No, no, I don't think money was the reason for recommending the exorcism. And I don't think Muttacchi's broke."

"I had the same thought. But Muttacchi is not broke." Anand paused. "I checked."

"You what?" Anita felt herself bristle. Had he actually gone into her family's finances?

"I have surprised you, it seems."

Anita felt herself flush from confusion, surprise, and perhaps even anger. "It feels — I don't know — invasive."

"Well, I learned this from you. Check everything and everyone."

"Those phone calls?" Anita grimaced.

"Hmm. To a few friends with the right computer access." Anand paused, and Anita knew he was waiting for her to work this out. Well, yes, he had surprised her, and yes, she had wondered if perhaps Muttacchi was having problems, so yes, he was right. But she didn't like it one little bit.

"Just warn me next time," Anita said. "But yes, we have to check everything out. So Muttacchi isn't broke, and Konan didn't want the exorcism to make money."

"Despite his obvious debts." Anand

slipped his hands into his pockets, and waited.

"No, I think he recommended the exorcism to control Gauri. She knows something, she's seen something, and she doesn't realize it. If she doesn't have another possession, and stays away from the estate, she'll be all right — at least for a while."

"And if she does have another trance?"

Anita winced. "I think she's made an enemy in Konan whether she has another possession or not. Which means we don't have much time to figure this out." Anita paused. "Why does he care if she has possessions at Muttacchi's house?"

Anand leaned against the white car. A light breeze rustled the leaves overhead, and the dappled shadows shimmered on the ground. The heat that was transforming the new urban landscapes was merely a topic for the evening news for those resting in the shade of hundred-year-old trees. "What are you smiling at now?"

"You," Anita said. "In your white slacks and white shirt, with the white car behind you, you look like an image of Kalki come to destroy the world at the end of the Kali Yuga and restore the Dharma, duty and justice."

Anand's mouth twitched. "I'll have the car painted red."

"I can't help it," Anita said with a laugh as she sat down on a nearby bench and stretched out her toe to tap against the shiny silver bumper while she reordered her thoughts.

"There is something we haven't looked at yet, also, something I've let slip by," Anita said, pulling off her dupatta from around her neck, shaking it out, and draping it around her shoulders. She could feel the evening settling in. Her blood had grown so thin over the years from living in the tropics that she wondered if she'd ever be able to live in a cold climate. She dreaded the thought of visiting Delhi in the winter months. It had been years since she had spent a whole year in the States visiting her parents; she couldn't imagine living through an entire winter again.

"Your cousin Surya?" Anand nodded. "Yes, that's been on my mind also."

"I want to know where she is and why she couldn't at least call us to tell us what happened, but all that seems unimportant compared to Bindu and Gauri." Anita wrapped the dupatta tight around her shoulders, then draped it around a second time. She liked the feeling of sitting inside a shawl, with the warm fabric hanging over her shoulders down to her waist, covering her hands. She felt shrouded and concealed, a way of expressing outwardly her private inner nature. "But in answer to the obvious implicit question, no, she was never this rude. She is a bit scattered. We were all a bit scattered when we were younger — we really were very indulged here, but not in a way that would have let her think she could just not show up without telling anyone. We were expected to be dutiful." Anita looked across the front of the house to a small shed where a red motorbike was propped up in the shade. The heartfelt anticipation had been replaced by disappointment and resignation, and someone had kindly moved the motorbike out of Muttacchi's sight.

"So you're thinking what I'm thinking?" Anand smiled down at her, the familiar warmth in his eyes, his slight amusement at her whenever she got caught up in some mystery involving her family or friends.

For a moment Anita felt herself flush, and was doubly grateful for the evening darkening around them. No, she thought, you don't know exactly what I'm thinking, which is probably good for me. I'd be embarrassed. "I think so," she said, answering the question that was intended. "Something must have happened that we know nothing about. I'm worried. I need to find out if she's all right."

Anand sat down on the bench beside her, then moved closer till their bodies touched. She was grateful for the dark. "I can check flights if you want."

"You can?"

He laughed and nodded. "All my pals are in the same line of work — we work on every computer system in the country. We could bring down government if we wanted. We could make paupers out of Tata investors, start World War III, redraw the maps of the world."

"I sure hope your ego is under control."

Anand laughed again. "My ego is very under control." He squeezed her hand. "I shall find out if she got on a plane and if she got off anywhere in the world."

"And to think that all I can come up with is a bus schedule."

"You can always pump the servants for information," Anand said.

"My favorite pastime." Anita reached for her purse. "Is that your mobile or mine?" She pulled out her mobile, opened it, and heard the familiar voice of Auntie Meena. When the other woman was finished, Anita barely had a chance to say goodbye before the call ended. She flipped the phone shut.

"What is it this time? A hotel inspector who wants a bribe? No water? No guests? Too many guests?"

"Just one guest in particular — the tour guide, Sophie." Anita sighed and dropped the mobile into her purse. "This is where my dark side starts rumbling, and I want to sabotage the entire hotel, ruin its reputation, drive away all the guests, shut the place down. But then I'd end up with no place to live."

"Or you and Auntie Meena would be sharing a flat in Trivandrum," Anand said.

Anita groaned. "I'd better leave first thing in the morning."

TWELVE

The early morning stillness was almost perfect — the clean smells of the air blending with the early morning warmth, in near total silence. Anita pulled open the cottage door, lifting it to minimize its creaking, and stepped onto the veranda. She hated to leave the estate, its serenity and beauty, at such a moment, but she had promised Auntie Meena. Resigned, Anita pulled out a chair and sat down at the small table.

Anita lifted the red-plaid cloth off the plate, ready for breakfast — warm *puttu* and a bowl of chickpea curry. She marveled at how perfectly rounded the tubelike form of rice and coconut was — Lata was an amazing cook. Anita reached for the hot coffee first — she was still tired, but the drink would invigorate her. Despite the hot breakfast, no one else seemed to be around. Anita heard nothing from the kitchen, though a shaft of light fell onto the veranda and splayed on the courtyard.

Anita cocked her head to listen, her attention more on her meal than anything else. When she looked up Sett was walking toward her. When he saw Anita watching him, he nodded, moved his small cloth bag from one hand to the other, and turned toward the servants' quarters. He must have been bathing farther up the river, Anita thought as she pressed the remaining curry and puttu into a tight little ball and popped it into her mouth.

An hour later Anita confronted her aunt in Hotel Delite. "You really must stop getting so worked up," Anita said. "Joseph almost knocked my brains out with his wild driving." She followed her aunt into the office. Meena closed the door behind her, crossed the room, and closed the door to the registration desk also. "Well, that's a first," Anita said. "I didn't even think that door worked."

"This is not the time for frivolity. This matter is most serious, Anita." Meena extricated a linen handkerchief from her choli and patted her face with it.

"I can see that." Anita pulled out a chair and sat down. A tray of tea things occupied the center of the table. She noted the sleeping mat rolled up in the corner, the pillow on a chair. "Have you been in here all night?"

Meena lowered herself into a seat, as though she were even older than Muttacchi. "I have indeed. You do not know my distress. I didn't dare leave the office."

"You'd better start at the beginning." Anita pushed away the tea, just now realizing that there might be more going on than she thought.

"This tour lady has come three, perhaps four years in a row. Always she is coming this month, with very specific requirements. We are accommodating. She is most appreciative, it seems to me. Good tips, no complaints, always adequate notice of bookings."

"Is it the tour guide Sophie you are talking about? How is she different this year?"

"This year she is arriving unhappy. She is saying she has heard the rooms are no longer as clean, the food is no longer as good, the staff is no longer as honest."

Anita swore softly. She had observed ordinary people turn into monsters when something didn't go their way, finding offense in a wastebasket not being emptied, dangerous neglect in a balcony that has no screen to block crows, fraud in failing to provide three fresh towels daily for a single room. But to accuse the hotel staff of dishonesty? Anita felt sick.

"I have done everything — redoing the rooms, giving free meals, calling back old staff — some too old to work any longer, but calling them still." Meena paused and ran her hand over her face again. Her skin was glistening and pink with the stress. "I am ready to throw them out."

"As well you should be, Auntie."

"But she is threatening to sue if we do not deliver the tour as promised." Meena leaned back in her chair and closed her eyes. "I have spent hours looking through the reservations. I can find no tours promised, but she is saying that the tour you, Anita, gave them last year of some temples is promised for this group every year."

"What tour?" Anita threw up her hands. When she saw her aunt's pained look, she quickly leaned forward and tapped her forefinger gently on her aunt's knee. "Listen to me. It doesn't matter, Auntie. I'll take them wherever they want to go — Trivandrum, Kollam, Kanya Kumari — it doesn't matter to me. And then, when they leave, we'll never let them book in here again."

"Nothing is the same now," Meena said, rubbing her eyes. Anita was afraid the other woman would start to cry from sheer exhaustion. "Before, nice foreigners would come and stay and swim and eat and pay and go. Now they come and harangue and complain. And there are more of them. And the ones from the boat! They are even worse because they cannot go back to the cruise ship any time for rest and safe water."

"Lots of change, Auntie, lots of change." Anita tried to smile reassuringly, but she too thought some of the tourism business was getting out of hand, wearing down even the hardiest of the hoteliers. "She'll be gone soon, and then you never have to deal with her again."

"This tour and one more, I am thinking," Meena said, looking glum. She wiped her eyes.

"You've really had a horrible night, Auntie. But don't give it another thought. I'll talk to this Sophie at breakfast." She glanced at her watch. "It's seven thirty. When did you promise them breakfast?"

"I have told her no one can take food before eight o'clock, the usual time, just as you said. Then I had to hide in my office. But she is already in the parlor reading the newspaper." Meena sighed and held back a tear. "I am so tired and so grateful, Anita. You are like my own daughter."

■ ■ ■ ■

Anita turned over the brochure and pointed to a tall temple *gopura* towering over the countryside. The middle-aged woman, her long blonde hair piled high on her head, leaned forward less than an inch, gazed at the brochure for a moment, then reclined in her chair.

"I don't want to go so far as Suchindram. Yes, it is very impressive, but my people are tired. They want something closer to the hotel. Didn't you show us some interesting features in this neighborhood last year?"

That was exactly what Anita had been trying to recall for the last half hour while she turned over brochure after brochure in an effort to organize a satisfactory tour and watched Sophie's expression remain unchanged. "There's nothing around here but little temples, most closed to non-Hindus, and as for beaches, other than the ones here at Kovalam, just some beaches where only the fishermen work."

"What about that one with all the lovely painted figures over the gate?"

"Most of them have painted figures," Anita pointed out.

"It's by a river, on the way to Trivandrum.

213

On a dirt lane away from the highway."

"Ah, yes." Anita named a small temple with unusual carvings, and then paused to wonder when Sophie had noticed this, because she was sure she hadn't taken anyone there last year.

"Yes, yes, that is exactly what you showed us last time." Sophie stood up. "That's what my group wants, that temple, the beaches, all those things you showed us before, although . . ." She leaned out the parlor window to look down at the terrace where the low murmur of voices deep in conversation over food was regularly drowned out by the crashing waves. "Some are inclined to spend all their time at the beach. It is very lovely so I can understand this." She let her gaze drift along the shore, perhaps drawn by a pair of goats working their way across the rocks to the next hotel in search of food. But then she turned to Anita. "All right. We will go in one hour and return for an early lunch."

Surprised at the abruptness of Sophie's decision, Anita watched her go, then she too went to the window and looked down at the diners. Sophie's tour members seemed well settled for a long and leisurely breakfast, judging by the tray one of the waiters was juggling as he tried to serve a number of plates. The goats bleated, and Anita watched them settle on a clump of grass. In the opposite direction the cruise liner lay at anchor, and a catamaran — the simplest of boats that was no more than four split logs tied together, more canoe than boat, not the least bit watertight though seaworthy — carrying two men skidded toward the shore and disappeared. But Anita knew where it was landing — on a small beach regularly flooded during the monsoon season. She sat in the window, wondering how someone got to be like Sophie, and vowing she would never personally find out.

"The only thing I can recall," Anita later said to Aunt Meena as the two women stood in the doorway watching Joseph supervise the driver of a second car, dusting out the back seat in preparation for the area tour, "is taking some woman to the ancient Pallava sculptures nearby after she missed the bus for the tour to Kanya Kumari."

"Does it matter? At least Sophie seems happier." Meena looked as glum as when Anita first saw her an hour earlier. "It is a relief."

"Well, let's get it over with. Where is everyone?" Anita stepped into the sunshine as Sophie came clumping down the lane.

"I had to purchase sunscreen." Sophie held up a small paper bag and swung it in front of her. "Are we all ready?"

Sophie and two other women piled into the back of the hotel car and Anita joined Joseph in front, wondering as she did so what had happened to the large group of foreign tourists who simply had to have a local tour by Anita. Her camera hung around her neck, and Joseph gave her several quick glances begging for reassurance as they set off, climbing the road to the highway. A smile pasted on her face, Anita turned around to face the back seat and begin what she hoped would be interesting enough to keep the troops in line but not so interesting that they'd ask question after question and prolong this tedious trip.

After an hour Anita had driven them past two modest bungalows (brief tour of one, thanks to the caretaker) designed by a famous architect, recently deceased and completely unheard of by all three women, and a small family temple not yet abandoned but so little used that anyone could walk in and stare at the delicate wood carvings, the slatted windows, the carved stone slabs.

"And this is the temple," Anita said, waving to a tall entrance with brightly painted figures atop the gateway at the end of a long dirt lane. Joseph drove into the courtyard and parked under a tree. Anita and the other women piled out and walked toward the temple entrance. The compound was empty except for a few beggars and almost silent except for the occasional conversation drifting through an office window. The highway sounds were dulled.

Anita had arranged for a temple employee to meet them and take them around the temple, explaining the iconography, temple history, and anything else that came to mind. After that, the women would be invited to enjoy a cup of tea and then a tour of the outbuildings, where artisans repaired woodwork, worked on tin decorations for special events, or mended festival costumes; scribes copied manuscripts; and small groups of students studied the ancient texts. It was the best Anita could do on such short notice and with such little inclination to accommodate a woman like Sophie. Privately, Anita thought it was quite a wonderful opportunity for the tourists, but she doubted it would be fully appreciated. When all three women disappeared around a corner, Anita felt a wave of relief wash over her and turned on her camera. It was an unexpected pleasure to have time for her own interests.

The temple was one of many situated along the Karamana River, not far from a lagoon and, farther on, a channel opening into the sea during the monsoon. It was an area Anita knew well, and she was glad of a few minutes on her own to revisit it.

"*Maaaa!*"

Anita turned at the sound of the familiar wail. A beggar woman hunched over and held up her hand, beseeching Anita. Her teeth were almost all gone, her sari mere rags, her staff nothing more than a sapling stripped of its young leaves. She was as frail and thin as they come in this part of India, and Anita found herself searching for a few coins. She liked to have her salwars made with pockets, to make life easier, and tried to remember to keep a few coins or small bills at the ready. She pulled out a rupee and handed it to the old woman, who took it, touching it to her closed eyes, before secreting it.

"*Ma,* such beauty that way." The beggar woman nodded to Anita's camera, then toward the thick growth along the river. Anita followed her gaze and noticed the beginning of a path. The old woman pointed to the camera and again to the path.

Why not? Anita thought. The temple guide was a garrulous man who was eager to show off his English, his love of art and sculpture, and his association with foreign lands — a cousin in England, another in New Mexico, a brother in Australia, and his sister's uncle-in-law in Africa. He knew the world and was ready to talk. Anita checked her watch — she had time to explore on her own. She could head east, moving upriver in the direction of the family estate.

The path ran along the river, but within seconds the thick foliage closed around her and at once muffled the sounds of cars and buses crossing the bridge and flying along the road. When she looked back, the white temple buildings glistening in the bright sun were all but gone. She could hear her own footsteps crunching on twigs and pebbles. The narrow path could not have ever been meant for more than one person to cut through private land to the temple, and Anita found herself imagining the old estates of past years along the riverbank, linked through the centuries by boatmen and their work, women washing clothes at the quays, children playing and running from house to house with their friends. She had to laugh at her romantic version of the past, but the empty scenery was always populated in her mind by the many lives that preceded hers.

The path continued on, and she sighted her camera through the trees. She turned toward the river and admired the view but found nothing of interest artistically. For Anita, nature was pretty but not much more. Her portfolio held the required photos of waterfalls, tea estates at Munnar, the maharajah's mountain retreat at Ponmudi, the abundant flowers of the winter season, but otherwise, nature was background for the narrative of lives being lived. She turned her camera upward, looking for the creature scurrying through the branches that signaled others had noticed her approach, but it was too quick.

The path grew darker and her feet crushed leaves underfoot; she looked down at the dry leaves. Odd, she thought, and looked up again but these trees were not deciduous. Then she saw it. A black snake with white bands moved sluggishly among the dead leaves. She gasped, held her breath, stepped back. Then exhaled loudly.

"That has to be a young wolf snake," she told herself as she prepared to step over it. She raised her foot, and it lifted its head and darted. She felt the fangs, like pinpricks on her leg.

"Omigod." She fell back. She pulled the camera from around her neck and dropped it onto the ground. The snake was weaving and lowering its head. It wasn't a common wolf snake at all. "Omigod." It was a common krait. Anita felt her body grow warm, her breath quicken. She was starting to panic. This was a krait. Its bite was toxic. And it had just bitten her, and it was trying to do it again.

Anita rubbed her calf. She could barely tell where the snake had struck, and maybe its fangs hadn't penetrated, but she couldn't take that chance. She knew there might be no symptoms whatsoever until she found she couldn't breathe, and then it would be too late. She continued to move back, into the darkness. The snake swayed like a drunk unsure which direction to go in.

"What is it doing here?" Anita wondered. The little she knew about the krait flickered across her consciousness — nocturnal, inhabits open scrub, likes to live with people. She waited, standing as still as the Universe would allow, trying to defeat by sheer will her body's intense desire to shake and tremble and flee. After a minute the snake lowered its head into the dirt. She imagined her leg beginning to sting, but she pushed the thought from her mind.

"I'm not giving in to fear," she repeated again and again to herself, using the mantra

221

to keep away all thoughts except what she had to do this very minute, to keep her mind focused, clear, calm.

She stepped to the right, into the brush, looking at the trees and other growth around her. Light barely penetrated here. Along the river edge was a single coconut palm growing out over the water, its bare gray trunk a muted contrast with its surroundings. But it was hard, clean, and nearby.

Anita moved gradually behind the snake, taking long seconds, almost minutes between each step, each lift of her foot, each placement on the ground. Then, in a nanosecond, she grabbed its tail and swung the snake as hard as she could, smashing the small narrow head again and again against the bare trunk. Like a dhobi smashing soaking wet lungis onto a rock to work out the dirt, she smashed the snake down again and again and again. The skin split, the head cracked, the body went limp. She threw it on the ground and waited, but the creature was well and truly dead. Her breath came fast, in great gulps now that she was free to make a sound. She pulled off her dupatta and knocked the lifeless body into it with a stick, then folded the fabric around it, tying it into a huge knot, grabbed her camera, and ran for the temple.

"Joseph!" She shouted his name again and again as she ran along the path until she reached the hotel car. Poor Joseph, standing and waiting, didn't know what he was supposed to do until Anita threw herself into the back seat and told him to head for the hospital.

"Hey! What about us?" Anita heard the calls behind her as the car sped out of the compound.

"They can wait," Anita said to Joseph when he gave her a worried look in the rearview mirror. "They can wait."

The young nursing assistant sponged Anita's leg carefully, rinsing off the mild soap one last time, then dropped the sponge into the metal basin and stepped back to evaluate her work. Anita too looked at the spot on her leg, its two tiny puncture holes clean, the leg not swollen, no sign of necrosis. She didn't dare give in to the wave of relief surging within her, but she couldn't take her eyes from the site of the bite either.

Anita looked up at Dr. Premod, who was standing beside her recording Anita's vital signs on a chart. The doctor looked over at the assistant, then at the site on Anita's leg, and nodded her approval. "Yes, thank you, that is all." The assistant slipped quietly from the room. The silence thickened, and Anita thought it had to be bearing the weight of her barely controlled terror.

"It looks clean," Anita said. "I mean it doesn't look like . . . I have no idea what I'm trying to say."

"Most important is calm," the doctor said. She was a little older than Anita, a down-to-earth woman who had returned from studying in the States to join one of the new, advanced hospitals in her home country. She rested her hand on Anita's arm. "Calm."

Anita took a deep breath. "That was a krait that bit me — in the middle of the day!"

"Yes, most unusual." Dr. Premod frowned. "Most common is the farmer or laborer coming to us with a stomachache or weakening muscles, or complaining he cannot keep his eyes open. He does not remember being bitten because, most probably, he was asleep, lying on the dirt floor of his little house." She rested the chart against her hip.

"Are you going to give me an antivenin shot?" Anita was doing everything in her power to remain still — she knew enough to know that excessive movement of the bitten limb would only make matters worse — but she wanted to bounce up and grab the doctor and tell her to get on with it. Get that shot! Do it now! That was her irrational side. It was time to let her somewhat more rational side, if she could find it, run the show for a little while at least.

"A shot? No, not yet, until I am certain." Dr. Premod frowned, then suddenly smiled at her. "Cough, please."

Anita coughed.

"Again, harder."

Anita coughed, harder.

"Very good." The doctor bent over Anita's leg. "Is there pain?"

"Not really. Just a little soreness."

"Excellent." She straightened up and rolled her watchband so that the face was visible to her. She reached out and took Anita's wrist. "Excellent pulse."

Anita could feel herself growing calmer. Her toes relaxed and her leg fell to the side, leaving her lying on the bed as though she were sunning herself on the beach. She took a deep breath and sighed with relief. "You're relaxed, so I'm relaxed, I guess."

"I am very glad." The doctor turned to a rolling table and picked up a small vial filled halfway with blood. "Twenty-one minutes since taken," she said, holding up the vial. She tipped it to one side but the red liquid was too thick to flow and appeared to be a solid mass. "Very nice, Anita, very nice. Excellent coagulation."

"Then I'm all right?" Anita said, feeling like she was going to cry with relief. So this is what it's like to come back from the dead, she thought. "I thought a bite was almost a done deal."

Anita fell back against the pillows and closed her eyes. For the entire frantic journey from the temple parking lot to the hospital on the other side of Trivandrum she had tried to be calm, to not think about what this careless encounter might mean. She could not shut out of her mind the shock of being lifted out of her life, pulled violently from her family and her world, and nothing she could do about it. From deep within her came a burst of passion. I want to live, she thought. I want to live — live live live. And now, here she was, lying on a clean bed in a modern hospital, with a doctor who mostly smiled and joked with her, allaying her terrors. "I feel like I must have been foolish — but I wasn't. *Ayoo,* I am so relieved."

"No, no. You are right to be concerned. Certainly we are having a high rate of deaths by snakebite in this country — some estimates are as high as twenty thousand people each year — but these are often poor farmers who do not know they have been bitten, and they are slow to reach the clinic. And the clinic may not understand the problem or it may not have the antivenin serum. All these are complications. But not you, I think."

"Do you think I should have an antivenin shot just in case?"

Dr. Premod frowned and pursed her lips. "I am thinking no, not at all. But we are waiting for a few hours to see if you remain as you are at this time."

"What's wrong with erring on the side of caution?" Anita asked, propping herself up on her elbow.

"Snake antivenin is not without its problems. Some people are allergic to it and reactions can be very serious. It is after all derived from the plasma of horses that has been hyperimmunized to snake venom. If we can avoid using this, it is good."

"How long before you know?" Anita looked down at the snakebite again. She felt disconnected from her limb and even heard a voice in her head saying, Maybe she could just leave it here for a while and come back for it later. *Ayoo,* I'm rattled, she thought.

"Let me say this. At this moment, you appear not to have envenomation from this bite. It does happen occasionally that a progression of envenomation is slow in some cases, rare but possible, but you show no signs. Also, I have heard from colleagues that a bite during the day may carry less venom, and we also know that not every bite includes venom." She replaced the vial on the table. "Your muscles are strong, your blood is coagulating, there are no signs of envenomation. But we will err on the side of caution and keep you here for a few hours. I want to be confident. I will test your blood again in an hour. And now you should rest."

"I don't think I can," Anita said, leaning back again. "I'm exhausted but much too wound up to rest."

"You have had a fright, but you are all right." Dr. Premod smiled again, but this time she paused as she pulled a mobile phone out of her pocket. "Hmm. Your Aunt Meena is at the registration desk demanding to see you. A foreign woman is trying to calm her. Shall I protect you from her hysteria?"

Anita opened her mouth to thank the doctor, then closed it.

"No?"

"No. I think I have a better idea." Anita pushed herself up and glanced at the door. They were in a wing of the hospital, at the end of a long corridor; other than the assistant, Anita hadn't seen anyone pass by.

"Shall I close the door?" the doctor asked. Anita nodded. The doctor did so. "Now what?"

"The snake." Anita thought back to the path along the river.

"Yes, I was going to ask you how you came across it."

"It was on a path along the river, more jungle than anything."

"Hmm. Not the usual environment for the krait." The doctor pulled up a chair and sat down. "And you saw it there?"

"Just as it bit me," Anita said. She continued to stare at her leg, and in the silence the doctor waited. "Can you keep me here?" Anita asked abruptly.

Dr. Premod had a young, sweet face, but as she absorbed the question and its implications, her expression grew shrewd. "If you are thinking this is a good idea, then I can order you to remain."

"Good." Anita nodded and tried to think of exactly what she wanted to do. "Good. I want you to tell Auntie Meena out in the registration area that I have to remain in hospital, then bring her here. The foreign woman is Sophie, I think, the tour guide I was with at the temple. I want her and anyone else out there to think I'm stuck in here and possibly quite ill." She paused and looked around. "The hospital has a back entrance, doesn't it? Don't you have ambulances coming in around back?"

"Why are you wanting to know this?"

"I want you to let me out the back," Anita said. "But I want everyone to think I'm still here, lying quite sick and not to be disturbed."

"But you must remain, for blood tests." Dr. Premod sat bolt upright, her eyes wide.

"For a while I'll remain, but then I have to leave. If the krait didn't inject me with venom, then I have nothing to worry about, right?"

"Well, yes, but . . ." The doctor sighed. "After some hours and more blood tests, then you can go."

"Good. Then I just have to make one phone call." She flipped open her mobile, scrolled down to Anand's number, and hit dial. While she listened to the tone, she said to the doctor, "Do you have a sari I can borrow?"

Anita rested her head on her drawn-up knees, balancing on the chair seat, as she let the cool of the stone interior of the small room seep into her. So much had happened in the last few hours that she barely knew herself where she was. Her dash out the back door of the hospital and down the narrow lane to the temple compound had left her sweaty and tired. She was still weak from the emotional roller coaster of the snakebite and Dr. Premod's happy diagnosis — a bite but no venom. Inside the cool of the monk's cell, she felt safe and savored the feeling of relief.

The temple was closed at this time of day, only the priests in the office finishing up the usual paperwork. She could hear voices in the distance, two men sitting on the stone steps reading newspapers aloud and chatting over reports of an investigation into a state office. The flower vendors were gone, not expected to return until later in the afternoon, and the tea wallah was probably asleep inside his little shop.

At the sound of voices closer to hand Anita raised her head and stared through the open doorway, the bright sun creating a wall of shimmering white outside. Anand, wearing a mundu, circumambulated the sanctuary. He passed out of her sight. When she saw him reappear, she moved to the doorway of the small room long enough for him to notice her. Then moved back into the darkness. Anand continued his pious walk around the central image until he came to the doorway, pausing before stepping inside.

Without even thinking about it Anita went to him and wrapped her arms around him, resting her head on his shoulder. She was still trying to come to grips with the fear and stark terror of what she thought was going to happen to her. She had just begun to sense how deeply the fear had penetrated her view of the world and herself. Anand wrapped his arms around her and said not a word. After a while, Anita pulled away and sat down at the table.

"Nice digs," Anand said looking around. A single lightbulb dangled from the ceiling, giving barely enough light to illuminate the small space. In the center of the room stood a small wooden table, and two straight-backed wooden chairs. He pulled out a chair and sat down opposite Anita. A banana leaf with the remains of a meal had been folded up and set aside for collection near the door. A small mat lay rolled up along the back wall. "Are you planning on staying?"

Anita laughed, but without humor. "The hospital backs onto a lane that leads here. It seemed the safest, most discreet way to get away. I didn't want to run into anyone in the hospital waiting room."

"Does anyone know you've left?" Anand asked.

Anita explained her diagnosis and added, "So, I'm not poisoned, and I didn't need an antivenin shot. But I'm not going back to show myself till I know what's going on."

"You've told your aunt?"

"Yes. She didn't like the idea of me leaving the hospital, but I really am all right. Just scared. How's she doing?"

"Auntie Meena? She is driving everyone crazy — she's offered to donate just about every organ she has — and to put up the hotel as collateral for anything you need, including a private jet to New York for medical care." He let a wry smile settle on his face. "This has led to the usual chauvinistic arguments about India versus the world."

"So she has everyone convinced I'm lying near death's door in a hospital bed?"

"Everyone, including herself, from the sounds of it."

"Who's the audience?"

"Other than the other patients waiting to see someone?" Anand tipped his head back as he recalled the scene. "Well, there's Sophie, of course, who is going on and on about how awful this is and how distressed her tourists are and now they'll never come to India again. And what can she do to help?"

"Other than go away?" Anita said.

"Other than that. And Joseph, who is literally in tears — he adores you, did you know that? — and the two women who were with Sophie. They look pretty stunned, and I'm not sure they know what they're doing there."

"Protective cover?"

"Cynical woman," he said as he ran his fingers over his sacred thread.

"I'll bet that cost you something," Anita said, nodding to the three thin pieces of string draped across his chest. She hadn't seen him wearing a sacred thread before, even though he was a Nambudiri, and had attended temple festivals with her, but then there was no reason why he should. Other than the priests working in a temple or in connection with pujas, most twice-born men, as upper-caste Hindus were traditionally called, just didn't wear the sacred thread anymore on a daily basis.

"Who would have ever thought that a few pieces of string could put my future on the line." He looked down at the object lying across his fingers. "I had to promise my father that this was really only a disguise, and I was not reverting to a past life. And you really were in danger. I thought he was going to burst out with, 'Oh goody.' "

At this Anita did manage to laugh, and her eyes lit up. "Where do these people come from?" Anita shook her head. "I hope Auntie Meena isn't too too upset. It is an act, isn't it?"

"Some of it. Despite Dr. Premod's repeated reassurances — Dr. Premod even went so far as to show your aunt the vials of clotted blood — your aunt is not entirely convinced you really are all right." He paused and grew serious. "It is very unsettling, Anita."

"I know." Anita glanced away, recalling the morning hours. "I was shocked — I was absolutely terrified."

"Did you bribe her to get her to release you?" He looked so serious that Anita felt a strange chill, that he meant what he was saying.

"No, but I trust her. She wouldn't have let me go if she thought there was a danger. But I need to use this time well." She glanced back at him. "I know you don't like this idea, but I need you to help me. So, we have to get past that worry and deal with this."

"And what exactly is 'this,' as you put it?" Anand looked tired, as though he had just run a marathon. Anita winced — she should have given him more information over the phone. Her call had been rather cryptic.

"You do deserve more of an explanation, Anand." She took a deep breath, explained the tour and the respite along the path while Sophie and her clients went into the temple.

"That sounds pretty innocuous," Anand said.

"I agree," Anita said. "But you don't find common kraits in the middle of the morning on a path in a dark jungle." She looked up quickly. "And no, it was not a wolf snake. The lab man was quite definite about that. And so am I. I know the difference. But I brought in the carcass just to be sure."

"That's pretty grim, Anita." Anand leaned forward. "If what you're saying is true . . ."

"I was lucky, Anand. Lucky I saw it. Lucky it was too sluggish to release any venom." Anita shivered.

"You are convinced this was not an accidental encounter." Anand reached out and rested his hands on hers. The coolness of his fingers soothed her.

"The snake was sluggish, out in the middle of the day and confused, and sitting on a bed of dried leaves, and those leaves didn't fall from any of the trees above it — that was not a rubber plantation I was walking

236

through." Anita pulled her feet onto the chair and wrapped her arms around her legs. She sighed and rested her chin on her knees.

"Yes, you were very lucky, Anita."

She nodded, closing her eyes.

"So someone put it there." Anand tapped his clasped hands on the table while he considered this. To Anita it looked like he was holding himself in check, as though if his hands were free, he'd stand up and hit something.

"Exactly." She shut her eyes for a moment. "My first thought was, I hate to admit it, Sophie. Just shows you how much I dislike her. But she didn't know until this morning that I would be taking her tour group around. I could have taken them anywhere. But . . ."

"But?"

"She could have just as easily taken that path along the river with her tour group and run into the snake. Suppose I'd waited for them, as I usually would, and showed Sophie and the others the path." Anita sank into a deep quiet.

"And you're wondering if it was meant for someone else, either Sophie or someone on her tour?"

She studied him for a moment. He was

gorgeous and brilliant and always rational, and entirely his own person. If he hadn't agreed with his parents' politics, they would not have been able to do anything about it. That was one of the reasons she was so fond of him — she could count on him to listen and consider, and never dismiss out of hand, anything she said. His comments were incisive and his support unwavering. But he wouldn't rush to her side if he didn't think rationally it was justified. "I'm convinced it was meant for me. Sophie's annoying, but that's all. No, she wasn't the target."

"Do you have any reason for thinking you were — other than instinct?"

"Anand, look at the evidence. It would be so easy for me to think it was meant for someone else, or that it was just an accident. But how likely is it that a krait shows up on that path, just when I've been sent there by a beggar woman? Who, I might add, disappeared like a *yaksha*. I sent Joseph back to find her and no one, I mean, no one, saw her before or after the incident, no one saw her arrive at the temple — according to the vendors no old beggar woman entered through the main gate, and there's no way for her to get in through the back. No, she came in and out in a car, concealed, or she came in and out by boat."

"Why would the vendors care? You can't rely on them."

"Yes, I can. Beggars can be a real problem, and a beggar woman, small and slight, is one of the best thieves around. Worse, they drive away the tourists. Vendors watch them carefully. They don't like seeing too many around — it makes for trouble. *Ayoo,* I sound so mean." Anita pressed her hand over her eyes. "But they can be trouble."

"All right. I'll accept your conclusion about the beggar woman." He hunched his shoulders, as if getting ready for another round with her. "But who knew you were going there?"

"The temple officers — I called to tell them I was coming, to set things up. The tourists — Sophie and her clients, those two women."

"Anyone else at the hotel?"

Anita blanched. "I have to look at everyone, don't I?" She sighed. "Ravi on the desk must have heard me and Auntie Meena talking. The tourists might have mentioned it to the other guests. Joseph, of course." She paused. "But does that give anyone enough time to get a krait here and plant it on the path?"

Anita and Anand met each other's eyes.

Anand nodded. "Yes, I think you're right.

This was planned in advance. You were targeted." He let his palms fall open on the table. "Anita, I know you can't let an assault pass unnoticed, and you're used to sticking your neck out over all sorts of things for other people, but this krait business is just as serious. It seems so extreme. Is Gauri's problem the only thing unusual in your life right now?"

"That's it." The single lightbulb hanging above them flickered, its already dim light waning, then went out. The room went dark, despite the bright sun, but oil lamps soon appeared, carried about by acolytes. A young boy handed a plate with two candles in to Anand, who set it on the table. The flames shimmied in the draft, then settled to thin, undulating lights. "That attack on Bindu was vicious," Anita said after a silence.

"It's a miracle she wasn't killed," Anand said.

"She hasn't recovered yet." Anita took a deep breath. "Which means I shouldn't be surprised that whoever is behind it would try something like this."

"What's next?" Anand asked.

"Everyone thinks I'm confined to the hospital for the rest of the day at least, thanks to Auntie Meena's histrionics," Anita said. "That gives me a least tonight and maybe part of tomorrow, if I'm lucky, to go around without anyone looking for me. Things are coming to a head soon, if I'm right, and it will be harder to put people off. But . . ."

"But you can't do it alone — you can't let anyone else drive you around. Right?"

Anita reached across the table, took his hand, and held it in hers. "I need to talk to Gauri — soon. Like now. But I can't take a chance on Konan or anyone else spotting me."

Anand lifted her hand to his lips.

THIRTEEN

At four o'clock in the afternoon a shiny white Mercedes drove down a dusty lane and pulled over to the side of the road. Anand climbed out of the car and walked to the front. He popped the bonnet and raised it with one hand.

"Okay, you can get out."

The back door opened and a woman in a worn sari climbed out and squatted on the ground. She closed the door and rolled into the brush. Anand slammed down the bonnet, got back into the car and drove off at a sedate speed.

When the car was a mere speck in the distance, Anita stood and rearranged her sari, pulling the *pallu,* the long decorated end, around her shoulders, although in this case the decoration of the cheap, red-patterned sari was so faded and frayed it was hardly worth noticing. The beggar woman from whom they'd bought it had barely waited to understand what Anita was saying when she saw the three hundred rupees. She grabbed the bills and unwound her sari, grabbing the new white one lying on the ground in a paper bag. Anita had held her nose, promised herself a long hot shower, and tied on the red sari.

Her brown hair was darkened with coconut oil, her limbs dusty, her face dirty. She pulled the pallu over her head, a pretense of modesty that concealed much of her face, and worked her way through the scrub to the back of the little family temple used for the exorcism. When she heard the temple bell ahead, she turned away and moved through the trees parallel to the temple until she came to a road. As she drew closer she felt the flutter of anxiety and bent over. "No one looks at a beggar woman," she said to herself. "No one will notice me." But she felt uneasy just the same.

Anita stepped carefully, remembering she was a poor beggar woman, worn down in body and spirit. When she looked up she could see three young women in bright nylon saris coming toward her, three abreast on the road, their multicolored skirts billowing out around them, their voices rising into the air. The breeze brought a whiff of the sweet tuberoses tied into their braids.

Anita lowered her eyes as they passed, just in time to spot the coins dropping in front of her feet from one of the women. Startled, she remembered in time to stoop quickly and grab them, then had to pause for a moment to decide where to put them. It hadn't occurred to her that anyone would actually give her money. She slipped the coins into her choli and walked on, satisfied that her disguise was working.

As she drew closer to the temple, Anita slowed her step, looking for a good vantage point. A half-dozen worshippers climbed the low incline to the temple, an old woman was sweeping around the perimeter, a few children played in the dirt at the entrance. The bell clanged again and two older women worked their way up the hill. At the sound of an autorickshaw Anita turned, following its approach. The auto pulled up and stopped, and Gauri clambered out. The driver moved on to a shady spot and cut the engine. Gauri went into the temple. "Show time," Anita thought, rearranging her pallu.

Anita trudged up the hill, reminding herself she was a poor, weak woman, hungry, greedy, looking for someone to give to her. At the entry a priest in a dhoti came down the few steps, gave her a swift appraising glance, and passed on. Out of the corner of her eye she watched him, but he wasn't familiar.

Inside Anita studied the list of pujas available and prices for each. She had a few rupees stuck into her choli, but not enough for anything beyond a small donation. She pulled out a one-rupee note and wandered past the small shrines until she came to one with a bench nearby. She pushed her donation into a locked metal box, then sat down on the ground where she had a clear view of the entrance. Soon Gauri appeared, and lost herself in her puja at the inner sanctum. Some time later she began to circumambulate the shrine. Anita waited.

A few coins fell in front of Anita, and she leaned over and grabbed them. "Oh, Amma, Bhagavati has chosen you." Anita slipped the coins into her choli.

"Huh?" Startled, Gauri stepped back and leaned over to get a better look at the beggar woman. "*Ayoo!* Chechi!" She slapped a hand over her mouth and quickly looked around to see if anyone had heard her. "Chechi, this no good."

"Gauri, this is very good. You didn't even know me." Anita swung her head back and forth as if asking for more money. "Pretend to pray at this Ganapati."

"Pretend?" Gauri was shocked, but she stood in front of the image set into the wall and tried to pretend.

"Has anyone come to you since the exorcism?" Anita kept her voice low.

"No, Chechi. No one is coming."

"Don't look so worried, Gauri. This is only pretend."

"This no good, Chechi."

"You said that. Are you sure no one came to see how you were doing?"

"Only Konan." Gauri glanced up at Ganapati and began to pray for Anita's release from beggardom. "Amma sent him."

"How do you know that?"

"He is telling me. She is worried I am still unwell." Gauri smiled, pleased with the flattery of her employer's attention. "I am telling him, no, I am completely myself."

"How did he take that?" Anita wondered what it might mean to someone like Konan to be told Gauri was completely herself.

Gauri frowned, looking puzzled. "He is asking me again if I am hearing Bhagavati's call. But I am not hearing. Life is as it has always been."

"That was good," Anita said, hoping that this news might make Gauri of less interest to others. "Now, tell me, is the priest who carried out the exorcism here? I can't go looking for him without drawing attention to myself." Anita put her hands together to plead for money from a woman who passed by while Gauri lost herself in her prayers to Ganapati. *"Maaaa!"* The woman tossed a coin to Anita, who grabbed for it, pleased with how well she was doing in her role.

"Chechi!" Gauri hissed in disapproval.

"It's pretend, remember? Besides, the merit is in the giving, not in who receives it." She secreted the coin. "Is the priest here?"

"No, I haven't seen him. Only the other one, the one who helped."

"Where is he?"

"In one of the offices at the front, just a little room."

Anita pushed herself up and kept herself bent over. "One last question, Gauri. How did Konan arrive? By auto?"

Surprised, Gauri turned to her. "Yes, auto."

"What was the driver like?"

"Very bad driver. He is not turning around easily, and he is not strong enough to move the auto. Bad leg, I think."

"Bad leg," Anita repeated. She bent over and moved away, crying out *Maaa* as another worshipper came near. When the woman passed without tossing anything to her, Anita briefly cursed her, surprised at how much relief she felt before the inevitable guilt flowed in, then turned back to Gauri. "Go talk to the assistant priest, Gauri. Ask him if he can do the same exorcism for someone else you know, ask him how much it costs, just keep him talking."

"Another time? You want him to do more?"

"I want you to keep him talking; he'll be interested in talking about something that will make him money."

"Oh, yes. Yes, Chechi." Gauri went off, her step faltering once before she hurried on.

After a suitable interval, Anita followed Gauri to the offices and slipped into the smaller one. She immediately found what she wanted and began to turn the pages of the large ledger. Ten minutes later the assisting priest came through the office doorway and, seeing Anita hunched over the desk, began to rage at her, picking up a staff and smashing it across her back. Her fists clenched, Anita let herself be driven from the temple like a beggar woman caught in the act of stealing. As she fell down the last step she was chuffed to hear Gauri flinging out a string of vivid, somewhat terrifying curses on the priest and his family for abusing a poor beggar woman.

The hot water flowing over her body felt so
good that Anita stood in the shower for a
good five minutes, letting the water slide
over her, not caring if she used up every
drop in the tank. With her face turned up to
the shower head, she thought of all the beggar women she had given to and the ones
she had not, the ones she had passed by
when she was in too much of a hurry to
stop for them. Perhaps she'd start an orga-
nization, something like a union. She'd
charge the temples a fine if they didn't give
to a certain number of beggar women every
week. She'd agitate for laws to protect them.
Her eyes popped open. This was just the
thing for Anand's parents — they'd love this
kind of fight. Buoyed with these plans, even
if they were fantastic, she scrubbed herself
clean and shut off the water.

When Anand suggested they go straight to
his bungalow, to give Anita time to recover
from what he regarded as her ordeal, and
save Auntie Meena from the sight of her
niece garbed in a tatty, smelly sari, Anita
had no energy to protest. She hated the
odor that came from the sari and just
wanted to get out of it.

In the small tidy bedroom Anita unfolded

the white Kerala sari, its dark green border a perfect match with the green choli sitting beside it. She was close in size to Anand's mother, so her wardrobe, scattered over the homes of various relatives, including that of her son, was handy. Anita hoped the other woman wouldn't mind, but she couldn't stand the thought of tying on that beggar woman's sari again. Anita was seriously thinking of burning it.

Wrapped in the clean white sari, her brown hair soaking wet, Anita came down the stairs to the first floor, her bare feet telling her that the tiles beneath were not ordinary tiles. They felt like silk. The sensation so startled her that she studied the bungalow as she passed through the dining room to the sitting room — the casement windows with latticework grills, the arches over doorways, the way the doorways and windows channeled the breeze.

"You don't know how good I feel," Anita said as she came into the sitting room.

"I know how much better you look." Anand stood up as Anita entered. "I'd ask how you got that smell, but I don't really want to know." He leaned toward her, and his lips lightly brushed hers. "Now you smell wonderful."

"Yes, it was disgusting." She fell onto the

soft settee, closed her eyes, and leaned back against a pile of thick throw pillows. "This is wonderful, everything is so clean." She opened her eyes, and sat up straight. "I feel reborn."

"Luxury is not overrated sometimes."

Anita grinned. "Tell me about Gauri. She got home safely from the temple?"

Anand nodded. "The same auto took her home. It is someone I know. I've hired him to park nearby, as though he's waiting for a fare. He'll let me know if anything happens."

"She didn't like my disguise." Anita smiled and laughed. "But I made three rupees, all in coins."

"Cheap, aren't they?"

"Very. And I got a beating, too."

"She told me." Anand looked grim. "I don't like it when you take such risks."

"You mean you don't like it when you can't go in there and thrash the guy."

"That, too."

"I didn't like that part either, but it was worth it."

"You should report it to the police."

"You're serious," Anita said, amused. "First of all, they'd laugh at me for complaining that someone hit a beggar woman found in a private office. Second, they'd just tell me how much they disapproved of me going about in such a disguise — it's a dangerous game to toy with karma. Besides, I'm all right." Anita sat up and reached for the tea tray sitting on the table in front of them. She poured herself a cup of milky tea. "I'm starving."

"The maidservant left *irunnu* vadai for us. And fruit."

"Perfect." Anita reached out to a small covered casserole and lifted the lid, smiling appreciatively at the small savory doughnuts soaking in curd.

"What did you find out?"

"The office keeps a list of all the pujas performed, whatever sort. There was one last weekend dedicating a goat. We knew about that one. And there was a puja for fertility by a young couple, and a small puja for a grandmother's health. But there was no mention anywhere of an exorcism. And considering how much Muttacchi paid for it, you would think there'd be some record of it."

"Unless the temple proper had nothing to do with it."

"Or it wasn't a legitimate puja." Anita pulled her feet up onto the sofa and crossed her legs, resting her arms on them and holding her teacup.

"You have reason to think it wasn't legitimate?"

"You didn't see it, Anand." Her body tensed and little ripples broke the surface of the tea. "They really were beating her. It was horrible — no wonder she came out changed. It wasn't a light whip stinging her, it was a beating. I think they meant to do more, but Muttacchi wouldn't leave them alone with Gauri, and for sure wouldn't leave Gauri to go through the exorcism without someone to watch over her." She took a sip, but the cup still shook in her hand, and with effort she lowered cup and saucer to the table.

"These things are supposed to be frightening, Anita, to push the individual back into line." Anand reached for a cup, turned it about with its handle, but then pulled back, pushing himself back in his seat. "They're meant to impress with ritual and invocations and they drive away the tormenting god."

"The priest told us to leave in the beginning, but Muttacchi wouldn't budge," Anita said, growing calmer. "I was worried about her — she seemed so uncertain, so worried. I think she sensed something wasn't right."

"She's a smart woman," Anand said, "but these things, what's going on at her property, these are not the ordinary difficulties she's used to."

"You're right, and I think she knows that too. The priest tried to keep me away, telling me to sit out on the entry, small as it is. But I was watching everything along with Muttacchi." She looked up at Anand, who met her gaze. "I think that's the only reason Gauri survived."

"If the exorcism wasn't part of the temple services, then someone had to arrange for it to happen there," Anand said.

Anita nodded. "We need to know more about the priests."

"What disguise will you use this time?"

"No disguise, but I do want to avoid being seen."

"That's him." Anita pointed to a middle-aged man hurrying down the temple steps, a battered backpack slung over his shoulder. Behind him a younger man in slacks and a shirt pulled shut the heavy wooden door, shoved an iron bar through two slots, and hung a padlock through a slotted flap, pushing the shackle into the case. "I don't know who this other one is — he wasn't there. Probably some guy in the office." The evening puja was over; the temple was closing. "But the first one was only the assisting priest."

"He was part of it," Anand said. He watched the first man follow a dirt path across the compound, cross the road, then pick up the path through the trees until he came to a clearing. Anand slouched down in the seat as the priest's car pulled onto the road and headed away. Anand and Anita had parked several meters away from the temple, in front of a small house; throughout their vigil a little boy stood by the driver's window staring in at them, solemn, silent, still. "We're leaving now," Anand told the little boy. "Thanks for helping." The boy blinked in surprise and ran back across the street.

"Whose car is this?" Anita asked, sniffing at a new smell loosened from the worn fabric seats when a breeze drifted through the open windows. The old black Morris Minor was indistinguishable from a million other cars plying the Indian roadways. With the loosening of the coils on the economy, fewer of these cars remained as younger and wealthier Indians purchased new cars in many hues, but nonetheless the old car was nothing anyone would notice.

"My father's. He uses it for going to protests, just in case someone blows it up."

Anand leaned forward and turned the key. The engine grumbled and turned over.

Anand had no trouble following the priest's little red compact as it sped along the highway, flying north of Trivandrum, over the tracks, over the river, along the coast.

"You don't think he's heading to Kollam, do you?" Anita asked.

"I hope not." Anand glanced down at the speedometer and other gauges. "It's an old car — no telling how many miles it has left in it."

As the evening grew darker, the lights brightening along the road, the red car cut its speed but still moved along at a determined clip. Anand dodged out into traffic, caught sight of the car, and fell back behind a lorry piled high with coconut halves on their way north for processing into coir rope. The lorry's load swayed, Anand dodged, and buses honked furiously as they tried to pass in the blind night. When the traffic slowed, Anand dodged out again.

"He's turning." Anand nodded toward the red car turning west, toward the coast, onto a dirt road. Anita rose in her seat, craning her neck to get a better look.

"Where on earth is he going? Don't tell me he lives out here?" She settled back in her seat. "I didn't expect that." Anand slowed the car and drifted onto the shoulder, drawing up before a row of shops. Lights were strung from tree to tree, a radio blared, and men clustered in small groups. Anand stopped and climbed out, walking over to the nearest one. He returned a moment later.

"We can go along the coast from up there, come back down and be on the same road he turned onto. It's just a dirt road that connects the villages. Nothing special." He slammed the door and drove back onto the highway. "We're looking for a distant cousin who's just come home from Gulf last week and sent word to you about family problems."

"Lucky me," Anita said.

"They were very disappointed. They were hoping we were shopping for goods for a tourist shop." Anand gave her a wry look.

"We can't be that obvious." Anita sat up in her seat, genuinely worried.

"No, they're just hopeful. With all the tourism around Trivandrum, the dealers have been scouring the countryside for goods to resell. We won't find much, he said, just in case we aren't really looking for your cousin's family."

Anand drove along until they came to a

side road, turned onto it, and soon was driving south along the coast, with the roar of waves crashing to their right. Once in a while they caught a glimpse of the ocean through the trees, but mostly they drove along a narrow road with deep ditches alongside, goats bleating outside houses, a few cooking fires still burning. It was growing late, and the villagers were settling in for the night. The fishermen were out at sea, if they were going out, and the farmers had corralled their cows and goats.

Anand slowed down when they came to the road the priest had taken and moved slowly along. He let his car run into ruts, so that it bounced and swayed, giving anyone watching the impression that this poor old car couldn't go any faster if it wanted to. When he came to a particularly large pothole, he maneuvered around it at a mere two miles an hour, if that.

"Do you see his car?" Anand asked.

Anita shook her head. She had been peering through the windows, trying not to be obvious, her hair modestly covered, but so far she had not seen a single car. There were fewer lights, and the darkness thickened. "It sounds like the world's asleep, except for the ocean. Makes you feel how insignificant we really are." The waves rumbled and roared as they drove on.

"Anand!" She reached across and touched his arm. There, parked alongside a small house, next to an autorickshaw whose license looked vaguely familiar, sat the red car. "That's him, I'm sure of it." Anita strained to read the TC number on the house. "Go slow." She pulled out her binoculars and slumped down in the seat, steadying them on the windowsill. "Got it."

The car continued to bounce down the lane, then turned, driving out of sight.

"There!" Anita pointed. "There's always a path."

"You can't go back, Anita."

"One of us is going to walk back." Anita opened the door and climbed out. Anand climbed out on his side.

"All right. You stay here this time," Anand said.

"You're too obvious." Anita shook her head and pointed at his white pants and white shirt. "No one's going to think twice if I pass by." She pulled the pallu low over her forehead, concealing her face. "I'll just take the path to the edge of his property, just to see who else is there. That's all." Anita glanced back at Anand. "And no, you can't talk me out of it."

"Fifteen minutes and I'm coming after

you." He crossed his arms and leaned against the car.

Anita kept her eye on the path wending its way around coconut palms, past sapling fences, over tiny gullies that would flood and overflow in a few months. Every few feet she stopped to adjust the pallu, taking the time to orient herself and listen for any conversations nearby. She reached the house with the little red car out front and turned inland, taking cover behind a shed. Four men stood talking in the back yard. Their conversation was low, and it sounded like they were talking about the upcoming festival. One man stood apart, watching the other three.

"Oh," she murmured to herself as her eye passed from man to man. She expected to recognize the priest, but not the others. She crouched lower, holding herself as still as possible, more concerned than ever that no one spot her. As the men drifted away, Anita melted back into the jungle.

"Not so long," Anita said when she met Anand waiting for her near the car. "Let's go."

They got into the car with celerity and drove away, following the dirt road, until Anand came to a lane leading back to the highway.

"You've been very quiet, Anita." He glanced at her. "Are you going to tell me what you saw?"

"I'm recovering. It wasn't what I expected." She took a deep breath. "It's a relief to get away from there." Anand kept his eyes on the road, his hands resting loosely on the steering wheel, but she knew he was tense — his jaws were working as though he had a clove to chew on. "Four men, Anand. Four men. One of them was the priest, of course, but one was Konan and one was Mootal, the moneylender, the man who drives the auto. He was the one who brought Konan to Muttacchi's house."

"What about the last one?"

"I've seen him before — just recently, I think." Anita frowned, trying to get a fix on the fourth man. "He looks like a laborer — you know, plaid lungi, undershirt, *chappals.* He was standing off to the side. Oh! That's it."

"What is it?"

"Standing off to the side — that's where I saw him before — at the boatyard, where Bindu's father works. I took him money for Bindu's medical expenses, remember? The boatmen all came up to watch, his friends who were so sorry for him — except for one, the one who hung back among the boats. I thought it was because he must be new. That was the fourth man. I think his name is Gokul or something like that." Anita could tell Anand was thinking about this — the car slowed.

"Konan, an astrologer, Mootal, a petty moneylender, a lower-level priest, and a laborer." He spoke softly, reciting the names and descriptions, drawing out each syllable. "Could you hear them talking?"

"Some, but they only seemed to be talking about a festival, or something for tourists. It was hard to make sense of it, but how bad could it be if they were talking about it openly in the back yard?"

"Why was a coolie there?" Anand swung the car around the roundabout, dodged an oncoming bus, and pulled onto the highway heading south.

"I wondered about that, too." She lapsed into silence.

Anita spotted Muttacchi on the side veranda as the car drove up to the house. No lights were on, and Anita guessed that the old woman was the only one still up. Anita felt the old woman's eyes on her as she climbed out of the car, but Muttacchi only shook her head and hobbled away.

"I can't leave her here alone suspecting

what I now suspect," Anita told Anand. He came around to the front of the car and leaned close to her in the darkness.

"That's why I don't think you should stay here alone."

"I'm not alone — there are all those servants."

"None of whom you know personally — you don't know if you can trust any of them. Bindu was attacked here, remember." He glanced around, keeping an eye out for anyone who might overhear them arguing.

"How can I forget?" She felt herself growing anxious and lowered her voice. "Look, Anand. I can't leave her here alone, you know that. And you can't stay here either without raising all sorts of nastiness. I'll be all right. And you can get to work on finding out who lives in that house. Do you mind?"

"I don't like it." He started to move toward the house. "I think we should have a talk with Muttacchi."

"We can't, Anand. She's an old woman watching her world cave in."

"Anita, if she's anything like any of my old relatives, she's got a far worse opinion of human nature than we have. Come on." He led the way to the side veranda, kicked off his sandals, and waited for Anita to follow him.

After watching him watching her, Anita grabbed her bag from the back of the car and, with her sandals dangling from her left hand, climbed the steps to the veranda. "If this goes wrong, Auntie Meena will never let me forget it."

FOURTEEN

Anita took a deep breath and started over. She wasn't doing very well — she stumbled through the first few words, veered into inane talk about visiting relatives and old families and tradition, thought better of that direction, and bolted into the surprises life has in store for us. "I guess I don't know where to begin."

"That is obvious, Anita." Muttacchi lay on her mattress inside the mosquito netting, her arm wrapped around a long, thick bolster. Her white night shift blended in with the sheets, and every now and then rustled under the breeze from the ceiling fan. Anand sat in a wooden chair, one leg crossed over the other, his elbows resting on the chair arms. At first he had insisted on delivering Anita and then returning to his car, but Muttacchi had ordered Anita to provide him with a chair, so he could sit on the veranda and listen through the open door.

"She doesn't want to frighten you," Anand said.

Muttacchi raised her eyebrows as she turned to Anita. "Me?" Then she laughed, but only for a moment. "Just tell me what this is all about." She glanced at Anand. "You are not here for romantic reasons." She didn't wait for an answer, just lowered her arched eyebrow, sighed, and shifted on the bolster.

"No, Muttacchi, he's helping me." Anita shook her head. The old woman's comment was so casual, and seemed so obvious to all, that Anita was surprised at the pang — of what? — she felt. So intense was it that she leaned forward, as though what she was about to say required it.

"Well, get on with it," Muttacchi said, giving her bolster a punch and getting more comfortable.

"It seems to begin with Gauri," Anita said. "She knows something — she either saw something or heard something — and she doesn't realize it. I think she becomes possessed whenever she comes onto the area where something has happened, and that's the only way she can express the danger she senses."

"And Bindu was an accident — whoever attacked Bindu meant to get Gauri." Anand spoke softly. "To kill Gauri, I think." Even though the door to the front veranda was closed and bolted, along with the small window, the open walls above and the side door still could let their voices travel.

"I think Konan has something to do with this, too. He's not telling us everything." Anita waited for a reaction, but noticed only that the old woman's breath seemed to grow shallower, faster. "I think he wanted to remove Gauri from the property for a long period of time — that's why he recommended sending her north for three months to that mantravadi."

Muttacchi lay down on her back and stared up at the ceiling, her body still except for her large toe, wiggling back and forth.

"I'm sorry." Anita stood and began to pace the room. "I don't know what all this is about, but I think there's another man involved, a moneylender, and also a priest." She rounded the sleeping platform and came to the far wall, where a niche, cut into the wall, held drying tuberoses and a small image of Ganapati. The back wall was blackened with years of residue from small oil lamps. This evening a small modern brass standing lamp, the kind purchased for a few rupees in Chalai Bazaar, showed signs of recent use. "Has anything happened with the kavu?" Anita turned to her aunt. "I get the feeling that if you sold it for house lots no one around here would be upset."

"How perceptive of you." The old woman continued to stare at the ceiling. "Anand, you must know about this sort of pressure. Yes?"

Anand lowered his head to his hands, templing his fingers against his lips. "My parents have struggled with the rest of the family over the proper disposition of land, yes."

"Have they kept it?" Muttacchi asked.

"Most of it is still in their names." He sighed. "But there has been dissension over their plans to give it to an orphanage, clear it for poor people's housing, raise goats, you know the sort of thing they get up to."

"Ah, yes," the old woman said. "But the names are on the deeds." She fell silent, thinking her own thoughts. "It is sad, is it not, to preserve and protect and prepare to make a gift and then learn no one wants the gift. What is one to do?"

"So, you were getting ready to give everyone in the family a plot of land?" Anita said, trying to make sense of this rambling talk.

"Oh, no, no." The old woman laughed without humor. "No. Under some pressure

268

and on the advice of my man of finances, I adopted a stratagem to protect the land from overzealous governments by dividing it up into odd configurations requiring co-operation of all owners for its use by any one owner. Of course, at this point, I am the sole owner, fully in control." She smiled, a smile of satisfaction that briefly amused Anita.

"I had no idea you were so crafty," Anita said.

"She manages a huge estate," Anand said, with a grin. "I wouldn't expect anything less."

Muttacchi raised herself on her elbow and gave him a warm smile and a nod. "Large families are all alike, yes?"

"Do you think that what Gauri is sensing is something to do with fighting over the land?" Anita asked. "After all, the rest of the family can't possibly have been pleased about this."

"Your father was!" Muttacchi broke into a gale of giggles. "He understood com-pletely!"

"So, which parcel is mine?" Anita asked.

"Which one do you want?"

"I'll have to think about it. I'll take a walk with Kedar." Anita shook her head and tried not to laugh out loud.

"But you are right there is some disagreement in the household, and it may have something to do with the kavu." Muttacchi lay down again and resumed staring at the ceiling. Just as Anita was about to speak, the old woman turned to Anand. "Perhaps you know the answer to this. I am not satisfied with anything I have been told."

Anita moved to the edge of the bed and sat down. "What's the question? It sounds serious."

"Some months back I learned that Sett was making a rapid recovery from a serious illness — he was doing much better than was expected. I was pleased." She nodded but didn't look happy. "Then Lata made some comment, and I took note. Later, I asked her to explain herself when I got her alone. She sputtered that she had only been griping and meant nothing, but I pressed her."

"What was the comment?"

"His recovery wouldn't last. Bhairava would take revenge."

All three were silent. Anita stared at her aunt, and Muttacchi looked toward Anand.

Anita was the first to speak. "Lata could only be hinting at one accusation — that Sett had gone into the kavu to harvest something medicinal. If that is true, he has trespassed on sacred ground and done so for personal benefit."

"I wondered about that," Anand said. "Do you remember, Anita, when I brought you the binoculars and we looked into the kavu? My family has property in central Kerala with a kavu — actually with several small ones that were once one large one. My brother wants to reunite them if he can figure out how to do it. Anyway, he talks about them all the time at family gatherings, and mostly I offer to write a program for him. But he is more like my father — he wants to achieve his goals with a lot of fanfare and drama, a lawsuit and protest and people camping out on old family land. But he has talked enough about them so that when I looked into your kavu I expected to see certain plants flowering, and I did not. It surprised me, and I have meant to ask him about it. But now I don't think that will be necessary."

"You think Sett is still using the kavu for his medicine?" Anita asked.

"I think it is possible." Muttacchi's voice was a mixture of sorrow and anger.

"But would he kill to keep that quiet?" Anita asked.

"I don't know," the old woman said. "I do not want to believe such a thing of anyone

271

who works here. But he is unkind to Gauri, and perhaps he feels threatened by her." Muttacchi shifted on the bed. "Lata has already hinted as much. She thinks there is bad blood there."

"That wouldn't be enough to kill," Anita said. "No, you might fire him, or make him perform a special puja, but he wouldn't kill someone over this."

"How long have Gauri and Sett been enemies?" Anand asked.

Muttacchi closed her eyes and began to count on her fingers. "So many months," she said flicking her hands.

"That's as long as Gauri has been having trances," Anita pointed out. "But that can't explain everything."

"It might," Anand said. "Gauri catches Sett going into the kavu early in the morning or late at night, and instead of feeling able to come to Amma about it, she falls into a trance. No one feels they can complain about another, not seriously, so Lata gripes, Gauri has trances, and Konan is left trying to find a solution to a very simple problem."

"But that doesn't explain the beggar woman, the snake bite, the temple's record book, and the autorickshaw driver," Anita said.

"What snake bite?" Muttacchi said, sitting straight up. She grabbed Anita's wrist through the netting and began inspecting her arm.

"It was on my leg and I went to the hospital and got thoroughly checked out. I'm fine. Really." She lifted up her leg to show her aunt the tiny puncture holes from the snakebite and smiled reassuringly.

Muttacchi wrapped her hands around Anita's leg and closed her eyes, mumbling a prayer. "Oh, where is my Ganapati!"

"I'll get it for you." Anita started to move away, but the old woman held her leg with one hand and waved her other.

"No, no. My family Ganapati. It is gone for repairs." She cast a woeful glance at the niche. "Bronze disease."

"Bronze disease!" Anita and Anand spoke at once. Muttacchi started at their reaction.

"That Ganapati didn't have bronze disease, Muttacchi. It was installed here generations ago — it's never been mishandled, it hasn't shown any vulnerability to that, it didn't have any the last time I saw it — it couldn't possibly have developed bronze disease since then." Anita pulled away and hurried over to the niche. She picked up the small figure, obviously a modern reproduction, and turned it around in her hands.

"When did you send it out for treatment?"

"I don't know. I've forgotten. Not long past. A few days ago. Don't fuss about it." She waved to Anita to come back to the bed. "It is Gauri we must be concerned about. She cannot be afraid to return to work, and I don't want to send her away, and force her to find another job."

Anita replaced the image, but continued to stare at it, before turning away. "Then we have to catch Sett in the act and confront him."

"No, we cannot have anger or violence in the kavu." Muttacchi shook her head. "It is sacred."

"All right, we won't catch him inside," Anita said. "But if we observe him going in and coming out, with or without flowers or twigs or whatever, that will do it." Anita moved to the open door. "I can see it all from my room."

"You can see it all from here, too," Anand said.

Anita smiled at him over her shoulder as she moved to the door. "You worry too much, Anand."

"I agree with him, Anita. Yes, I too will feel safer knowing you are close by." Muttacchi pulled the bolster closer to her. "A snake bite," she whispered, arranging herself on the mattress again. "Now I am worrying."

"He'll be back in the morning," Anita promised her aunt after she had seen Anand return to his car and drive away. She closed and bolted the side door, folded the netting tightly under the old woman's mattress, and pulled a chair over to the small window.

"Lata has brought me my usual pitcher of warm *lassi*." The old woman lay on her back staring up at the ceiling. "There is enough for two."

Anita poured Muttacchi a glass of the spiced buttermilk, then lifted the netting and handed it in to her. After the old woman had poured half of it into her mouth without touching her lips to the rim, Anita refilled the glass and set it on a small table by the window. "I'm hungry, but I don't think I should raid the kitchen tonight."

"If Lata doesn't beat you to death, Veej will for sure." The old woman rolled over onto her side and in moments Anita could hear the soft purr of her breathing.

Anita settled herself in her chair, moving it a few inches to the left so she could see directly through the window to the kavu opening, where the image of Bhairava sat in warning to all who approached. At least it was supposed to be a warning. The idea of someone invading the sacred grove for personal gain was repugnant to her and to everyone else who understood the purpose of the grove and its dedication to the gods.

The moonlight rippled through the clouds, giving the entire estate a gentle, soft blue-black color. It hardly seemed the place for violence and theft. In the stillness it was hard to believe that any evil could find purchase here. But then she thought about Bhairava. Bhairava was, after all, a wrathful god. She leaned her head back against the chair and recalled the impression she usually had of this deity. What was the story? Shiva, in a great sorrow over the death of his wife at her father's sacrifice, wandered the earth with the dead body of his wife on his shoulders, a frightful sight of sorrow and rage. To bring an end to Shiva in this horrifying form, in this form of Shiva as Bhairava, Vishnu chopped up Sati's body with his discus and flung her limbs across the earth. The land where they fell became sacred sites.

But there was another story, Anita recalled. Surprised at how sleepy she felt, she reached for the pitcher of lassi, poured herself another glass, and sipped it. The evening was still, with not even a dog moving in the darkness looking for wild animals, not even a bandicoot out foraging for food. She put the glass down, pinched her cheeks to wake herself up, and in another minute was sleeping soundly.

Anita started awake, alert, listening. She felt stiff and cramped. Confused, she looked around her, wondering at her own wooziness. Then she remembered the lassi. The glass sat on the table nearby, more than three-quarters full, cooled by the night air. Under the netting Muttacchi snored, snorted, scratched at her great stomach, and shifted again into comfort. Anita raised the glass of lassi to her face and sniffed. Nothing. But there had to be something. She'd gone out like a crab into a sand hole.

Anita rose and carried the glass over to the armoire and slipped it into the back for safekeeping. Then she returned to the open window, raised the binoculars to her eyes, and scanned the property. Nothing moved except the occasional tree branch. She listened, and in the distance heard a cow lowing. It was close to three in the morning — she had slept for several hours.

She let the binoculars rest on her chest as she stretched her arms above her head. The wooden chair left her stiff and sore, and she bent forward and back, side to side, to get the kinks out. Her head was beginning to ache, and she thought again of the lassi. Lata had brought it to Muttacchi, apparently as a nightly ritual, and then gone away, not waiting to see if the old woman drank it. That could mean that Lata was not aware of a sedative or drug in the milk drink, or it could mean that she was fully confident her employer would drink it down as she did every night. Was it customary to give the old woman a sleeping pill in milk? Did she know about it, and just forget to tell Anita? Or did the entire household rely on pills to get a good night's sleep? There was one way to find out.

Anita pulled back the heavy wooden bolt and the side door creaked open. It should be oiled except that Muttacchi insisted such creaking assemblies were more protection than guard dogs and alarm systems. Anita was going to test out the theory. She slipped out onto the veranda and looked around. Nothing moved; no sound suggested an animal or person hiding nearby.

The front of the house lay in darkness, its doors and windows closed tight against strangers and the night. Anita passed by the front, moving quickly across the sandy parking area until she came to the corner. She peered around it. The three small buildings used by the servants were dark. As her eyes adjusted to the night, she recognized at least one figure lying on the back veranda outside the kitchen, a small mat hanging over the edge. It could be Lata or Sett or Veej, or anyone who spent the night here. But tonight it was Sett.

Anita moved back to the front entry and passed through. To her surprise the boy Arun lay asleep on the veranda facing the courtyard, but he was so sound asleep he failed to stir as Anita approached. She passed him and left him sleeping, reminding herself to mention to Muttacchi that someone else might be a better choice for night guard, such as one of the Gurkhas who worked in this area.

At each step Anita swept the ground with her foot, clearing away twigs and leaves, to avoid making any noise. She passed the kitchen door shut tight, the storage rooms closed and locked. At the end of the long building, she crouched down planning her dash to the next building where her room was. A frog jumped into the tank. Another croaked. The sound reverberated through the air, but then died, and all was still again. Anita moved cautiously into the open and hurried across to the shrubbery alongside the veranda. Again her thoughts went to the stillness.

It was too still.

She was used to nights full of life, when birds and bats and bandicoots and more went about their lives, when farmers tended their cows all night long, when goats got loose and wandered, and children were sent after them. Sometimes it felt as if the night was as busy as the day. Her mother had once said, We have to nap in the daytime; otherwise we'd be too tired for the nighttime. Anita looked back at the main wings of the estate — both lay in the moonlight, their whitewashed walls shimmering gray. Ahead, the kavu lay still also.

Anita moved around the side of the building, past the tank, and into the trees edging the property. Again the stillness remained. She moved through the trees, farther and farther away from the estate and its buildings, until she was in the forest, so thick that for a moment she worried she had trespassed into another sacred grove. That would make people in this area really angry, an anger that wouldn't pass easily. She moved deeper into the forest and eventually came to a path, crossed it, and moved into the brush lining the riverbank.

Here was the busyness of the night, of

animals moving, birds fluttering among branches, rodents scurrying from burrow to burrow. She squatted and listened, comforted by the sounds, reassured by the familiar. In the quiet came also the sound of water lapping. She leaned into the river and tried to see in the darkness. From somewhere upriver she heard a pole scrape the side of a boat, a small wave slap the shore, a person cough. She withdrew into the shrubbery as the boat drew closer, and waited. The fragrance of tuberoses came to her, grew stronger. Someone started to speak, but a second quickly shushed him or her as the boat drifted past. A tall figure poled languidly. Anita counted two figures plus the boatman in an ordinary working vellum, the kind she saw every day carrying sand or coir or any of a number of other goods up and down the river. The boatman stretched upward, leaned backward as he dug the pole into the riverbed, then pushed, stood, and pulled the pole from the river bottom. The two passengers remained still as death. Then the central figure put out his hand to push away from the overhanging branches, but the front one was still. A dupatta slipped off the front figure, dragging in the muddy water, until the man reached down, pulled it from the river, and draped it along the side. Anita hadn't expected a woman.

Anita stared hard at the boatman, watching the turn of his shoulder, the long hands on the pole, the bony knees. It was too dark to be certain, but something told her that she had just seen this man earlier, that he was the laborer meeting with Konan and the moneylender and the priest. This was Gokul, from the boatyard near the bridge. Was this what the meeting was about, to plan this trip down the river? And what was the point of ferrying two passengers at this hour of the night? Where were they going?

Anita thought about the woman sitting rigid and still, her dupatta trailing in the water. She was so oblivious to it that she let the man behind her — husband, brother, cousin? — take care of it for her. Was she unwell? Was she drugged? None of them had spoken a word. That too was unusual. There was always a word or two from the boatman and the passenger, always a comment about not leaning too far out, careful about shifting your weight, watch the oil coating the sides, or don't muss the load, watch the ropes — that sort of thing. But there was none of that on this boat. No one said a word, just that single motion of the man pulling the dupatta out of the water and laying it on the gunwale.

When the boat was gone from view, Anita stood up and leaned into the river to scan it for any other boats. She saw no other. A sound from above startled her and she lowered her binoculars.

But it wasn't above her — it was behind her. Something pulled tight at her neck, and she was jerked backward. She started choking. Her hands flew up, throwing the binoculars into the air. She clawed at the rope with her fingers but it was too tight — she couldn't get a grip on it.

"You should have stayed in your own home." The voice was low and harsh, rasped in her ear. He pulled the rope tighter and Anita felt her windpipe close. She gasped and wheezed for air. She swung her body to the side, bent her knees, and flipped the man over. As he slid down the riverbank he grabbed her hair and pulled her into the water with him. She was under water, in the darkness of a muddy river. He held her down, pushing her onto the mud bottom. She squirmed until her hand found a rock and with one hand holding onto his arm she shoved the rock into his face.

The hand released her throat, the feet that had pressed down on her chest and leg were gone. She thrashed around trying to right herself and clawed for air, until she broke through the surface. Anita scrambled to the riverbank, slipping in the muck, stumbling against deadwood and rock. She threw herself onto the dry bank and got to her feet, her knees almost crumbling beneath her. Adrenaline pushing her, she grabbed for a stick and turned to face her attacker, but there was no sign of him.

Waves spread out from where she had splashed, tree branches were wet and torn where she had grabbed at them, but she was the only one here. Her chest still heaving as she caught her breath, she stepped into the river and began jabbing the stick along the bank, into the mud. The river wasn't very deep in this part, and she walked several feet toward the center, but still there was no sign of him. She turned back to the shore. A chill ran through her as she wondered if he had made it to shore and even now was waiting for her along the path.

Anita tossed the stick away and plunged into the river, swimming upstream as quietly as she could, taking long strokes, and hoping she didn't meet any snakes along the way. She pushed out into the river, avoiding overhanging branches that might conceal her attacker, drifting quietly back toward shore.

When she came to the stone steps near the family kavu she swam up to them and waited, listening for her attacker to give himself away. In the silence she heard only the lapping of water against the stones and her own sniffling in the chilly night air.

"The safest place is the most dangerous place," Anita thought. She pushed off from the stone steps and again headed upstream, stroking as silently as possible, then pulling herself into shore by overhanging branches, moving among the plants untouched for hundreds of years. She used the waning moonlight on the tree trunks to guide her. After some distance she came to a break in the undergrowth — here she could see through the trees into the kavu itself. She drew closer and grabbed hold of a tree root to pull herself onto dry land. She was growing cold in the water, chilled in the night air, tired from her unplanned swim, and now that she could safely admit it, terrified that someone had tried to strangle her and almost succeeded in drowning her. Her only thought now was to get onto dry land and find safety. She clambered ashore, and lay exhausted on the riverbank, her legs dangling in the water.

Anita felt a cold, abject terror. This was the kavu. This was a forest sacred to

Bhairava. She might be safe from humans, but she would never be safe from Bhairava if she brought herself up onto land, this piece of land. Bhairava, a god of wrath, Shiva taking form as rage and terror after he snipped off the fifth head of the god Brahma, a skull that stuck to his palm and turned into a begging bowl. Shiva as Bhairava, wandering the earth with a skull on his palm, terrifying to behold. These weren't the stories of her childhood anymore — they were the warnings of the undercurrents of the world.

"I'm sorry, Bhairava. Truly. I'll atone for this," Anita said into the trees. She took a deep breath, and scrambled onto dry land. Sitting on the spongy ground, she tried to assess what had happened. She'd seen a boat with two passengers and a boatman pass by, and been attacked by a man on the riverbank. It was easy to assume they were connected, but were they? Had the second man been lying in wait for the boat to pass so he could get on with what crime he had planned? Had the boat put him off his course and put her in his path?

Anita pushed herself farther back from the bank, crawling backward on the dirt, until her hand landed on a plank. It was about four feet long and wet, very wet.

Anita rolled over on her stomach and began to crawl deeper into the kavu. She had no idea where she was in relation to the estate houses — as far as she knew she was at the farthest end, or she could be near the path Bindu had taken. It didn't matter. The only thing Anita wanted was to get clear of the kavu.

When she was ten feet in from the river she felt an indentation in the ground, something shaped like a half moon, and beyond it another shaped more like a square. She moved closer, but as she did so she noticed what looked like tracks, as though something — or someone — had been dragged across the ground, tearing up vines and tufts of grass and digging up debris. She ran her hand through the up-turned soil, then along the ground in front of her. Something had gone on here — something big enough to destroy the surface and tear up all the growth. She moved her hand across the soil and felt something scrape the skin on her palm. She ran her fingers over it — it felt like a piece of wood. She tried to pull it off the ground but instead it creaked and held. She crawled closer and brushed the dirt and debris away, and as she did so she could see it was actually the top of a large box buried in the

ground. She ran her hand over it — big
enough to hold two large loaves of bread.
Anita pulled open the box and peered inside.

FIFTEEN

Anita rested the wooden box on the ground as she stared through the trees to the house beyond. Confident no one else was about, she picked up the box, dashed across the open ground, and ran up the veranda steps. She pushed the heavy door open with her shoulder, twirled into Muttacchi's bedroom, and pushed the door shut behind her. The old woman's startled expression as she sat up in bed confirmed what Anita suspected. She looked awful — like a rat covered in mud, with a rotting, mud-caked box clutched to her chest, along with a few rotting twigs and leaves. She had a lot to explain.

She had crawled into the kavu after swimming upriver, found more than she ever imagined, pushed herself back out of the kavu — covering her soaked and torn salwar khameez in dirt and grass stains — then slipped into the river, where she only made things worse by swimming through algae and dead branches. She swam to the stone steps, holding the box aloft and praying she didn't run into anyone else before she got safely out of the water and onto dry land. The servants would be up soon, and she didn't want any of them to see her and ask what she was up to. She was drenched, muddy, covered in slime, her salwar practically turned into a rag, and there was a bright red rash along her throat where the coir rope had chafed to the point of near strangulation.

Muttacchi watched Anita deposit the box on the floor, then slip out of her clothes. She grabbed a sheet and headed back outside, to the nearest spigot, where she poured buckets of water over her head and limbs, wishing she could sluice away her guilt as easily. Every time she thought about what she found in the kavu — about how magical it was to be inside this place for a brief minute before her discoveries nearly sank her — she felt a creeping sense of guilt and uneasiness.

"Where did you get this?" Muttacchi asked as Anita rummaged in the old woman's armoire for a sari. "Anita, if you are looking for something to wear, see that parcel, there. That is — was — for Surya.

Choli readymade and sari. It will fit you." Muttacchi returned to the box, gazing at it, flicking away the dirt with the nail of her index finger.

Anita pulled out a dark green cotton choli, slipped it on, fastening it in the front, and then pulled out a white sari with a green and black border. She tied it around her quickly, rotating her right hand rapidly to make the folds that draped in front, then she wound the rest of the sari around her once more, again making pleats, and draping the pallu over her left shoulder. The old woman barely glanced up, her eyes fastened on the box.

"I've done something wicked, Muttacchi." Anita pulled her wet hair away from her face and knelt down, studying the old woman's expression for a clue to how she might react.

"This box." The old woman spoke as though she were naming it, drawing it into reality as if from a dream, touching it to make sure it was real, now rubbing her fingers over the dirt-encrusted surface. The wood was rotting, and Anita had half-wondered as she carried it home if it would disintegrate along the way, leaving a trail of rotted bits along the path for anyone to follow. Afraid to hold it too tight against her chest lest the mere pressure of breathing crush it, she had held it with her open palm beneath the bottom, like a servant carrying a silver tray. "Where did you find it?"

"That's what I have to tell you, Muttac-chi." Anita took a deep breath. Get it over with, she told herself; no one in your family is going to be really surprised you did something so outrageous. "I found it in the kavu." She spoke as matter-of-factly as she could manage, then waited. It occurred to her that by kneeling, she had brought her face level with Muttacchi's hand, so that if the old woman was so inclined, she could merely reach out and slap Anita, and that would be her answer. Certainly it would be understandable. Anita had violated some-thing sacred. Poor planning, Anita thought, glancing around for something to sit on.

Muttacchi's eyes flickered from the box to Anita and back again, with no effort made to conceal the conflict and confusion and surprise she felt. The value of the box to her could not have been made clearer to Anita as she watched the old woman absorb both the recovery of this treasured object and the place where Anita had found it, a place where no one should have gone to find anything. After a long minute, the old woman turned an increasingly stern eye on Anita. "Tell me."

Anita swallowed, looked down at the floor to gather her thoughts, and began. She told about falling asleep, and then suddenly waking and sensing something she couldn't put her finger on, hiding the lassi in the armoire. She described the trip to the river, the boat and its passengers, the encounter in the forest and fight in the water, and then the impulsive swim up the river and the escape into the kavu.

"You are injured!" The old woman leaned forward, touching Anita's shoulder lightly with her fingertips, scanning her body for wounds.

"No, no, I got away. I fought back and got away."

Muttacchi shook her head. "It is not worth it. Whatever has happened, let it go. I cannot have you harmed."

"I won't be. I know now to be more careful. I will not take any more risks, Muttacchi." She gave her a reassuring smile.

"I want to believe you, Anita, but you are not so pliable as other girls."

"I promise, I will be careful."

Muttacchi studied her and seemed to resign herself to having to take Anita's word. She looked down at the box and said, "Where did you find this?"

"The box was planted in the ground." By

now Anita was speaking normally, though softly, and Muttacchi had folded her hands around the box, pulling it onto her lap, opening the lid and running her fingers along the inside edges. Dirt smeared her nightshift and the sheets, and fragments of wood clung to the mosquito netting.

"This was my uncle's money box." Muttacchi peered into it. When she said this, Anita understood the depth of emotion the old woman was experiencing; she was thinking back to a childhood spent in a manner no longer lived in Kerala, of the communal family where the oldest woman's brother was the head of the household. The uncle was both feared and revered. "You see here?" She pointed to the remnants of hinges along one side. "This is where the false bottom began — there were smaller cubbies here for coins and other valuables, precious stones, deeds, gold."

"Was it very old?"

"It was old when I first saw it, and Uncle guarded it as though it were the oldest treasure in the household." Muttacchi paused, her face softening with the memory.

"When did you last see it?"

"I used to go into his office as a child and he let me sit at the wooden desk on the floor and pretend to be his clerk. If I was very good, and he was happy, I could open up his boxes and he would show me what was inside. I was a girl, but I knew everything that was in his office. My mother encouraged me — she adored her brother, and he admired her, too." She paused and drifted deeper into her reverie. "He sent me to school so I would understand the work."

"Muttacchi?" Anita rested her hand on the other woman's, to bring her back to the present. She looked at Anita, a wistful, almost secretive expression on her face.

"In the kavu, you say?"

"I'm sorry, yes." Anita opened her mouth to say more, but the old woman rested her fingers on Anita's lips. For a minute they held silence, their breathing soft and low, the night sounds distant.

"So much is different now, Anita. I see my relations in the hills cutting down hectares of kavu without so much as a puja to appease the gods." Tears began to fill her eyes and rest against her lashes. "In my heart I know you did not go there with ill will, and you have been rewarded with this. Bhairava would not have given you this if he had thought you were engaged in evil. No, Bhairava wanted you to find it, and it was your duty to bring it to me. You honor the kavu by making it pure again, removing from it something that should not have been taken there in the first place."

Anita could not conceal her relief. For all her impulsiveness, her flippancy about the old ways fighting the new ways, there was a part of her that believed deeply in the traditions of the Nayar culture, of her family heritage and the world that was shrinking and fading around her. And she was secretly grateful that Muttacchi, a woman she respected and sometimes stood in awe of, did not despise her for this violation of a sacred tradition.

Then, much to Anita's surprise, the old woman smiled.

"A puja, a real puja. We shall now have cause for a real puja for Bhairava. Now we have reason to offer Bhairava as is his due." The thought pleased the old woman so much that she began to list the many gifts and the priests she would invite, until Anita again rested her hand on her knee and leaned closer.

"Tell me what you know about it — the box. When did you last see it?"

"Oh, yes." The old woman peered at the box, studying it hard. "I am getting old. I think it was Lata told me Veej had used it to transport the images with bronze disease. There is much of that here now."

Anita cringed. "This is the second time you've mentioned bronze disease. When did all this start?"

The tone in Anita's voice must have sounded a warning to the old woman because she lost any trace of sentimentality and zeroed in on Anita. "You are doubting this?"

"Well, it's just that, well, I never noticed any bronze disease before." Anita frowned. "Who said they had bronze disease?"

"Surya examined some of them. She told me." Anita felt the old woman watching her. "Was she wrong?"

"I don't know." Anita tried to recall if she and Surya had talked about any of this during her last visit. "Most of your images have a patina from years of use and being handled — that nice deep dark coating that's part dirt — and sometimes there's a part of the image that's shiny because that's where someone rubs Ganapati's stomach for good luck, for example. But none of them looked like bronze disease — that's when you have those tiny bright green grains, like bright green sand, breaking out in specific spots on the image. That's oxidation, and not every image is vulnerable to it." Anita rested her head in her hands, trying to think back to what the images had looked like. "Do you remember what they looked like?"

"Not like that," Muttacchi said, shaking her head. "Nothing bright green."

As much as Anita hated the idea of bronze disease and what it could do to an image, she liked this answer even less — it suggested something worse. "You said Veej took them. Did he just gather them up and take them, or did you give them, or what?"

"Surya seemed to choose when she was here last year, but then I don't know."

"Surya picked them out?" Anita considered this. "But Veej took them? What did he do with them?"

"He took them for cleaning," Muttacchi said.

"Oh, no!"

"You sound like Surya. She called soon afterward, I think, and she was very upset. She said the Ganapati was not diseased — only dirty. Quite put out, she was."

"This doesn't make any sense. First, Surya says they have bronze disease, and then she's upset that Veej has taken them for cleaning for just that problem." Anita shook her head, wondering if she was missing something else here. "How many times did this happen?" She didn't want to think of how much antique sculpture had been spirited away from the property under the

298

guise of treating supposed or even real oxidation.

Muttacchi's hands clasped the box in a vice, pressing tighter and tighter. "Surya was very angry about it. It has made me unsettled. I don't know how many times, once or twice, maybe more."

"What about the Ganapati?" Anita turned to the niche, where the large murti had always stood. "When did they take that one?"

"Recently. Just days ago Veej is bundling it up." The old woman frowned and began to count on her fingers. "It was just after the man who said he was Lata's cousin came by."

"Lata's cousin? I thought she had no family," Anita said, surprised.

"She has lost a husband and a daughter, and all others except a sister who lives nearby." Muttacchi looked old and worn as she recalled the sorrows that had pummeled Lata. "But one day this man came by — she was not here, out shopping — and said he was her cousin. When she returned I mentioned this to her, but she is turning away, taking the talk back to who she saw in the market."

"Did he come again?"

Muttacchi shook her head.

"I did not know she had a cousin around here," Anita said, adding more to herself, "There are too many people popping up around here, and no answers about anything. I'd like to know who he is, just for my sanity."

"Oh, that is easy," Muttacchi said. "He is a tour guide at East Fort in Trivandrum. I have seen him there often. He does not remember me, but I remember him." She went on to describe him in careful detail.

"You're wonderful!" Anita said, reaching out to squeeze her hands.

"Don't be foolish. It is my duty to know who comes here — but the murtis. I am troubled for my images." Muttacchi leaned over and brushed her hand across Anita's cheek. "You will get them back for me, yes?"

"Yes, I will," Anita promised, or get killed in the process, she added to herself.

Anita decided she had better see for herself just what was happening with property from the old estate. She took Muttacchi's keys to the office and storage rooms to see what was missing, what was oxidizing, what had been returned. Over the years the accumulated wealth had been locked away, partially forgotten about, and Anita was increasingly uneasy about what she was beginning to suspect.

Anita opened up the storeroom, and then stepped back as the heavy heated air poured out of the room. Old rope beds were shoved against the back wall, two small tables were piled one on top of the other in front of them, intricately carved teak chairs lined the left-hand wall. Anita pulled open the window shutters and noted the small amount of dust on everything.

The largest piece of furniture was an armoire that looked too big to move. Anita worked her way through the keys on the chain hanging around her neck until she came to one that seemed right. The big key jammed in the lock. She wiggled it a few times, then listened as the rusted metal gave way, the key turned, and she heard a bolt move. The door fell open easily, soundlessly. Surprised, Anita pulled it wide to get a look at the hinges. She ran her fingers over the wood and iron work, feeling the oil on her fingertips. Someone had oiled the door hinges in the last few months. Then she looked closer — the bed in which the hinge was set had been cut deeper, and a new hinge fitted with a post that pulled out, releasing the two parts. Anita swung the door back and forth. Someone had replaced the old hinges with new ones whose parts could be separated, so the doors could be lifted off, obviating the need for a key.

The shelves held an assortment of small images, brass oil lamps of various heights, most of them new, a dozen medium-sized brass water pitchers, seven brass trays, and a small metal coin purse. Lying on the bottom shelf were two tridents and a tall spear with a crescent moon at the top.

Anita picked up the coin purse. About the size of a small eggplant, with its top cut off to serve as a cap, the brass purse was encrusted with dirt and black with age. In her hand it felt familiar, heavy. The weapons were similarly unattractive — weapons made for religious use rather than war. She replaced the purse and recounted the other items.

What she feared most had come true — someone in the household was stealing from Muttacchi, and not just pilfering foodstuffs and cheap goods. The family images gathered over centuries were gone, and the puja things also accumulated over the same period were also gone. Aside from the weapons and coin purse, everything was new, made in the last five or ten years. Gone were the hundred-year-old lamps, images, pitchers, and trays. Old bronze had been replaced by new brass.

Anita felt sick. She hardly knew where to begin. When she thought about it, she felt helpless, then angry, so angry it frightened her. As she turned around the room, thinking of the generations that had lived here, she thought about the family Ganapati that had also been taken away, ostensibly for cleaning. Anita felt like she'd been kicked in the gut.

The loss of Muttacchi's Ganapati was bigger than the loss of everything else combined. A gift to an ancestor, in gratitude for his service during the ministership of Raja Kesava Das in the 1790s, the Ganapati represented the long and illustrious history of the family, and its supremacy over generations. The gift of the image of Ganapati symbolized the greater gift of land, and with it power. The image was carried to this part of the region, the lands put under cultivation, and the family prospered.

To have the image of Ganapati removed from the family home meant more than an audacious theft, more than the loss of an eighteenth-century bronze, more than a cruel deception of an old woman. The loss of Ganapati would signal the end of the family fortunes. Anita had to get it back.

Anita stepped onto the veranda and pulled

the door shut behind her. Through the gate she could see a man on a bicycle wobbling down the driveway, almost to the road, a wooden box teetering on the back rack. His knees stuck out perpendicular to the frame, and his rubber chappals looked like they would slip off the pedals, but he pushed on. He rang the little bell when he turned onto the road. He looked a comic figure making his way shakily down the road.

Anita idly wondered who it was, but she pushed that aside. First on her list was questioning Veej on where he had taken the images for cleaning. She tried to recall each bronze image she had seen here — the ones in the cupboard, those hidden under silk and flowers during a puja, the individual murti in a relative's private room — so she could confront him about each one.

When Anita had a list of more than a dozen images, she headed for the kitchen. She had skipped breakfast with her aunt in favor of searching the storage room, and now she was hungry. She'd settle for whatever was left over.

The kitchen was tidy, the cooking materials from breakfast put away, the dishes done. Anita pulled out her keys and began to work her way through the cupboards. She knew Lata had made idlies that morning and made a double batch. There should be some of those around.

Anita ran out of keys the same time she ran out of cupboards to investigate. But no idlies. She checked the small refrigerator, the tins lining the shelf, the modest store-room — no idlies. Confused, Anita stepped onto the back veranda looking for Lata.

"Gone shopping," Sett said, without being asked a question.

"All right," Anita said, annoyed. "I'll make myself a cup of tea, and then I want to talk to Veej. Where is he?"

"Gone shopping," Sett said, who rose, grabbed a broom, and tottered away.

Anita peered after the laborer, who seemed to do almost nothing these days. Sett was skilled at avoiding work, Veej skulked around the property, never there when you needed him, Lata cooked up a storm but seemed to hide the food. Bindu was in hospital, Gauri was almost in hiding, and Kedar was about as cold and suspicious of Anita as anyone had ever been. Even Arun, a mere boy, looked askance at her. Anita calculated she had alienated just about everyone on the estate, but one of them, she was sure, had preceded her into the kavu — and one of them might have been waiting for her at the river.

SIXTEEN

The autorickshaw turned into East Fort and pulled up behind a row of tour buses, just what Anita had been hoping to see. If Lata's relation was in fact a tour guide, he'd be working today. The temple was closed to all but born Hindus and members in good standing of the Ramakrishna mission, which seemed to make it twice as attractive to tourists. Even so, those who wanted to see the inside of the famous temple — which was still considered the property of the royal family — had to be content with peeking through open doorways. Guards were placed at all entrances, lest anyone wander in accidentally or try to sneak in.

From Muttacchi's description, Lata's relation sounded like one of the many unofficial tour guides found hanging around popular tourist sites. This was the kind that latched onto one or two foreigners and walked them around the palace, then the temple, and at the end took each one aside separately to thank them for their interest and generosity, his hands clasped in front of him, palms upward, like a bowl ready to be filled. Anita removed the lens cap on her camera, slipped it into her purse, and began to wander. She had a pretty good description of the man — Muttacchi hadn't liked the shape of his head and recalled it in detail along with her disdain. The whole description intrigued Anita — she rarely had such insight into an older relative's thinking.

After half an hour Anita spotted her quarry. He emerged walking backward out of the palace gate, leading a group of three elderly women in colorful skirts and floppy-brimmed hats, their cameras dangling down their chests. His shoulders stiff, the guide motioned them to follow him as he turned and walked briskly to the temple steps. There he waited impatiently for them. Anita followed along.

"Mind if I just listen?" she said, with a broad smile. The other women welcomed her, peppering her with comments.

"You should see inside the palace. No furniture at all. Not a stick."

"I wouldn't want to sit on the floor. I'd never get up."

"Can you imagine havin' to watch a whole

play through a window?"

The guide went quickly through his spiel, every now and then glaring at Anita as he turned to gesture to the gopura rising high above the temple entrance, the tank nearby, and the massive stone blocks of the temple foundation. At the end, he drew the women away one by one, collecting his tip. Anita moved in behind him, to block his path into the temple.

"You're Lata's relation," she said. "I was just with her, and I want to ask you something."

"You're mistaken." He glared at her with such venom that for a moment Anita wondered if she had made a mistake in approaching him.

"I don't think so." Anita took a step closer. He jabbed her forearm, the third time pushing her back. "You don't know me, I don't know Lata, you are only making trouble for yourself. Go back to your hotel and play with your guests." He gave her arm another shove and sprinted up the stone steps. In the seconds it took Anita to regain her balance and charge after him, he disappeared around the side of the temple.

She lunged after him, but just as she rounded the corner her path was blocked by a guard, who informed her she was entering a private area. "Off limits," he said, waving her back.

"I just want to look."

"Off limits."

She leaned around him, ignoring his growing anger, but all she could see was the guide's back as he walked away, hunched over and holding a mobile phone to his ear.

Frustrated, annoyed, Anita went over the man's words again and again. She was so absorbed in repeating his threats to her that she ignored the autorickshaws honking at her to get out of the way, the taxis swerving around her, the buses and cyclists slowing and their drivers cursing her. By the time she got to the gate for East Fort, facing Chalai Bazaar, she was no closer to figuring out what was going on with him than she had been at the outset. He knew who she was and still threatened her. Distracted by the ring of her mobile, she pulled it out and flipped it open.

"I have some information for you." Anand got right to the point. She liked that about him, because he managed to do so without seeming abrupt or curt. "About the house we passed the night we followed the priest with the backpack?"

"The priest from the temple that was part

of the exorcism?" Anita forgot her current problem and stepped out of traffic, letting the cars whiz by out onto MG Road. "You mean he doesn't live there?"

"The priest lives there, yes, but he doesn't own the building. The owner is someone else."

Anita struggled to turn her thoughts back to the chase of the red car. She had made all sorts of assumptions about him and the others that night, but she'd been wrong. "Who? Who owns it?"

"His name's Chuthan."

"Means nothing to me." Anita repeated the name to herself several times. "Nothing. Who is he?"

"Surprise, surprise, Anita. You know him. At least you've met him." Anand paused, and Anita heard him talking to someone else at the other end of the line. "One of my clients is having a meltdown. Fixable, of course. The house. Chuthan. He's the newsagent in Pattur."

A vision of the newsagent came into her mind — the man behind the stacks of newspapers and magazines who hadn't known anything or anyone, whose vagueness Anita had chalked up to discretion for his clients and suspicion of a strange woman asking questions. But nothing ominous behind it.

"Are you there?" Anand called her back to the moment.

"I'm pulling myself together," Anita said. "Of all the possible answers, that wasn't one that even crossed my mind."

"Nor mine," Anand said. "He seemed fairly innocuous when I saw him."

"I suppose there could be nothing to it — just one man renting property to another."

"Do you really believe that?"

"Not for a second," Anita said, with a laugh. "I'm just trying not to jump to conclusions. This is part of my effort to be open-minded and not make rash decisions. I'm not doing too well, am I?" The traffic officer waved, and Anita hurried across the street. "I need to rethink everything. I wasn't expecting Muttacchi's problem with Gauri to become so complicated. Can you come to the hotel? I have to tell you about what I found in the kavu."

"Anita?" Anand's tone of voice told her he guessed exactly what she had done and what it meant.

"Exactly. Lunch at Hotel Delite? We have to talk." Anita glanced at the policeman waving pedestrians across the street. "I have one more thing to do before I leave Trivandrum."

■ ■ ■ ■

Anita crossed into Chalai Bazaar, following the pedestrian traffic down the left, dodging cyclists and autos loaded down with goods — long stacks of sugar cane dangling from the back of a bicycle, an autorickshaw packed with stalks of bananas, another with steel pots in nets tumbling out the open sides. Street vendors offered oranges and limes, plastic combs, children's frocks, and more. Anita kept walking, past the flower vendor's fragrant display, shop steps crammed with gleaming aluminum pots and pans and smaller kitchen utensils hanging from a roof in bright red netting, past small specialty bakeries, past sari shops, until the large milling crowds of shoppers and wildly careening vehicles were behind her, the noise dulled.

The shops became smaller, and Anita was soon among the goldsmiths, the tiny one-roomed shops of jewelry makers working on special orders. Muttacchi, like Auntie Meena, had her favorite shops, and Anita knew these were farther down Chalai, where the older, more stable ones had lived for decades. The goldsmith she was looking for recognized her first.

"Alloo, alloo!" A skinny man in a short white mundu came hobbling out of his shop toward her, bobbing up and down, his hands pressed together in *anjali.* "You have come on an errand for your family." His smile could not have been wider, Anita thought, with a twinge of guilt.

"So good to see you, Raman." Anita returned the greeting. She liked him especially for his cheerful spirit — she knew he could be testy and harsh with apprentices, especially if he thought the young man a fool — but to his customers he was buoyant and bright, and, surprisingly, never obsequious. "Actually, I've come for some advice."

"Advice? Aha! Yes, I have much advice. And it is all yours, all yours. You are only to be asking." He led her to the doorway of his shop, which was really no larger than a small closet. A young man, probably only sixteen or so, sat cross-legged inside, leaving just enough room for the low worktable and Raman. The goldsmith called to a near neighbor, who trotted over with a wooden stool. Anita sat. After offering a few tidbits about her family, bringing him up to date on newly engaged relatives, which meant future commissions for him, Anita got down to business.

"You say his name is Mootal? He is

moneylender Pattur side?" Raman pursed his lips, drew down his brows, and hummed while he thought. "Yes, this name is known to me. Why is this name of Mootal known to me?"

"You've heard of him?" Anita leaned forward, praying he could remember what he had heard. She'd come into Chalai on a hunch that one of her family's goldsmiths would know about most of the moneylenders in the area, and she was right. She waited, gripping her mobile phone.

"Ah, yes. Yes, he is a moneylender." Raman nodded, smiled, glad to be of service.

"Is that all you know about him?"

Raman shrugged. "That is all. He is moneylender Pattur side. What else is there to know? He must be a moneylender for some time before we know what kind of man he is." He lifted his hands, palms up, as if to demonstrate the emptiness of his memory.

"What do you mean for some time? Is he a new moneylender?"

"Ah, yes, new. Very new. I think only this past year he is taking up this business." Raman turned to his neighbor. "Have you had dealings with Mootal?" The neighbor walked over, nodding. "Another goldsmith, very good colleague," Raman explained.

The man introduced himself. "Only once am I meeting him. He is bringing customer who is wanting bracelet made to particular design, and Mootal is advancing the funds. I am showing quality of workmanship. He is giving loan."

"How did you know he was new at this?" Anita asked.

"Customer is telling me. Last year Mootal is auto driver; this year he is moneylender." The man shrugged and strolled back to his shop, his eye on an older couple passing by, potential customers.

"I wouldn't have thought an auto driver would make enough money to go into this kind of work," Anita said.

"Ah, perhaps it is not his own money he is lending." Raman leaned closer and lowered his voice. "You are not needing his services, Amma. You are only needing to tell me what you are wanting and I am making for you. You will pay me in time. I know this. Tell me. What do you want?" He reached out imploringly, and Anita blushed. She quickly tried to tell him she didn't want to commission anything, she was not short of funds, but he smiled warmly, with a knowing look on his face. "When you are ready, then you are asking. Then I am ready." He closed his eyes and nodded reassuringly.

SEVENTEEN

Anita dropped the parcels onto the bed in her suite over the garage at Hotel Delite. The minute she walked into the room she tingled with a feeling of affection for her modest flat — she was glad to be home. There was something about coming back to this little apartment after a harrowing encounter, a trip away with friends or to visit relatives, that drew from her a sense of peacefulness and relief. Whenever she closed the door behind her on her way out, she knew how she'd feel in a few days' time on her return, and to protect that feeling alone she always made sure to leave the flat tidy and clean, almost pristine as it waited for her return. Now, she dropped her little shopping bags made of newspaper and felt that almost physical sense of escape from the rest of the world.

She opened the windows and stepped out onto the balcony, leaning on the parapet and gazing down on the sandy terrace and rocks below. It was close to noon, and two waiters arranged chairs and tables for lunch. One of them looked up, saw Anita above, and waved the tablecloth before he unfurled it. Anita waved back.

The tide was low, and no one was swimming in the small cove to the right. A goat grazed along the path, two catamarans carrying fishermen sailed by on their way to the small harbor. Close to the horizon a cruise ship lay at anchor. Everything seemed ideal, as though there couldn't be anything ugly or mean anywhere in the world. But Anita knew the falseness of that. Sadly, she pushed herself away from the parapet and went back inside.

An hour later she found Anand waiting for her at the far end of the hotel dining terrace, in a nook that allowed only one table but held the best view of the ocean ahead and the sandy beach to the left. The waiter reached the spot the same time as Anita.

"Great service here," Anand said. "I hear the food's pretty good too."

"I have a feeling Auntie Meena is in no mood for levity right now, even cheerful humor." Anita declined the menu and ordered prawn curry.

"She didn't blanch when I came in," Anand said. "Even though I'm sure she saw me at the desk. She looks a bit grim."

"I haven't had much of a chat with her," Anita said. "She's got that glassy-eyed look of terror she gets whenever a particularly difficult tour is in residence." Anita paused and glanced partway over her shoulder. "I'm not looking forward to this discussion."

"Why don't you begin with me?" Anand quickly picked a vegetable *kurma* and handed over the menu. "I'm feeling a bit grim myself. No, don't ask yet. Tell me your news."

So Anita told him — about falling asleep in the chair at midnight, her suspicions about the lassi, about the kavu, the boat passing by with its passengers, the box, the odd marks on the ground, about Muttacchi's Ganapati and other images being taken away for bronze disease treatment, Anita's search through the house for the images, her encounter with the man at the temple, and her conversation with the goldsmith at Chalai.

"What were you doing in the river?"

"You got that, did you?" Anita winced. She thought she had gracefully sailed past that little detail. Anita told him.

"*Ayoo,* Anita, you could have been killed."

Anand paled and his eyes grew wide.

"But I wasn't, I'm fine." Anita tried to reassure him, leaning forward and lowering her voice. "But it tells me I'm on the right track. Something is going on in the kavu, and Muttacchi is being drugged so she doesn't hear or see anything at night."

"Did you challenge Lata about this?"

"Not yet. Both she and Veej had gone shopping when I was looking for them." Anita unrolled a cloth napkin and draped it on her lap. "I can't figure her out, and I don't want her to know how much I suspect until I'm more confident about where she stands."

Anand nodded.

"She's confusing," Anita added. "I went out to the kitchen to get something to eat — I skipped breakfast and went straight to the storeroom for the images — but when I went to check out the kitchen, she was gone and I couldn't find the leftover idlies." She positioned the cutlery on the tablecloth, giving the pieces a little pat. "So, I'm starving."

Anand listened, his head tipped to one side, not saying a word.

"What do you have? Anything on Surya yet?" When Anita saw his expression, she moaned. "What?"

"About Surya? I had my friend check and recheck. He was right the first time." Anand paused, pulled out a small notebook and flipped through it. "She got on flight 520 in Dubai and landed in Trivandrum on Sunday morning, at 3:30 A.M., right on schedule."

"How long to get her luggage and get through customs? An hour?"

"She had a carry-on bag — nothing checked."

"Not surprising," Anita said, leaning back in her chair. "She doesn't need to bring a lot of clothes here — she can buy whatever she needs and probably left half a wardrobe with every relative. We all wear each other's saris and salwars. She doesn't need to bring much, just jeans maybe and a skirt if she wants one." She dropped her head into her hands. "Oh, Anand. I don't want to think about it."

"She disappeared when she left the airport." Anand slipped the notebook back into his pocket. "Didn't anyone plan to meet her?"

"She makes her own arrangements. We all do — if we can get away with it." Anita rested her arms on the table. "We're so used to being met by a dozen relatives that when we get the chance to go on our own, we take it. It's so liberating to get off a plane and be so free in a new city, to be able to go anywhere, take your time, start and stop. She and I both grew up with a thousand relatives around us all the time.

"You know, I never closed my bedroom door until I went to the States? I didn't know people did that. She and I talked about it once — she felt so strange, she said, not knowing some of these customs, even though she grew up in the States. But she was an only child. And she didn't spend that much time at her friends' houses, and most of her friends were first-generation Indians. Then the family moved to London, and she was even more confused. How would she know what the rules were?"

"What are you talking about? Closing bedroom doors?" Anand looked bemused.

Anita strangled a laugh. "Foreigners like a lot of privacy, so kids have their own rooms and keep the parents out. Children close their bedroom doors, and their parents have to knock." Anita shook her head at Anand's expression. "It's their way, Anand."

"Yes, it is and it is nonsensical." He frowned. "Where're her parents?"

"Still in London, I think."

"Do you want to call your parents, get them onto this now?" He struggled to remain calm, licking his lips and shifting in his seat. "Getting off a plane and enjoying a few minutes of being alone is not the same as not showing up at all."

Anita shook her head, worry turning her face gray. "Yes, you're right, of course. Maybe she just went off to see someone and forgot to call." She glanced up at Anand.

"You wouldn't do that. Would she?"

"Well, yes, she would, but she would have called by now." Anita pushed away the salt and pepper shakers as the bowls of food arrived. "I need to work out what's going on, and we need to find her, find out what happened to her. I wonder if Muttacchi knows more than she's telling me."

"What do we actually have?" Anand pulled out his notebook again and a pen.

"You're right," Anita said. "We should focus on what we have already. We have a lot, too."

By the time Anita was nearly finished with her prawn curry and Anand with his vegetable kurma, his list of points beginning with Surya's failure to arrive and Gauri's trances had filled two pages. Anita studied it while the waiter cleared her place and brought the dessert menu, which she declined. She reached for the large water bottle, poured the remaining few ounces into the glass and drank it down.

"So Lata is stealing food from Muttacchi, and Sett is stealing from the kavu," Anita said. "Would herbs and such really be worth the effort, do you think?"

"It depends." Anand leaned back while the waiter cleared his place. "Some ayurvedic practitioners will only use wild-growing plants, and others use the cultivated varieties without concern. I don't know if there is a difference in efficacy, but there could be."

"But if you believe there is a difference?"

"Ah, then, yes, of course. You would want the purest available — even if it meant violating a sacred space." Anand ordered coffee for them. "I have to work this afternoon, but on a day like today I wish I could have the afternoon nap. What about you?"

"I'm going into the village to find out what I can about Veej and his family." Anita stirred her coffee. "But I feel like a nap, too."

She sipped her coffee and listened to the waves crashing below. Sometimes at night, the breaking waves were so loud that she lay there wondering at the explosions, and at other times they were so gentle, it seemed like another coast. Three fishermen were collecting mussels in the small cove below. Members of this group had appeared at least once a week for the last few weeks, and even though their members varied, the old man who knew the best spots and did most of the work appeared every time. He was unusual in that he had shocks of white hair and a grizzled chin, and his body was mocha colored. Anita wondered if it was a layer of salt lightening his skin.

She liked watching him time the waves before he jumped into the small cove, worked his way to the rocks, and began chopping off clusters of shells. He carried his harvest in his lungi, holding it out like an apron, over to the rock pool, where he dumped the shells. He did a quick sorting before returning to the water. Through the morning he moved from site to site, and she had grown used to his methods. She sensed where he would go next, when he would show up during the week, how long he would work. She was so used to seeing him that if he was sick, she'd know it and send an offer of help to his village.

"He's going to deplete the cove with such thorough harvesting," Anand said.

"Yes, he is." Anita paused. "Oh! You're right."

"Anita?"

Anita stood up as though in a dream. "I'll be right back." She pushed away her chair, hurried around the side of the hotel and down the stairs to the beach. She climbed the rocks and clambered carefully as close to the edge as possible. She squatted down, waiting. A wave came in, broke, and sent spindrift ten feet into the air, soaking her hair and salwar. The fisherman continued to sort through mussels in the rock pool. When he was finished, he refolded his lungi, picked up his knife, and returned to the edge of the cove. When he judged the time right, he jumped into the water and waded across. Anita called out.

The fisherman looked up. *"Shari, shari. Nallatu."*

"Yes, I know it's a good site. But isn't there another one farther south? You haven't used that site for weeks." Anita motioned to the coast behind her, waving her arm and talking. The fisherman looked where she was pointing, gave his head an affirmative shake, and slashed his knife between the rock and shells. They fell into his hands, and he scooped them into his lungi.

"Enikku venda. Enikku rupa tannu."

"Who? Who gave you money not to go there?"

"A man, just a man."

"A fisherman?"

He shook his head. Just a man. "He is sav-

326

ing them for himself." The fisherman gave a sly smile, chuckled, and began to move away. "What does he know? If he hires a man to harvest them for himself and his hotel, then he is paying more than he has to. But a fisherman will make more money." This seemed to amuse him the more he thought about it, and he went off chuckling to himself about the foolishness of city men.

Anita ran up the stairs to Anand waiting at the top. She explained what the fisherman had told her as they walked back along the path.

"I was just thinking about his harvesting when you pointed out that he was overdoing it," Anita said. "He didn't used to. He came occasionally, then he went off and harvested somewhere else. But this month he's been here only or in this area." Anita followed Anand back into the cool of the hotel parlor.

"Is the cove in front of a hotel? Are they claiming it as their property? The coast is supposed to remain open for the fishermen."

"He didn't say that, just that a man paid him not to harvest there. He took the money and moved on," Anita said.

"That's not a good sign for you, is it?"

Anand said.

Anita shrugged. "There's a lot of pressure on the coast, and the hotel owners are doing everything they can to protect their property. Some hotel owners share and others don't like it. It's hard on the fishermen."

"And this is where your hotel gets some of its seafood, yes?"

Anita nodded. "But it seems odd that we haven't heard about this. Why that cove? I hope that isn't the beginning of problems up here."

A group of foreigners had initiated a volleyball game at the point where two beaches came together, and their high spirits and shouts of encouragement were attracting a small crowd of tourists and shopkeepers. Anita was glad to see the resort and her colleagues prospering, but this time, as she passed the shops selling souvenirs, she took a closer look at the images in windows. She wasn't sure she'd recognize her family's pieces, but she would know if the displays featured old or new sculptures. And as bold as these thieves might be, she was sure they wouldn't be so stupid as to try to sell an ancient Ganapati so close to its home.

Anita turned onto her lane and waved to the tailor Chinnappa as she reached her photo gallery next door. The metal shutter flew up with a light touch, and the heat inside barreled out on top of her. Before she had reached the air-conditioned closet where she stored her photographs, Peeru, the young teen who helped her, pushed past her into the tiny room.

"Am I not here? Am I not here?" Peeru wrapped his thin arms around a set of easels and dragged them into the gallery. Anita followed with another set, and soon the two had her photographs arranged throughout the small space.

Chinnappa ambled over and sat on the gallery floor, which was raised almost a foot above the lane. "We have heard about the attack at your ancestral home." He crossed his legs and rested his folded arms on his thigh, and then gave a loud harrumph, as though blaming Anita herself for this indelicate matter.

"A maidservant, Bindu," Anita said, coming to the edge and joining him there. A pair of young women on their way to the beach passed by, trailing their brightly printed wraps behind them. The breeze caught the end of the woman's wrap, and it brushed across Anita's face. She sputtered and waved the cloth away. Chinnappa chuckled.

"The season is quiet. Gossip is necessary," the old man said. His frail limbs could fold up like a chair, his voice wrapping around him like rough coir rope.

"What gossip have you heard about the coves where fishermen collect mussels?" Anita leaned back and stretched out her legs to protect herself from the various items swinging out from tanned arms as beachers passed by.

Chinnappa raised an eyebrow and studied her. He had a finely shaped head and with the right look of arrogance might have passed for an aristocrat. Of course, he'd need better clothes, Anita thought. He sewed beautiful pants and jackets, but his own were practically rags.

"Fishermen again, is it?" He sighed and raised his head in thought. "Yes, we have heard things, fishermen pushed aside."

"Not good," Anita said.

"Temporary." Chinnappa nodded.

"And that means what?"

Chinnappa glanced around him as though this place were unfamiliar to him, a new place possibly worthy of study, but then he seemed to decide that no, it was ordinary, and he turned to Anita. "Temporary. Once or twice a month at most fishermen are pushed aside. And compensated."

Anita stared at him. "How do you know this?"

"I am poor. The fishermen are poor. The poorer we are, the more we know what should not be known. What does it matter if we know these things? Who will listen to us?" Chinnappa shrugged.

"Once or twice a month," Anita repeated. "That works." She nodded. Yes, she thought, that works just right.

"No, no, it does not." Chinnappa snapped at her, and Anita, startled, blinked at him. "It is a bad thing they are doing. You are not to go there, not to go there."

Anita climbed the hill past Hotel Delite, jumping from stone to stone. She had continued to chat with the tailor Chinnappa, but he refused to explain himself — he just kept repeating his admonition. She was to stay away from the fishermen's cove farther south.

Anita was used to Chinnappa, especially the way he could turn from sweet and easygoing to a snappish, hostile old man, but this time he was the worst she had seen him in some time. She couldn't make any sense out of it except for his longstanding but usually silent hostility to the way developers encroached on the land of laborers and fishermen. Frustrated at his behavior, Anita closed up the gallery early and headed out to the nearby village, to learn what she could about Veej.

The household servants who had been with Muttacchi for decades were turning out to be the least reliable and trustworthy of the many characters in the old woman's life. It was painful for Anita to think of Muttacchi being taken advantage of, it made her angry, but she reminded herself to keep a calm head and keep learning what she could about them.

If family treasures were missing, could Veej be the one who suggested sending them out? Was he part of a plan to steal little-used images, the ones that might have been set aside and forgotten? Anita surely hoped not, but she was going to find out for herself. If Veej's wife and child had expensive household goods, he would have to explain them. As generous as Muttacchi was, she would never buy anyone a television.

The dirt lane was rough, used only by villagers going back and forth to work at the hotels or on the beaches, and it rarely attracted foreign tourists. At the top Anita wound her way through the brush, past the empty liquor bottles, rags, and occasional plastic bags left behind by young men with time and money and boredom. Part of the scrub had been torn away by motorcycle tires, from the looks of it. This was the flip side of the resort, the part the tourists weren't supposed to see.

Anita crossed the road and picked up the path, following it down into a gulley and up the other side, emerging at the back of a row of small houses. She crossed to a narrow lane, and climbed the low hill until she emerged onto the main street leading down to Vilinzham harbor.

The heat of the day was waning, and shops were opening up for the evening. The hand-painted sign announcing Homely Meals was still standing on the sandy shoulder, and Anita headed straight for it. At the doorway, a man on a stool slouched against the wall, watching over the cash register.

"Veej?" He repeated as he leaned forward and studied Anita, apparently less interested in answering her question than in getting a good look at her. "The resort?" Anita nodded, and he did, too, pleased to have his assumptions confirmed. "Why do you want him? A better dhobi is there." He tilted his chin toward another part of the road.

"I know him," Anita explained. This didn't

seem to impress the man, but he tried once more to throw business to someone he preferred, then relented and pointed up the hill. "Take the fork, cross over the lagoon, up the hill. Near the cathedral. The back of his house borders the plaza." Anita thanked him and waved down an auto. She wasn't going to walk up the hill through strangers' yards.

The auto pulled up in front of the cathedral and an empty plaza inside the compound wall. Opposite the church was a school, quiet in the late day. Straight ahead were the backs of houses on a slope falling to the harbor. The village had crept up the hill when the new church had been built. The old one, built on the beach by the Portuguese centuries ago, still served a portion of the village.

Anita explained to the driver who she was looking for; the driver sought out a man lounging in the shade of a nearby tree and returned with directions. He pointed to the narrow lane, and Anita set off.

The hard-packed dirt path led down the hill. The cove and ocean came into view between the tightly built houses before vanishing behind walls and trees. She turned right onto another lane and worked her way between the one- and two-story houses, their low doors keeping the interior shady and cool. At the fifth house she stopped and raised her hand to knock.

"*Ivite illa.* Not home. Not home." A small boy ran up to her, repeating the news that no one was at home. "Veej is away."

Anita brushed her hand over the door and the shiny new lock. Up and down the lane women went about their business, giving her a quick appraising glance before they dodged into a house, picked up a sheet to hang on the line, watered a row of plants, or served a child a handful of rice. The quarter was full of quiet activity, but only one door, Veej's main door, sported a shiny new lock.

"How long is he away?" Anita asked. "Do you know when he's coming back?"

The boy frowned and shouted down the lane to the women. *"Epool tiriccu varum?"*

Once engaged, the women drew closer, eager to trade information with Anita. Who was she? Where did she live? Who were her people? How did she know Veej? Yes, they knew him, his family. No, he was no longer here. He went away, and he took his family with him.

"Someone must know where he went," Anita said.

"No one knows," said a woman who was

the age of Anita's mother, with leathery skin and a torn red work sari hiked up around her knees. "He makes so much money he can leave, so he leaves. Now he rents his house to a stranger who puts such large locks on the doors. Who can steal here? Do we not have eyes in our heads? Can we not see who is coming and going?"

"When did he leave?" Anita asked, wondering if they were talking about the same man.

"This morning." The woman took a step closer. "Veej comes on his bicycle after breakfast time. Why do you want to know?"

"I want to hire him, for my family." This was as good a lie as anyone needed. Immediately she was overwhelmed with suggestions of better dhobis, cheaper dhobis, cleaner dhobis, leaving Anita with the clear impression that the women didn't like Veej at all. "But he has a wife and child to support, doesn't he?"

"Everyone has a family to support, but yes, this is true." The woman shrugged.

"You must miss your friend," Anita said, probing hopefully.

The women glanced at each other. "What do you want to know?" the woman asked, moving even closer. "You don't need a dhobi." She lifted the end of the dupatta draped over one of Anita's shoulders and let the thin cotton fabric float in the hot air.

"All right," Anita said, getting the message. They were poor, but they wouldn't tolerate patronizing. "I want to know if he came into a lot of money." That set the women buzzing among themselves — the surprise of the question, the suspicions around who was asking, the curiosity of the women about someone whose secrets had escaped them.

"They left in the middle of the morning. That one," the woman said, pointing to a young woman holding an infant to her breast, "saw Veej carrying a bundle down the lane. And then she saw his wife and child going after him."

Anita fingered the new lock, trying to figure out what it meant. "Did he have a lot of new belongings inside? Some expensive things?"

The woman who had appointed herself the spokesperson shook her head. "He is poor like the rest of us. He puts his little bit of money in the bank, like the rest of us." She looked hard at Anita. "But he has other friends. Not people from the village, from outside. He does favors for them."

"And so sometimes he needs a good lock," Anita said.

The woman shook her head. "He needs to make himself feel safe. A guilty conscience."

"What does he have to feel guilty about?" Anita asked.

She waved her arms around, motioning toward the other women. "We are Catholic. Veej is Catholic." She pointed to the cathedral towering behind them. "But he works for your people."

Anita started, wondering if even in this small village they knew her family, then realized they meant Hindus — Veej worked for a Hindu family. "Does that matter here?"

She shook her head again. "No, not that. But the old woman he works for gives him old brass things — pots and plates and such. He feels guilty bringing such things into this village." She crossed her arms over her chest and flicked her chin at Anita for punctuation.

And that, agreed Anita, explains the lock.

EIGHTEEN

The auto driver chatted with Anita on the drive back to Hotel Delite, curious about who she would know on such a lane, whether or not she had spoken to the priest or one of the women always hanging about the church, but Anita could muster no more than an occasional *shari, shari,* right, right, whether it suited the question or not. After a mile of bumpy road and no interest, he turned around fully to the windshield and sped up.

Anita didn't notice the driver's disappointment. Something was obviously happening — she knew it. She was sure of it.

The auto climbed the hill and the driver swerved around a cyclist and pedestrians, jolted over speed bumps, and turned left onto Lighthouse Road. The heat of the day was abating, and goats were wandering across the road heading home. Farther along, where the road split, the left fork heading to the Muslim village and the right down to the resort hotels, shops were doing a brisk business. The driver turned right, jounced over a speed bump, and downshifted. The road was filling up with tourists out walking, gazing into shops for something interesting to buy, looking for a chemist's shop or newsagent. But Anita barely saw them.

"Come into the office with me, Auntie Meena," Anita said as soon as she walked through the door of Hotel Delite. Surprised, the older woman abandoned the mail she was sorting and followed her niece into the small room. Anita reached behind her to shut the door and then shut the second one, in the opposite wall.

"You look very worried, Anita. Has something happened?"

Anita gave a harsh laugh. "You mean in addition to Bindu's assault, Surya going missing, Gauri having possessions, and most of Muttacchi's murtis being taken away to be treated for bronze disease?" Anita fell into a chair.

"Bronze disease!" Meena gasped and leaned over her niece. "You are joking, yes?"

"Horrible, *illee?*"

"Worse than horrible, Anita." Meena lowered herself into a chair, staring hard at something beyond Anita. Anita couldn't remember ever having seen her aunt look quite so shaken. Meena Nayar was a woman whose histrionics erupted before anything serious could happen, masking whatever her deeper emotions might be, but right now, on this news, she was different. "Not the murtis, Anita. Tell me you do not mean this."

"Ganapati, the large one that is so old, it is gone." Anita rested her elbows on the table and dropped her head into her hands. "Gone."

"Not the —"

"Yes, the family Ganapati."

Meena grew silent. Anita felt her staring at her, waiting for something more. But there was nothing more. "Anita, we must do something."

"I'm going to see Gauri — right now."

"Gauri? This is more important than Gauri. Why are you —" Auntie Meena paused and peered at Anita, searching her face for understanding. "What are you saying? Gauri would not do such a thing! Gauri is difficult, but she is Gauri. She is dutiful and good and and and . . ."

"It's all right, Auntie," Anita said, squeezing her aunt's hand. "I am not accusing Gauri. I feel exactly the same way you do

341

about her."

"Then why? You are confusing me, Anita."

"I am confused myself, Auntie." Anita slipped her hands under the end of her dupatta and lifted it to her face, dabbing lightly at her perspiration. "I went to see Veej and his family, but they have disappeared." She dropped the dupatta. "Gone, completely gone. They went in the middle of the morning, in daylight. A neighbor said they just packed up and left."

"Why would they do that?" Meena lifted her hand and jerkily brushed a stray curl away from her face. "Veej is Muttacchi's dhobi — he has been so for years."

"He put a lock on his house — a shiny new lock that you need a special key for. Not like one of the usual cheap padlocks. This was special." Anita felt her shoulders sag, and her legs ached — both a sign that the worry and confusion of the last few days were getting to her.

"Why would he run away?" Meena said. "If he is in money trouble, why not come to Muttacchi and ask for a loan, for some little help? She is always helping her servants. It is our way." A look of distress came over her. "It is an insult to us that he has done this. It tells people he cannot seek help from his employer. This is very bad. Why would he do this?"

Anita watched her aunt's face twist in shame and understood every emotional step in her progress from loyal employer to betrayed benefactor. Yes, Anita thought, Auntie Meena grasped the question at once. Why would a longtime trusted servant run away instead of asking for help? What does that tell us about the trouble Veej is in? But instead of saying all this, instead of probing and asking Auntie Meena to probe also, Anita said nothing about it. Instead, she said, "Something is going to happen. I'm sure of it." Anita stood up. "I'm going out to see Gauri. I think she can help."

"Poor Muttacchi!" Meena said, slumping into a chair.

"I need Joseph and the car," Anita said.

Joseph, the hotel driver, pulled up alongside the sapling fence and put the car in park. Anita climbed out and went in search of Gauri. Anita had passed boys in white shirts and navy shorts on their way home from tutoring sessions, women out shopping, dhobis delivering laundry — the business of the evening was picking up, and the streets were growing crowded. Anita would have to manage her business with as much discretion as possible. When she looked back, Joseph had slid down in his seat and settled in for a nap.

Anita rattled the door.

"Araanathu?" Gauri's voice came from the back of the house.

"Gauri? It's me," Anita called as she walked around to the back. "There you are."

Gauri folded the sari over once, then again, laying it on a stack of similar items sitting on a cloth on the ground. She was dressed in a shabby work lungi tied up around her waist, the folds dangling to her knees. A small white dish towel was thrown over one shoulder, concealing part of her choli. Anita had interrupted her at work in her own home, in her least presentable attire, but that didn't seem to bother Gauri. She had an inimitable dignity.

She gave the pile of clothing a little pat and turned to Anita with a broad grin. "You are coming. Chai? Come." Anita accepted the invitation and followed Gauri into the house. "You go that way." Anita walked through to the front room and settled herself on a chair. When the tea was ready a few minutes later, Gauri appeared in the doorway with a tray and two steel cups in flat-bottomed bowls. She deposited the tray, which also carried a plate of freshly fried bananas. Anita guessed that Gauri, like many villagers, kept one burner in her wood stove smoldering throughout the day, to keep the milk simmering.

"This very nice," Gauri said as she pulled up a chair and smiled at her guest. "Nice visit."

"I'm glad you think so," Anita said. "I have a reason for calling."

"Trouble?" Gauri tried to look serious, but Anita knew that unless it was a matter of starvation or immediate violence, there was little that could dampen the maidservant's spirits. She'd been irrepressible all her life, but what was happening now might change that.

"It's about Muttacchi and her murtis and the kavu." Anita's words had the desired effects. Gauri grew pale, and even looked a little sick.

"This is big trouble." The teacup was inches from her lips, but she lowered it to the tray and waited. "Tell me about the murtis. She has sold them? And the big one?"

"*Ayoo,* no, Gauri, never. Muttacchi would never sell her Ganapati." Anita was surprised at Gauri's reaction. "Why would you think that?"

"People sell them for money. We are all having these things, but over time we are growing poor and foreigners want them, so we are selling them."

"No, she hasn't done that." Anita felt a chill pass through her. It was hard to believe that Muttacchi could be so poor that she'd sell an image that practically defined family and its history.

"No? That is good. But it happens." She pointed to a small shelf high up on the wall behind Anita. "There, you see? Empty. For many years I am having my Bhagavati there, but now I am poor and Bhagavati is gone."

"When did you sell her?"

"Many years ago, after my mother die." Gauri glanced up again, somewhat wistfully, and without any apparent resentment. "Perhaps Muttacchi did this, too, and is not wanting to tell anyone."

Gauri's diffidence as she repeated her suggestion that the old woman would have sold her murtis to escape a financial difficulty stalled Anita. It seemed completely unlike Muttacchi but also more pointed than a mere suggestion. "Why do you think she would do this?"

Gauri shrugged.

"Did you hear something?"

"No, no. I am only thinking if someone sees I have need, then perhaps she sees that Amma has need."

"She? You're not talking in generalities here, are you?" Anita waited for Gauri to deny it, but instead she looked embarrassed and shrugged. "Tell me! Who is this 'she'?" Anita waited while Gauri glanced at everything in the small room, its whitewashed walls streaked with rainwater from the leaky roof, the brightly colored calendar stained and torn.

"Surya?"

"Surya!" Anita gasped. "My cousin-sister Surya came to you about selling your murtis?"

Gauri nodded. "Nicely offering, nicely offering. But," she shrugged, "I have none."

"When did this happen?" As far as Anita could recall, Surya had never shown any interest in traditional Indian objects — folk art, sculpture, painting. It seemed completely out of character for her to express interest of any sort in a murti, old or new. Anita tried frantically to fit this new piece into the puzzle; she felt like she'd been given a lamp with no handle. "Gauri, I don't understand this. Muttacchi says her murtis were taken away for treatment of bronze disease." Anita glanced again at the empty shelf.

"Bronze disease!" Gauri scowled, then sneered. "What is this bronze disease?"

347

"It's when a bronze image or object starts to oxidize — it emits little green grains, like green sand. Not the patina that these things usually have, but something bright green that shows something is eating away at the bronze. Sometimes an image loses a hand or fingers, or some part of the body is eaten away." Anita looked around for something in the house that might demonstrate, but Gauri was truly poor — there was nothing to point to.

"This is a disease?"

"It's just a term in English that I translated into Malayalam — it sounds odd, I guess."

"I am not seeing this. Ganapati is not having a disease." She waved away the idea, and picked up her tea.

"But the image is gone, along with several others, smaller ones." Anita grew insistent.

"Who has done this?"

"That's what I don't know," Anita said, not sure how Surya was involved, "but I have to find out, and I think you can help me. Please, Gauri, I want you to help me."

Gauri grew still, no longer the insouciant maidservant who was willing to try anything on her employers. She watched Anita before tsking and looking away. "What do you want me to do?"

Anita wondered just how far she dared go.

Muttacchi had spent a small fortune to relieve Gauri of the burden of spontaneous trances and possessions, to bring her back to her normal state, even though that was sometimes more trouble than most employers would put up with. Gauri had been willing, even eager, to go through with the exorcism and get her normal state back. And here was Anita on the verge of disrupting her family's efforts and Gauri's health and sanity.

As unexpected as it seemed, Anita had the uneasy feeling that she was now dependant on Gauri and Gauri's unpredictability. To carry out the plan that was coalescing in her mind now, she had to present her request in such a way that Gauri would understand she could say no and would say yes if only she saw no danger to herself.

"What is troubling you?" Gauri asked. Her tea rested in her lap, her small fingers gently holding it upright. Her little gray cat bounded in the door, and Gauri leaned over to pet it. *"Puccha!"* she said, laughing at the animal's antics.

"Is that what you call her? 'Cat'?" Anita asked.

"Cat!" Gauri giggled and leaned over to pull the animal out from under her chair. It was then Anita noticed her hair. Gauri's normally neatly combed and well-oiled black hair wasn't tied in its usual sleek knot at the nape of her neck. It looked matted and flat, as though she hadn't combed it in ages. Gauri gave her a shy, almost embarrassed smile when she caught the expression on Anita's face.

"Your hair . . ." Anita began.

"Yes, it is as you see it." Gauri blushed and gave the cat a gentle pat. "I am combing my hair but the comb is getting stuck. Ah, I understand." The cat dived for Gauri's wriggling fingers. "Bhagavati has called me. I understand." She nodded, lowering her eyes. She seemed embarrassed as she played with the cat, letting it latch onto the end of a cloth as she twirled it around. Gauri had taken the knots in her hair as a sign from Bhagavati that the goddess wanted her to take on the role of devotee — Gauri would have matted locks now, for as long as the vow lasted.

"But the exorcism," Anita said, hoping to remind Gauri of her earlier resolve to recover her nature.

"Ah, yes," Gauri said, still smiling. "But this morning it comes to me."

"What happened this morning?"

"Bhagavati speaks to me." Gauri let her eyes fall shut as she nodded and smiled, reliving the moment.

"Tell me what happened, Gauri."

Gauri stared at her, as if awaking from a long sleep, a bit confused, not sure where she was or what was going on. "Happened?" She creased her forehead in thought, still smiling. "I took irunnu vadai to Amma. She loves my vadai." Gauri stopped, apparently deeming that explanation sufficient. But as tasty as the small savory doughnuts soaked in yogurt were, Anita knew there had to be more.

"And something happened then?"

"Bhagavati is calling me."

"You mean you fell into another trance?"

This confused Gauri, and she stopped. "No, no, not that. Bhagavati is not angry, not in the same way. Bhagavati is telling me she is near, she is calling me. But she is not angry." Gauri paused, thinking this over, decided it was accurate, and relaxed into another warm smile. "You eat," she said, pointing to the banana slices.

"When you say 'Bhagavati has called you,' what do you mean exactly?" Anita said, hoping against hope that this didn't mean exactly what it sounded like.

"Bhagavati has called me." Gauri smiled, and in her expression Anita saw the young girl she must have been, shy, willing, accepting. "You eat." Once again Gauri pointed to the bananas.

Resigned and also feeling adrift, Anita reached for a banana slice and felt her heart sink. Her dilemma was getting worse by the minute; a solution to the mystery surrounding the kavu as well as Surya's disappearance had seemed to be within her grasp, needing only one last stretch. But now, with Gauri telling her she had given herself over to Bhagavati, Anita felt the solution to her family's troubles and the secrets of the kavu slipping further and further away. If Gauri had adopted the stance of a devotee, the only person who could persuade the maidservant to help Anita would be Bhagavati herself.

"Will you be doing puja here this evening?" Anita asked.

"You staying? Talk to Bhagavati?"

Anita nodded. There was no other way. She went over Gauri's recital of her visit this morning, and hoped against hope she was interpreting it correctly.

Gauri sat bolt upright in the front seat of the hotel car, her eyes fixed on the road ahead and the headlights veering past them in the dark. She pressed herself hard against the seat, but gave no other sign of her anxiety. Anita thought about how brave the maidservant was, beneath that odd mixture of mischievousness and sweetness, how willing she was to join with Anita in tonight's gamble, knowing how dangerous it could be.

"Right here." Anita ordered Joseph to pull over to the side of the road, near the end of Muttacchi's driveway. She pushed open the door and climbed out.

"Go straight to hospital, ask for this doctor. She'll know what to do. And then return." Anita handed Joseph a chit of paper with a small note. "Make no stops along the way, Joseph." Anita leaned in through the passenger-side window and repeated her instructions.

"Oh, Chechi. One stop at Chalai." Gauri screwed up her face in delight at the prospect of a drive into Trivandrum, and began to wheedle for this one digression.

"Joseph, if I find you have done this, you will lose your job." Anita sounded so serious, as indeed she was, that Joseph blanched, swore at Gauri to impress on her the seriousness of the matter, and promised profusely to obey. Anita slapped the door twice, and sent him on his way. She prayed he didn't disobey — it could cost Gauri her life. Without a prophylactic antivenin shot,

Gauri would be even more vulnerable than Bindu had been.

Anita turned to the lane. The sun had set some time ago, in the sudden way it did in this part of the world. One moment it was bright and golden and fiery in the sky, and then it felt like a cloud had swept in and covered it, and soon it was dark. The moment of pink rosiness in the air lasted barely half an hour in the best of seasons — sunset, like sunrise, was dull. Unlike some parts of the world that could claim a dramatic twilight, Kerala had nothing but a dawn and dusk that disappointed in their brevity. But they did have moonlight. Anita looked up at the sky, thankful the moon was on the wane, almost a crescent.

Once in the parking area, Anita could have turned to the right and headed to the veranda outside Muttacchi's room, but instead she went straight to the main entrance and climbed through the gateway, knowing as she did so that Sett was watching nearby. If she turned to look at him, she knew he'd quickly engage in some menial task; it was enough to know he was keeping an eye on her. And it was what she expected. She would have to be careful over the next few hours not to raise suspicions.

"No word," Muttacchi said when Anita

joined her in the courtyard. "I think I am getting it all wrong. Surya is such a quick young thing and I am so old now. I am certain she is telling me she is going to Mumbai first and then she is coming here, and I am getting this all mixed up. I am telling Meena that Surya is coming here first and then to Mumbai, and it is all turned around. What will she think of me?"

Anita leaned over to touch the old woman's toes with her fingertips. "She will think you are trying hard to find a way to excuse your beloved granddaughter's bad behavior." Anita fell into a chair. "But I think she didn't do this. I think," Anita said, upset when her voice caught in her throat, giving away her deep feelings about the situation, "we shall find her safe and sound and with a good reason for not showing up when expected."

"You think this?"

The desperate hope in Muttacchi's face pained Anita, and the old woman turned away and began to pluck at imagined stains on her sari folds, perhaps embarrassed at the naked need she had revealed. I should have dealt with this sooner, Anita thought. Of course, Muttacchi would have imagined the worst, and would be worried sick. I've avoided facing up to how she's been feeling through all of this, thinking she was deceived by my pretense of confidence. "I'm sorry, Muttacchi, for not sitting down with you sooner and telling you everything I've been thinking." She leaned forward in her chair and took the old woman's hands in hers. "I know you have been searching for an understanding for all this."

The old woman squeezed Anita's hands in her own, and shook her head. "They are feckless, these young ones. These are not our ways, not our ways at all — to show such disregard for their elders. My daughter has given up, I fear. She has taken a different way, and it shows in Surya." Muttacchi sighed. "Sometimes I am glad I am old. But you!" She looked up at Anita and a twinkle came into her eyes. "What has brought you here to me at this hour?"

Anita spoke in a barely audible whisper as she lowered her head. "You're right — something is going on. But I don't want anyone else here to know what I'm doing, Muttacchi. Things will happen tonight."

"What things?"

"Things, just things. But I am ready. And you must listen to me, just this once." Anita leaned forward and whispered. "Don't drink the lassi." Anita leaned back in her chair and resumed in a normal voice. "Have you seen Gauri since the exorcism?"

"Ah, Gauri!" The exclamation came after barely a moment to grasp the implications of Anita's warning. The old woman leaned back in her chair and waved her hands, putting all her attention into brushing away an insect. What a good sort she is, Anita thought. "She came by this morning, to bring me irunnu vadai. I have had it for my supper."

"Sounds delicious. My favorite." Anita let her head fall back and rest on the cushion; she stared up at the darkening sky. "I'm glad she seems better."

"Ah, well, somewhat." Muttacchi sighed. "She had a mild trance this morning. Not as bad as before but enough of one to tell me the exorcism has failed." The old woman suddenly looked very sad. "She has taken this call from Bhagavati to be true." The old woman smiled. "She will perhaps bring us good fortune, with Bhagavati's blessings."

"I'm sure she will," Anita said, and meant it.

NINETEEN

Muttacchi leaned heavily on Anita as she climbed the steps to the veranda, muttering a prayer for Gauri and for her grand-daughter Surya. Anita left the old woman settling into her room and crossed the courtyard to her own room. The evening was quiet, the darkness soaking up the sounds of Lata and the other servants putting the estate in order for the night. It always seemed to Anita that the tranquility and orderliness she saw around her were the most deceptive parts of life anywhere, in any country. In the quiet of a dark night animals stalked their prey and behind the brightly painted doors and neat lawns, husbands and wives stood at a kitchen table wrenching their lives apart.

In her own room Anita rooted around in the armoire for something light but warm, trying different dupattas and shawls, until she found one with the right weight. With the shawl in her hand, she closed her door and headed down to the river path. She looked back a few times, but no one seemed to notice her, to care that she was heading out at this hour for a stroll.

The occasional voice drifted to her on the light air, but otherwise the household seemed far away from her and her plans. That seemed especially odd to her, because now that she was convinced something was going to happen, she half expected others to appear more intense, louder, angrier, sneakier. But they didn't. They seemed to be going about their business as usual — Lata in the kitchen knocking aluminum pots into each other, Sett grousing as usual as he did the least amount of work, Arun shouting replies in the hyperenergetic voice of a young boy growing up fast, the sounds of traffic from the road nearby, the occasional voices from a neighbor's house. Only Veej's voice was missing from the usual evening chorus.

The river was quiet, the water still, with little sign of any activity either up or down the banks. Satisfied there was no one nearby, Anita stepped into the water, and in a moment was swimming along the riverbank toward the kavu. Quickly she slid under the overhanging branches and pulled herself along, confident she was fully concealed.

When she reached the spot where she had last climbed ashore, she pulled the shawl out of the water and pushed it onto the land. The soggy cloth fell away, revealing a large plastic bag, and from inside this Anita extracted the wooden box she had found here and taken to Muttacchi. Anita nudged everything farther ashore and climbed onto the riverbank. If she had miscalculated both the time and the events she anticipated for the evening, her efforts would all go for nothing. And worse, she might be tipping her hand to people who cared nothing for the life of another. Bindu was proof of that. But Anita was certain she was right about the timing. She reviewed the history of Gauri's trances, Konan's eagerness to be rid of the maidservant, the influx of tourists from the ocean liner and the guide's chronic complaints this year, the disappearance of Surya and of the murtis, and Veej's abrupt flight with his family.

Anita studied the ground, making sure to keep the flashlight beam low, looking for any sign that someone else had been here recently. Everything looked just as she had discovered it the other night — the hole for the box, the indentation in the soil, the large sweep of ground cleared of debris toward the water. Whatever had been going on here, tonight she would see for herself. And then she would atone to Bhairava — if such were possible.

Anita pushed deeper into the kavu. She came to the spot for the box, cleared away a few leaves, and shined her flashlight down. The carefully cut hole was intact — with no sign anyone had been near it. It was still empty, just as she had left it. Anita slid the box into its hole. She sighed with relief — the sides hadn't caved in, the box was intact, it fit where it had been originally. She had a theory about the box and what it was used for, and tonight she expected to find out if she was right. Objects handled by humans often had food residue on them, something that could make them tempting to wild animals coming upon them in the forest. A small animal could drag a murti anywhere if it promised the taste of milk or ghee. Better to hide the image in a box.

Her next task was to get out of there without leaving any signs of her visit. Anita began to crawl backward, brushing leaves and other debris over the disturbed ground as she withdrew. Several minutes later she slid back into the water and worked her way down the riverbank. She swam through the darkness past the stone steps, past the beginning of the path leading west, and on to the next set of steps. There she climbed out, dragging her shawl behind her.

Anita took the path back to the estate, and crept up behind her cottage. A few minutes later she was standing under a hot shower.

The evening meal called for very little conversation. Muttacchi had insisted it be served late, claiming she didn't feel very well. She studied each morsel before popping it into her mouth, and Anita was so distracted by trying to follow the behaviors of the servants without turning around to stare at them, she could barely remember to eat at all. When she glanced up at the sound of the old woman's voice, she found Muttacchi studying her.

"You have learned things you have not told me," the old woman whispered. "So I am waiting. And I am thinking I know some of these things. Watching and observing are more fundamental to wisdom than rushing about."

Anita blushed, then looked away. "I guess I'm just nervous."

"Is your friend coming to visit us this evening?"

"My friend?" Anita frowned, trying to think of who that would be. "Oh, you mean

Anand? Possibly. I'm not sure." Anita glanced toward the gateway, half expecting to see a crowd of villagers climbing through, wanting to know what all these water excursions were about. Villagers could observe supposedly secret conduct for weeks before coming forward and asking what all the skullduggery was about. "He may be busy."

Anita tried to smile, but instead she just looked crookedly around her. She was uneasy, not so much frightened as fearing she might have miscalculated. It made her edgy, her mind flighty. She could so easily be wrong — the connections between Konan, the astrologer, and the moneylender could be nothing more than the usual prudent behavior of a businessman making sure he got his money, even if it meant traveling around with the debtor. But the newsagent puzzled her. How was he involved? And the priest? What was he up to? And who planted that snake along the path near the temple?

Suddenly the old woman sat up and pointed. "What is she doing here?" Muttacchi continued to stare with a cold eye as Gauri pressed her hands together in anjali, a mischievous grin on her face.

"Ah . . ." Anita felt her heart sink. "I have no idea." She's not supposed to be here now, was what Anita wanted to say, not until much later, when she was supposed to come in through the trees so no one saw her. She certainly wasn't supposed to wander in like she owned the place, calling out greetings to everyone within earshot.

"Ah, Amma!" Gauri bowed to Muttacchi, looking happier every minute. The maidservant turned to Anita, offering a similarly warm greeting. "Bhagavati sent me."

Anita groaned. Gauri had her cornered. After a brief puja at Gauri's home, when Anita had the opportunity to address Bhagavati directly, through Gauri, Anita had left with the impression that Gauri would appear later, when no one knew she had arrived. Apparently, Bhagavati had changed her mind, and Gauri's along with it.

Gauri cast an appraising eye over the table, decided certain dishes were lacking, and headed off to the kitchen.

Anita lay in bed in the darkness, staring up at the ceiling and the mosquito netting tied up in its daytime knot. Outside, Gauri snored on her mat on the veranda. The maidservant had insisted on sleeping as close to the kavu as possible, on instructions from Bhagavati, apparently, and Anita could do nothing about it. This was not part of her plan, and as she waited for the night to advance, she wondered if she would awake tomorrow to a greater sadness than she had known in years, one that could not be assuaged by a walk into the jungle, to stand among birds and flowers and gentle silence.

Anita rolled over and patted the chair seat, looking for her watch. When she found it, she picked it up, pressed the button, and read the time in the soft green glow. Almost midnight. She shouldn't wait much longer. She sat up and straightened her salwar. Again she waited, moving closer to the open side window — nothing stirred, no sound came. She passed into the bathroom, walked over to the high window, and lifted the plain cotton curtain. Again, silence. She folded the curtain over the thin string, and with an abrupt tug, pulled the wooden bars out of the window opening. She rested the frame and bars against the wall and stood on a stool.

Sitting on the windowsill, with her legs dangling out the window, she leaned forward, measured the distance to the ground, and pushed herself out, landing in a crouch on the dirt. She was surprised at how little noise she made, and congratulated herself on remembering to clear away leaves and other debris earlier. Her soft thud wouldn't travel far in the night air. She paused, waiting just in case, before moving along the wall to the corner. She bolted for the woods and there took refuge in the undergrowth. For a second she wondered if she should warn Gauri, but decided against it. Now that the maidservant was in the service of Bhagavati, there was no telling how she'd react to anything Anita did or said. She pushed her way through the growth and headed to the river.

The evening had been hot, and the river felt good on her feet and ankles as she slid into the water. She had chosen a starting point west of the stone steps, if only because she was afraid of being seen by someone from the house. Veej was gone, but there were still Sett and Lata to worry about, and Anita couldn't be sure which one she could trust, or neither. She slid deeper into the water and began to swim toward the kavu. She went underwater as she came to the stone steps, pulling herself along the deeper stones. She hadn't realized how far down they went, and wondered if the river had been so much lower in previous years. But at least they served as a reliable guide.

When she surfaced, she drew closer to the kavu and quickly moved in to shore, using the overgrowth for concealment. She moved slowly, methodically, creating as little disturbance in the water as possible, one ear cocked to the river behind her, the other to the noise and activities going on inside the sacred grove. She could hear small animals scurrying about, a branch squeak and brush against another, something heavy fall or land on the ground. The kavu was alive this time of night, its inhabitants safe from the outside world — at least that was the theory and the belief all these years, until now. Anita moved slowly but relentlessly until she judged she had passed the eastern edge of the grove. Now, safe beyond the reach of Bhairava, unlikely to offend him here, she scoured the darkness for a place to conceal herself while she waited.

With her arms wrapped around the trunk of a palm tree growing almost in a straight horizontal over the river until it turned and grew upright, Anita let her thoughts drift. The river was wide enough here for images on the other shore to be indistinct enough to confuse any observer, and the level of development was still low. The riverbank was still lush growth, much as it had been for centuries. The burst of growth that was Trivandrum was located farther north, along the highway to Kollam and Kochi.

The moonlight lit up the river, picking out crests and ripples. A moment later a series of clouds drifted across the sky, and the night grew darker and chillier. Then she heard it. Anita tensed, waited, listened. Yes, a wooden pole scraped along the side of a wooden boat — someone was poling a vellum nearby. She drew in her legs and pulled herself closer to the riverbank, lowering herself into the water until only her head from her nose upward was above water, and that shrouded by a cluster of branches and leaves.

The vellum came from the opposite shore, the boatman pushing off from the land and guiding the boat across the river in short, fluid strokes. Despite the growth of Trivandrum and its fluorescent tube lights burning throughout the night, this part of the area didn't have enough ambient light to illuminate the surrounding countryside. The vellum moved in and out of patches of darkness as it crossed the river. As the boat took on a more precise shape, Anita could make out three people — the boatman and two passengers. The first one seemed to be no more than a child, a young girl shrouded in her nerid.

The boat drew closer, and Anita recognized the men — the boatman Gokul and

Lata's relation, the supposed guide from East Fort in Trivandrum.

Gokul locked his pole to the side of the boat and the bow turned toward the shore, coming almost directly at Anita. She felt the adrenalin rush through her chest. But then Lata's relation waved his hand and hissed at the boatman, who corrected his steering and headed the boat farther down the riverbank. She followed it with her eyes, not daring to move. Barely fifty feet away, the bow drove into the brush and crashed into the river-bank. With a few choice accusations of the boatman, the second man pulled the boat closer in to the bank while Gokul pressed the pole into the river bottom, pushing the boat inshore. When the boat was as close to the bank as he could get it, Gokul planted the pole in the water, slanting it against the side.

"Take it, take it," the second man said.

"Don't boss me, Pidar," Gokul said. "We are partners, isn't it?" Gokul clambered into the water, grabbed a bag from the boat, and climbed onto the land. He peeled back a few branches and slid deeper into the forest. Anita could hear him moving about, yet he was remarkably quiet. She knew she hadn't been that quiet on her two forays into the kavu — he must be familiar with the ground.

A few minutes later he slithered back into view and down into the water. Then, with a suddenness Anita was unprepared for, he grasped the woman in the front of the vellum and hoisted her out of the boat — only it wasn't a woman, it was an image standing in the bottom of the boat wrapped in a sari. Anita strangled a yelp, clamping her lips shut. Pidar hissed at him, and Gokul swore back. Anita watched as Gokul climbed back onto the land and pulled the statue with him.

Anita hadn't given much time to thinking about who these people were who would steal murtis. They were just more of those who had a path different from hers. But at this moment, as the night breezes chilled her as she held onto a root on the muddy river bottom to keep herself from floating out into the open, kept half her head below water, kept herself from calling out, she also felt a deep antipathy for what she saw before her.

The boatman's legs came into view again, and this time he had something to say. He grunted and whispered to Pidar.

"What?" Pidar jumped up from his seat in the middle of the boat and arched over as though he were going to dive off the boat.

"Go back. You're stupid. Go back and get it."

Gokul protested but gave in, working his way back into the forest, swearing and huffing and hissing. Pidar leaned over and grabbed at a root on shore, pulling the boat in closer, watching intently in the darkness. A few minutes later the boatman returned, shoving something along ahead of him, making his way out from under the branches and palm trees and vines.

"There. See for yourself." Gokul shoved something at the other man.

What is it? thought Anita. She didn't dare move, but the curiosity was killing her. And if she gave in to it, that very angry man would probably kill her.

Pidar grabbed at it and held it up. The box. The rotting wooden box Anita had pulled from the ground hung from his hand as though it were a serpent. He held it against his chest as he opened it. He turned it upside down. Empty. He threw it onto the shore.

"Where is it?"

"It's not there." Gokul worked his way forward until his feet touched the water. Then he turned and stepped into the river and then into the boat. "We are being cheated."

"No, no, he always paid." Pidar fell back onto the seat. "The money is always there. There must be trouble tonight."

"What trouble?"

"I don't know. Perhaps we are too early."

"You are wasting your time. We are being cheated, you will see." Gokul sat down and began to brush the dirt and debris off his arms and legs. "Tonight is the last one, so why should they pay? It is more for them."

"Go back and get it," Pidar said.

"What?" The fear in Gokul's voice was unmistakable. "No, no, I cannot do that. What he will do to me . . ." He lowered his voice and said, "You go back in. You do this sin."

"No!" Pidar's answer came fast, sharp. So, thought Anita, he's also afraid of the one he works for.

"Then we leave it for now," Gokul said.

Pidar swung around to glare at him. "All right, but I will not be cheated. If it is not there when we return later, I will find them and get my money. If they take the image and leave no money, they will know my wrath." The sweat on his face picked up light reflecting off the water.

Gokul stood up and reached for his pole. He pulled it from the muddy bottom, swung it over his head, and drove it into the

372

riverbank, pushing the vellum away from the shore. Then, before the boat moved out into the river, Anita heard one more time, "I will not be cheated."

She watched the boat cross the river and disappear in the darkness, but the determination in the voice lingered. Anita had no doubt, hearing him speak now, that Pidar, Lata's relation, if that was what he was, meant what he said: they would be back once more this night. That didn't give her much time.

Half an hour later Anita crawled around the corner of the veranda of her small room and peered over the parapet. There, to her surprise was Gauri, her legs dangling over the edge, peeling a banana. She was supposed to be asleep. Anita stood up, shaking from cold and distress.

"Did something happen to you?" Anita asked. "Did Bhagavati speak to you?"

"Bhagavati is calling Gauri. I am listening. Bhagavati is happy, sort of." Gauri frowned while she considered this apparent incongruity.

"What do you mean, sort of?" Anita moved to the veranda, remembering she had left the door bolted on the inside, and sat down. "Did you have a trance?"

"Bhagavati is calling." She smiled and took a bite of her banana.

Anita sighed. "Is anyone else about?"

Gauri shook her head. "Amma is watching through her little window but is not coming outside. Lata and Sett are sleeping, there." She nodded toward the back of the kitchen wing. "And you?" she said as she lifted the sodden sleeve of Anita's outfit.

"I haven't much time, Gauri." Anita crossed the yard to Muttacchi's room, knelt below the window, and spoke quickly. A moment later she reached into the window, then moved across the veranda to the storage room. She unlocked the door, went in, and a minute later emerged with a large object in her arms. She returned the key to the old woman, and crossed the courtyard again to her own room.

"What is that?" Gauri asked.

"Never mind. Just sit here and watch it." She set the object on the veranda and headed around to the back of the building, where she crawled in through the bathroom window. Inside, she stripped off her sodden clothes, and gave herself a quick hot shower, taking off the chill. She grabbed a clean salwar set, dressed as quickly as possible, her fingers fumbling and stiff. What she really wanted, however, was a flashlight. She rummaged through her suitcase and found one, no larger than a carrot. Anita opened the door and stepped out onto the veranda.

"It might be better if you stayed inside," Anita said.

"No, Chechi. No." Gauri smiled warmly, sweetly. "Bhagavati has called me here, not inside asleep. Gauri sit here." She patted the veranda twice, sweeping her hand wide each time, to emphasize her point. Anita sighed. She knew better than to argue.

"All right." She jumped onto the ground and gathered up the parcel. "I don't know how much time I have."

"Bhagavati is not angry with you."

Anita paused. Ready to hurry back to the river, she leaned toward the water, but Gauri's words held her, unable to move. Gauri's statement was a simple one, but it made Anita wonder about something else: Would Bhairava distinguish between those who invaded his sacred grove for good and for ill? It was a thought, a question, she had pushed from her mind most of the time. She had no business meddling in Muttacchi's affairs, except that Anita loved her, loved her family, and hated to see anything bad happen to them. But entering the kavu as part of an effort to protect them? It was her duty, her obligation to help them, but did that justify breaking a sacred rule? Surely Bhairava, Anita reasoned, could understand her sense of duty to her family, even if it meant violating the sacred space. All her life she had struggled to reconcile her duty with her life as it unfolded before her.

Anita clung to her belief in duty in a larger sense even while she felt repelled by the little acts of duty her family tried to force upon her. Surely Bhairava could understand that. But this debate within herself had been innocent, painless, academic — until now. Gauri was telling her Anita was allowed to do what she was doing. It both exhilarated and disturbed her, but in the end she let it comfort her.

"I only hope Bhagavati will help us as we need it." Anita clutched the parcel tighter to her chest. "I don't know what's going to happen."

"Bhagavati knows perhaps." Gauri picked up another banana and began to peel it.

TWENTY

Anita lowered herself into the river and began to swim upstream, holding the parcel aloft. Her progress was much slower this time, and her arms soon grew tired, even though she switched positions frequently. She turned onto her back and tried to swim with only her feet propelling her. As soon as she could, she grabbed hold of branches with her free arm and pulled herself along. At the spot where the vellum had docked, she moved closer to the bank and shoved the parcel ashore, pushing it as deep as she could into the forest. Then she climbed in after it. Silently she offered a prayer to Bhairava and pulled out her flashlight.

By now she had a pretty good sense of the lay of the land inside the kavu, but she had to be sure she got everything right. She moved the light over the ground, her vision blocked by vines and shrubs, branches and debris thick wherever she looked. She had seen Gokul leave two parcels — one almost as large as a child and the other a bag that might contain one or many smaller items. Since he hadn't gone long into the kavu each time, the parcels had to be nearby. When the thin blade of light fell on one parcel, she crawled toward it. She reached it quickly, no longer worried about leaving evidence of her presence. The next visitors would expect to see signs of activity here.

To her great relief, the parcel she had brought and the parcel in the cloth bag Gokul had left were almost identical in size. She drew closer to the one Gokul left and began to squeeze it, trying to get a sense of what was enclosed. She felt from the bottom to the top and then back again. It was as she expected — a tall figure standing straight. She turned to her own parcel and squeezed it in the same way — yes, it felt very much the same. Anyone who didn't know wouldn't pick up on the differences right away.

Anita passed her flashlight over the first parcel inch by inch, looking for an opening to expand. She found a fold and wriggled her hand into it. Moving about, her fingers reached close to the top and she felt along the surface. Yes, a face of metal covered in soft clay. She moved her fingers along and felt the elephant trunk gently ridged as it curved down over his big belly. This was a Ganapati — no doubt of that. She moved her hand deeper and down the back, feeling for a design she had long seen on Muttacchi's Ganapati. Yes, there it was, a fold in the dhoti, the sign of a brilliant artist centuries old. Anita felt herself beginning to cry. It was here, the treasured Ganapati, the soul of the family's history, insultingly wrapped and ill treated, but here, whole and safe and still on family land. She laid her head down on the parcel and felt a wave of relief, joy, exhaustion wash over her.

The sound of voices in the distance brought her back to the moment. A boat was approaching. Anita looked about her hurriedly — it was too late to slip back in the water and conceal herself there, and she couldn't let them find her here. Anita raised her head and looked toward the estate, a building she couldn't see through the thick forest — but she had no choice. She flicked off her flashlight, shoved into place the parcel she had brought, and pulled the first one close to her as she crouched under branches and made her way through the brush. She stretched out her legs where she could and took long strides over vines and shrubs, frantic just to get out of range of another's flashlight. A tangle of shrubbery almost stopped her until she crawled underneath it and curled into a ball on the ground, pulling up vines to conceal her.

Anita waited, listened, and soon heard the brittle crunch of a vellum gliding in among the brush and grinding to a halt. The voices were low and sounded harsh, one man scolding another for his inept docking. Did she imagine it, or did she also hear the impatience of greed, that testiness when ordinary life comes between a man and his temptation? She kept as low as she could and listened for the sounds of someone crawling through the brush. Behind, probably not far, sat the image of Bhairava, and she suddenly felt surrounded by the anger of humanity when things go awry.

"It is here already. I got it!" The man's voice was buoyant, excited, but also tense. He pulled at the parcel and began to tug at it, drawing it toward the river. "There's two this night."

"Good. Let's go. And don't make so much noise."

"Don't shush me."

"Someone from the house will hear you."

"Ahh! No one will hear me. Who are you afraid of?"

"That maidservant is back, the one who

hears Bhagavati."

"So? She will have a trance in the morning, and then so what? We are gone."

"She is here now. I saw her on the road this evening, going in. If she hears us, she will go screeching and yelling."

The other man continued to tug his treasure to the water, grunting and swearing every time it became entangled in a vine or branch.

"Did you hear me?"

"Yes, yes." He swore at a branch and worked his way through some time in silence.

"She came today, to see the old woman. And she returned this evening." Silence fell after this announcement. For a while Anita heard only small twigs snapping. "It is time to be rid of her." The statement was stark and seemed even louder for its finality and coldness. "I will take the murtis. You come on later by foot."

"Eh? What?" Something hit the side of the vellum and Anita heard waves lap against the shore.

"Yes, do as I tell you. You find her here, and finish it. Why else did I come prepared? A troublesome woman." Anita heard something scrape along the edge of the vellum and surmised the man was pulling the parcel into the boat. "I know how to pole a boat. You come after me."

"Now? But it is done. You have the murti. We are through with this place. I have left the money."

"Do what I tell you. What is your weakness?" The voices hissed through the night. "It takes but a moment when you find her. Did Bindu trouble you? No. Will Gauri trouble you? No, of course not. But this time, see it through. End it."

"But she is chosen. Bhagavati did not leave her." The man began to sound unsure, even whiny.

"She is a crazy one. Do it. Here." Anita heard a thud muffled by the ground, as if something heavy had been thrown onto it. The man on land swore. "When you're done, be rid of it all."

The next thing Anita heard was the scrape of a pole along the side of the vellum as the man took up the task of guiding the boat down the river. As he moved away, silence fell again. Anita was sure the one remaining man could hear her breathing, her short quick breaths and twitching limbs as she grew stiff and sore from crouching so long. But it didn't matter — he wasn't going to stay there. He was going after Gauri, and Anita had to stop him.

■ ■ ■ ■

A gentle splash, breaking branches, swearing. He must have gone back into the water, Anita thought. And if he's going to follow orders, he's going to go down to the stone steps and then go after Gauri from there.

Anita untangled the vines around her and relaxed her grip on the parcel. What on earth was she going to do with it? She couldn't take it with her, and she couldn't abandon it here in the kavu. Or could she? Anita managed to stand partway up, pushing away tree limbs and feeling like Alice in Wonderland, towering over a forest yet crushed by one from above. There was only one thing she could do — and still help Gauri. Anita closed her eyes, recited a prayer taught her by her grandmother many years ago, and then turned and knelt. She shoved the parcel underneath the shrubbery and pushed, stretching out as far as she could to get the murti as far away from the shore as possible, as deep into the kavu as she dared go, as close to Bhairava as was humanly possible for her. When she was resigned to what she had accomplished, she turned in the direction of the lane and began to bushwhack her way through the forest.

Anita had little sense of distances at this point, but she was certain that she was closer to the buildings than to the river. She tried to move as quietly as possible, ducking under branches, scaring away small animals, trying not to cry out when a branch unexpectedly slapped her in the face or her foot landed on something soft and furry. The darkness seemed to change after a while, and she paused to get her bearings. She laid flat on the ground and peered ahead, then moved forward. She was within a few feet of the path to the river. She closed her eyes and thanked Bhairava and Bhagavati for guiding her.

Other than the noises of the kavu surrounding her, no sound reached her. She listened intently and pulled herself closer to the forest edge. The boatman had not appeared on the path, and she couldn't hear him moving through the brush if he was on either side of the path. To her left, toward the house, she could see Gauri, but something was wrong. Anita moved almost to the edge of the kavu to get a better look.

Gauri was standing at the end of the veranda of Anita's bungalow, unmoving. Her stillness began to give way to swaying, her head fell back, and then she raised her arms to slap against her chest. She swung her arms out and back, slapping her chest with increasing ferocity. Then, suddenly, she turned and grabbed a bucket of water and lifted it over her head, letting it pour down on her. She threw down the empty bucket and continued swinging her arms, flinging them wide and letting the momentum swing them flat against her torso. The arms moved faster and faster, and Gauri's expression grew stranger and stranger. A lacy whiteness from the moon drifted down on her, and Anita could see the maidservant's head tilt back with her eyes closed.

Then, what Anita feared happened. To her right came the sound of someone moving cautiously through the darkness — a twig snapped, tall grasses brushed and swayed, heavy breath. Anita froze. Her mind slowed, and she saw herself rise slowly as the boatman came into view. She was ready to throw herself at his knees, to knock him flat and beat his head against the ground until the others came running. But in those seconds that seemed like minutes, the sounds coming from Gauri transformed the night.

The boatman held in his left hand a long thin snake that waved and wriggled in the air; a small cotton cap covered its head. The boatman's head was also covered, but not so benignly — it was the mask of a demon flickering in the moonlight, frightening, inhuman, irrational. Anita heard herself gasp. No wonder Bindu had been trying to flee. In the boatman's right hand appeared a mallet. Before Anita could move, Gauri roared. Anita turned at the sound.

If a human being could puff herself up like a peacock, Gauri had done this. But she wasn't beautiful — she was hideous, wrathful, wild and demonic. Every muscle in her face worked and twisted and raged against the boatman. Her shoulders seemed made of iron, shiny with the heat of the sweltering ovens, her legs stretched apart like the gigantic stone pillars of a temple. She roared and the voice was that of Bhairava. And the god condemned the man to suffer, to die a painful ugly death, to be reborn as an ant again and again and again, enslaved and mindless and hungry. With every word Gauri spoke she seemed to grow larger and larger, and she moved closer and closer to the boatman.

"Hi, ha!" She slapped her hands and jumped in front of him, the words of Bhairava ushering from her mouth faster and faster, cursing and terrifying.

The boatman fell back, his mask askew.

He lost his footing and collapsed onto the ground, the hammer flying out of his hand, the snake twisting away, the cloth cap slipping off. The mask fell, revealing the face of a man in a panic, overwhelmed with fear. He turned and scrambled to his feet, then lost his footing in the sand, and fell again. He screamed and stared at his right hand. He had been bitten.

He struggled to get to his feet, get away from the snake, but he was too unsteady now, too frightened. The snake darted at him a second time, hit his bare leg, then slithered away into the darkness. The boatman wailed, and tripping and running and tripping again, he fled to the water's edge. Anita heard a splash and the sounds of someone thrashing through the water. She had no idea which direction he had taken, where he had gone. Anita ran to Gauri.

The maidservant stood in the same place, but another transformation was taking place. Her head fell back, the muscles of her face seemed to relax, her eyes closed. Her arms hung limply at her sides. Her bare feet were once again those of a woman who had never worn shoes. She seemed to shrink until she was returned to the maidservant she had always been. Then her head fell forward and swung from side to side.

"Gauri?" Anita took a step closer.

"Chechi?" Gauri tried to focus her eyes on her. *"Ayoo!"* She raised her hand to her head as though she had a headache. "Bhairava very, very angry. *Ayoo!*" She slowly turned around, moving toward the veranda. When she reached it, she leaned on it and pulled herself along to the steps, where she sat down with a thud. "*Ayoo,* so angry."

"He sure is." Anita touched Gauri lightly on the shoulder. "Let me get someone to help you."

"No, no," she said, shaking her head. "You go. You find this bad man."

"Yes, him and a few others."

Anita ran to the front of the property, found the motorbike Muttacchi had purchased for Surya, and got it started. The deep night stillness magnified the sound of the small engine, and Anita looked around expecting to see someone coming forward to complain about the noise. But no one seemed to hear. She kicked away the stand and pushed the bike ahead, climbing onto the seat and revving the engine until it picked up speed. The headlight picked out the ruts in the driveway and she swung around them as best she could, then headed down the road.

This hadn't been part of her plan at all. None of this had. Once she had figured out the kavu was the drop for Hindu murtis, probably most of them sacred images stolen from temples, she had only wanted to capture them and turn them in to the police, for return to their owners. Let the police figure out who the thieves were, let them trace the murtis to their temple homes and the thieves responsible, let them find and punish the thieves. But the boatman's plan to murder Gauri changed all that. And the second man's escape with what he thought was a magnificent Ganapati concealed in clay and paint enraged Anita so much that she was caught up in the need to stop him. The bike swerved around a corner, and she told herself to remain calm.

"Don't drive the way you feel, idiot!" She was on the verge of crashing into trees or flying off into the brush or into a house. "Take it slow. Well, slower."

She downshifted as she came upon a sharp curve, slowed, turned, and sped up again. A man leaning against a tree, keeping a casual eye on an ailing cow, watched her with mild curiosity and turned back to his animal. Anita barely noticed him. She turned again and passed through a cluster of shops, continued on, and soon came along the row of shuttered shops that marked the entrance to the Parasurama Temple.

Anita followed on the dirt lane to the entrance, cut the engine, and drifted toward the gate. She couldn't think how long it had taken her to get here, but there was a chance, a slim one, that the boat had not yet passed, or was still within sight. The passenger, Pidar, wasn't a boatman, and for all his bravado about being able to manage a boat as well as the boatman, Anita suspected he didn't really know what he was getting into. It was one thing to push a pole into the ground once, lean against it, and propel the vellum forward; it was entirely another thing to control the heavy wooden boat along the river, poling and steering and keeping up your strength. Anita slowed to a stop and listened. And listened.

She propped the bike up against a tree and crept to the riverbank. To her left the highway rose and crossed over the bridge. To her right brush and a small tea stall marked the riverbank. Nothing was moving under the moonlight. It was hotter here, away from the thick growth that cooled the air on the hottest days and filtered the monsoon.

And then she heard it — a short grunt,

long sigh, a splash. This boatman was truly inept, a passenger who should never have bragged. Anita crouched low on the ground, concealed by the brush, as the bow of the vellum came into view. The man pushed the pole into the river bottom, facing toward the stern as he pushed away, then pulled the pole out, turned, and moved forward a few feet as he prepared to pole again. Pidar was worse than inept — he was dangerously unsafe, looking like he was about to lose his balance and fall in himself.

Pidar rocked on his feet as he tried to get a purchase in the middle of the boat, then turned and pushed the pole into the water again. He miscalculated and the bow veered into shore. He grabbed at the pole, pulled it out, and stuck it into the bank, pushing the boat back out into the river. The stern pointed to the opposite bank, and the man was all but turning the vellum around. The bamboo pole wobbled at the awkward maneuver. The man pulled it out and picked another spot and pushed again, trying to get the boat headed in the right direction. Anita prayed he didn't knock himself into the water — she had to follow him to his final destination if she had any hope of finding Surya. In ways that could be awful or innocent, Surya and this business of stolen murtis were connected. Anita didn't know how, but she was convinced they were.

After some time, the vellum passed under the bridge. Anita hurried back along the path to the road, ran across, and crouching low again, made her way along the flyover toward the riverbank. The man was struggling but kept the vellum moving. From here, Anita knew, he had to pass the small boat club set up for tourists, cross a lagoon, and follow the river as it meandered to the coast, and from there he could cross to the ocean through a narrow channel through the barrier beach.

Would he dare?

He wasn't skilled enough to do that, and a skilled boatman couldn't do it either. The vellum was for a river, the poling for shallow water. Anita lowered herself to the shore and watched the vellum move across the river. But he had to deliver his cargo, the parcel that was such a valuable murti that he was willing to kill for it. How could he deliver this? And where?

Small homes dotted the far side of the lagoon, and on the near side, behind the streetscape of shops and new homes and the dozen lorries parked for the night, was a private estate turned into a resort. Anita sometimes saw the guests riding about the lagoon in new and painted vellums, nothing like the tar- and dirt-plugged working boats this man was using. His was nothing seaworthy, that was for sure. But for most of the journey, the river ran through undeveloped land, with occasional homes and old paddy fields.

It would have been much easier for him to dock here, near the bridge, and transfer the parcel and himself to a car or an autorickshaw. But he hadn't done that. No, he'd gone on down the river. Anita began to sweat, thinking hard. If he had another drop site, she might never be able to stop him without following him on the river — which he was sure to notice, since he couldn't pole the boat without looking backward. But if he had no drop site, where was he going in a vellum? Why wasn't it safer and faster to travel on land?

She had to follow him. She thrashed her way out of the bushes and hurried to her motorbike.

Twenty-One

Why hadn't she put the pieces together sooner? Anita raced down the new highway, thankful for the straightaway that replaced the twists and turns and hills and dales that used to lead the traveler along the coast. Of course he wouldn't want to travel by land if he didn't have to, and this way he was closer to getting rid of his parcel — and of escaping any danger on land from police.

The motorbike sputtered and Anita glanced anxiously at the fuel gauge — half full. Relieved, she double clutched but then slowed to listen. Behind her came the sound of a motorcycle — something large and fast. She swerved off the road onto the soft shoulder, cut the motor, and drifted into the trees. As soon as she was behind the shrubbery, she laid down the bike and crouched behind the undergrowth. The sound of the motorcycle grew louder. It whizzed past her — black machine with black rider and black helmet. She could hear it racing ahead, into the night. When she reached out to her bike, her hand was shaking.

Suppose she hadn't heard it? Suppose he had come up behind her? Was this just an ordinary fellow who'd pass her and drive on, or was it someone warned to find her, track her down? Was this one more person in the long chain of marginal figures smuggling holy images out of India? Because it was a long line of helpers, a network of men who each took one step in the long journey ferrying a sacred image into the hands of unbelievers. She would not have believed there were so many, but she had seen them, each one at his own station, ready to catch the image and toss it on to the next. And each one melted back into the crowd when his role was played. It infuriated her and confused her — there were so many — how could anyone stop them all? Anita pulled her bike upright, pushed it back up onto the road, and headed out again, shaking and swearing as she rode.

After another mile or so, Anita down-shifted as she came along a straightaway with dirt paths leading off right and left. She was about fifteen hundred feet from the ocean now, but she wasn't sure which dirt path led all the way to the ocean, which one would let her ride all the way, without passing through a home's private compound. She stopped, and scanned the landscape for some sort of landmark. When she saw the old and bent tree near a deteriorating gateway, she turned the bike onto the lane, and sped on. Just ahead was the beach that is typical of Kerala — a long narrow strip of sand unbroken by gushing rivers or rocky outcroppings. She stopped at the top of the beach and looked northward. She shut off the bike, and the night silence was thick.

Anita propped the bike against a palm tree and headed north along the edge of the sand. Deep in among the palm trees she spotted the occasional light telling her houses were nearby, though not yet crowding the shore. She walked on, crouching low to stay within the bordering trees. She had to be sure. If she was wrong, she had to change her tactics — and chase down the parcel and the man back on the river.

But she wasn't wrong.

To her left the waves came crashing ashore. She moved deeper into the trees and peered through the vegetation. Ahead was a small lagoon, the end of the winding river. The thin strip of land that separated river from ocean here was little more than a sand bar blanketed with green ground cover that would be washed away in the monsoon. Anita crouched, waiting. Time seemed to mock her, and she began to fear she had been wrong. What could she do? Should she go back and find him?

After a while — she couldn't have said how long — she heard a voice, not speech, but the sounds of grunting and muttering. She pulled a branch away and was rewarded with the sight of the vellum and the passenger poling awkwardly. He pushed the pole in and leaned, and let the boat drift toward the shore — and again and again. With gracelessness and weariness, he pushed the vellum into the land and stumbled out, almost falling onto the ground.

The man was exposed to anyone in the area, but he seemed too exhausted to care. He pulled the vellum onto the sand and fell onto his side, mopping his face with a handkerchief. He rested his hand on the gunwale, apparently relieved all was well. A moment later, after catching his breath, he walked across the bank to the beach and scanned the shore, looking up and down the coast. Soon Anita heard the sound of a motorboat moving up the coast. He fell back, squatted, and waited. Anita did the same.

The motorboat came from the south. Anita could see it clearly through the branches — painted blue with red and yellow stripes, a motor clamped to its starboard side, one man managing the tiller. When he drew close, he cut the engine, and the boat drifted onto the beach. Pidar crept forward and called to the other boatman.

"Braj." It wasn't a question. The other man nodded, and Pidar continued. "It is here. Take and let me get out of here."

"Why are you sweating?" Braj asked.

"I had to do the poling. I sent Gokul to rid us of that troublesome woman." He took a deep breath. "It is here. All as promised."

"You will bring trouble down on us," Braj said, his voice a harsh whisper.

"She is crazy. They will think it is the goddess's doing."

"No more. Don't speak of this. It is not good. Let me have the parcels." Braj raised his hand, palm up, and motioned with his fingers for the other man to bring them to him. "It is late. The timing is now. I am going."

Pidar returned to the vellum, gathered up the parcels, and walked into the ocean to hand them over. For a moment, the men paused, as both grasped the parcels in their hands, before one let go and the other held them safely. Was this the moment when both men understood the transaction in all its ramifications, when the act of passing a parcel from one to the other became what it really was — a sacrilege of their beliefs, a moment of regret, of conscience, a turning point that neither one was ready to take but knew was passing before them. The point of no return was barely a second. The parcels moved from one man to the other and were laid gently in the bottom of the motorboat.

"Going." Braj turned, pulled the starter, and the motor caught.

Pidar waggled his head and stepped back onto the beach, grabbing the ends of his lungi and waving them in the night air. He walked backward up the beach as the motorboat turned, heading out to sea, before turning south.

This time Anita was sure she knew where the boat was going.

The engine sputtered as the little motor bike pressed upward to the top of the rise, turned, crossed a short bridge, and coasted down the hill, turning right toward the water. She passed no other vehicle, no cows or goats wandering. She had no idea of the exact time nor how long it had taken her to get here, but she could feel the fluttering in her chest telling her that it was all coming to a head. Why hadn't she thought to plan better? Why hadn't she at least called Anand and told him where she was going?

She cut back on the throttle and downshifted as she came into a small village that ran at least four houses deep along the ocean, the grassy grounds surrounding each house sitting just below sea level but sheltered by a sandy berm running the full stretch of the beach and village. She had brought tourists here to spot birds, visit a nearby shrine.

The dim moonlight draped a soft sheet of creamy yellow over the low, rocky promontory ahead, casting an old-fashioned capped gateway in dark shadows. Beyond it was a small cove favored by fishermen collecting mussels, the one the old fisherman had been paid to leave alone. She had come closer than she meant, and now, fearful the noise of her bike might serve as a warning, she made a sharp right turn down a dirt track running between one-story houses. She continued on until she came to a narrow road, crossed it, and rode on. She reached a house that seemed empty and stopped, shut off the bike, and propped it against the house. If anyone on the rise had been listening, she hoped they were thus persuaded she had been on an errand elsewhere.

Anita had little time to waste. She ran back along the path, cut through the dirt-packed yards, and headed again for the gateway. On this side of the rocky headland stood a small chapel to the Virgin Mary. Anita crawled along the rocks toward the coast, keeping low, checking the landscape as she went. She had to get this right — if she didn't . . .

She didn't want to think about what might happen if she failed. Somewhere among these rocks, among this lush edging of a resort with its quaint cabins with more amenities than the entire village she'd just passed through, somewhere in the darkness was Surya or someone who knew where she was — Anita was sure of it. But where? She was counting on the boatman leading her to Surya, but suppose he didn't? Suppose it was too late for Surya?

No, I won't think like that. Not now. Surya is out there, and I'm going to find her. Anita kept repeating this to herself over and over as she crawled among the rocks, ignoring the scrapes and cuts as she slid and lost her footing, stepped too far into a crevice, kept looking up instead of where she was placing her feet. But nothing hurt so much that she'd risk crying out. Surya was up there, somewhere, and silence was safety.

At the end of the headland Anita could see the lights on the water. But these weren't just the kerosene lanterns of the fishermen luring fish into their nets. Brightest among them were the lights of the cruise ship rocking gently off the coastal village. Anita scanned the water, reassuring herself that no small boat was moving toward the ship from this part of the coast. She squeezed her eyes shut and prayed she was in time. *Shivayanamah.*

Anita pulled back and crouched behind the rocks, listening. Above her came voices, indistinct but coming closer. She moved back, getting behind them, watching. Two men came down a path single file, one carrying a bundle. They stopped near the end of the headland and seemed to be discussing the motorboat and the distance to the cruise ship. One of the men didn't like the size of the boat, and the other said it was fine.

"Big enough," the first one said.

The second man shrugged. "If not big enough, dump some overboard. Who will care?"

"*Shari, shari.* So much trouble we are having this time," the first one said.

"Just the women are troubling."

"How soon?" the first one asked.

"Soon. He's coming. Look." He pointed to the water, and the two men peered northward.

"Ah, yes, yes."

The men muttered agreement and climbed back up the hill into the darkness. Anita slid around to see what they were pointing at, and in the dim light she saw a lantern cut off from the rest of the fishing boats. A single motorboat was coming toward her. That would be the boat with the parcels taken from the kavu. She had time.

Anita climbed back over the rocks and made her way up the hill. Just over the rise, in a sheltered hollow, sat three men, and beside them one large parcel and a small parcel about the size of a shoe box. Anita couldn't take her eyes off the large parcel — it was the size of a large child.

Or a small woman. The size of Surya.

The men's words echoed around her, rattling in her head, slicing through her brain. "Dump it overboard."

"Who will care?"

They couldn't mean that parcel, could

403

they? Was it Surya? Did she cause trouble like Gauri? Would they really throw her overboard? Was she dead already?

Anita felt like she was going to retch. She was too late.

Anita worked her way down to the beach, crouched among the rocks, and shivered. The thought of Surya wrapped in that parcel, about to be thrown overboard, was almost too much to contemplate. But the thought of Surya's body being taken out to sea on that cruise liner was even worse. No one in her family would know what had happened to Surya — no body to sprinkle with flowers, no final farewell, no peace for anyone.

No, thought Anita, I won't let it happen. She crawled among the rocks again and scanned the beach. Most of the boats were out on the water, their teams of two or three waving the lanterns to attract fish, then drawing in the nets. The catch was smaller every year, and sometimes, when she watched the boats land and saw the puny amount of fish, she wondered how the families survived. The sea, for all its grandeur, was growing poor.

Anita looked over the rocks behind her, judged the time safe, and sprinted for the nearest boat. This was the simplest of those used along the western coast — a catamaran, barely four logs tied together with coir rope at either end, sometimes with a simple mast and sail. They might look like a canoe, but they were unfinished — with nothing making the logs watertight. Nearby was a vellum, larger. She rummaged through it, looking for something she could wear. She could use her dupatta as a turban, giving the impression to the men on the rocks that she was just one more fisherman sailing out late at night to be with the fleet, but her salwar would give her away; she needed a man's shirt to complete the disguise. Anita reached in farther, and pulled at a piece of cloth. She inspected it briefly and threw it aside.

"Eh?" A man popped up on the other side of the vellum and glared at her. Anita gasped. He must have been sleeping on the sand, hidden between the boats. He jerked his chin at her, calling on her to answer. Anita fell back and thought fast. How much should she tell him?

"Your friends?" he said, nodding to the headland behind her. Anita turned and looked, and realized what he was getting at.

"No, no." She shook her head violently. She took a deep breath and decided to gamble. "They're up to something, something not good."

"Ah, *shari, shari*." His expression softened and he leaned away from her, no longer baring his teeth like he might attack. He didn't seem the least bit surprised at her words.

"I need your help," Anita said. She had no idea if this man was a lookout, part of the chain of helpers, or just a fisherman too drunk to go out earlier with his friends. She sniffed and felt her heart sink when she smelled stale alcohol. "I think they have — they have someone." She stopped. She couldn't bring herself to say it, that Surya was probably dead. She gulped. "And they're going to take her out to the cruise liner and dump her overboard." *Ayoo*, Shiva, why am I telling him this? I sound like I'm crazy. She watched his face, wishing she hadn't jumped into asking for help. "I think they're stealing images." But you're not Hindu, are you, she thought, glancing at the cross hanging around his neck.

The man spread his arms wide and then brought them together, palms a foot apart. "This big?" Anita nodded. "Wrapped?" Anita gulped and nodded again. She cringed as his eyes sharpened, glad she wasn't on the receiving end of his ire. This was always the worst part. Whenever she needed help, or wanted something unusual, she had to state her case, and then wait, while the other party stood there and thought about it. She had no idea what he was thinking, just that he was thinking it over. Did he believe her? Did he care? Would he bother?

"Shari, shari," he said. To Anita's surprise, he reached into his pocket and pulled out a mobile phone, flipped it open, and punched in some numbers. In rapid-fire Malayalam, he told the person on the other end that he was heading out to stop "that boat." Anita felt herself leaning closer. "That boat?" Did everyone around here know about this chain of thieves and smugglers? Were she and her family the only ones who were surprised to find them in their midst?

The next second he snapped the phone shut. He waved her back and stood up, walking around the vellum to the catamaran. He pushed the heavy boat onto its side and pulled out two oars, handing them to her. He grabbed one end of the boat and started dragging it down to the water, nodding to her to follow him. Anita watched him without trying to help. She knew just how heavy those little boats were — four solid, dense logs. She'd never have been able to launch one on her own.

The boatman hurried back to another vellum and reached in, grabbed something, and returned. He threw her a vest, undershirt, and motioned for her to put it on over her salwar. She did so, pulling off her dupatta, which she then wrapped around her head like a turban. From a distance she'd easily be taken for a fisherman starting out late. The boatman pulled the canoe into the water and held it while Anita climbed in at the bow. The boat sank an inch and water sloshed over the logs, but it wouldn't sink. Then he walked it deeper into the gentle waves and, after waiting for an especially strong wave to crash and ebb, climbed on. She passed him a paddle and they headed out to sea.

TWENTY-TWO

The catamaran moved ahead slowly, passing over waves beginning to gather before
rising and rushing onto the sand, with their
thunderous crashing and reaching, then
ebbing with a swiftness that could be frightening. Once they passed the headland, Anita
could see the motorboat approaching, with
its one passenger lying trussed and still in
the bottom of the boat. The boatman Braj
struggled to move closer to shore without
getting knocked about by the waves, fell
back, and tried again — and again. Anita
tried not to look over her shoulder too often
but it was all she could do to pretend she
wasn't interested.

The motorboat managed to make it closer
to the rocks, and one of the men on shore
reached out to catch a line and pull the boat
in between two boulders, where it rocked.
Braj hurried forward to keep the boat from
crashing against either one while the two

men carried down the bundles.

But those weren't the only bundles handed aboard. One of the men crawled down among the rocks, pulled out a line, and tugged. Hand over hand, he drew up the line. At the end was a nylon net bag and from that he extracted another bundle. He did this three more times, filling the motor-boat with a small collection of bulging plastic bags. Anita watched astounded as the largest bundle, what she believed was Surya's body, was covered with smaller bundles. But they were so absorbed in their work and keeping themselves and the boat safe from the waves that they paid no attention to anyone else on the water.

"Amma!" The boatman poked her to get her attention, then pointed to the south. A small motorboat moved toward them, the man on the tiller standing tall in the stern, another sitting in the bow. Ahead of her was the cruise liner, as far out as the fishing fleet, but from farther north came a number of small fishing boats, their kerosene lanterns moving across the waves like jumping fish, in and out of sight, brightly shimmering. Anita's boat continued to move forward. When she looked back, the motorboat carrying Braj and the bundles had moved out from the rocks and was turning seaward.

She dipped her paddle into the water and pulled.

"We'll never catch him," she said over her shoulder to the boatman.

"We are not catching him." He nodded to the other boats when she turned to object.

Unaware of how fast the others were moving, Anita was surprised to see the fishing boats closing in fast, a small fleet heading home after the night's fishing. Dawn was still an hour or more away, but not all the boats in the fleet would wait until daylight. She pulled on her paddle and tried to reckon how soon the motorboat would move out of reach, cutting through the waves to the cruise liner. But then it happened.

The motorboat moving up alone from the south cut across Braj's bow, almost close enough to knick it, and that seemed to infuriate the boatman. He raised his fist and yelled at Braj, turned the tiller hard, and headed back to Braj's boat. When the boatman drew closer, he cut across the stern, yelling and threatening. Braj waved him off, telling him to move on, go away. But the boatman wouldn't let up. He turned again, kept on yelling, accusing Braj of trying to scuttle him, and turned the black-and-red-striped motorboat straight into Braj's. Braj

411

yelled, screamed out an apology as he glanced again and again at the cruise liner. Was he looking for help out there, so far away? The boatman was closing fast. Anita turned to her partner. He smiled, nodded to the other boats closing in from the north.

Braj was starting to panic. Surrounded by fishing boats and angry men yelling at him, he couldn't get past them. Each one headed straight at him, getting closer and closer, then dodged aside at the last second. It didn't make sense, Anita thought. Why doesn't Braj just turn and drive out of there? As the fishing boats drew closer she had her answer. Braj's boat was lighter and smaller but loaded down with the bundles of metal images, no match for any of the fishing boats. When he loaded up, he must have thought all he needed to do was keep up a steady pace and he'd make it safely to the cruise liner. But now, loaded down and surrounded by lighter, faster boats, he was in trouble.

Now it was Anita's turn to panic.

"We have to get closer," she called to her partner. "My cousin's body." She motioned to the boat.

"No, no, let them have him."

"No, you don't understand. He'll throw her overboard, to lighten his load, so he can get out of there." Anita threw her paddle onto the other side of the canoe and began to pull with all her might. "I can't let him throw her overboard."

The boatman caught her panic and maneuvered the canoe so they too were headed straight at the motorboat.

Braj saw them coming, and he must have seen something else. For a second he stood motionless in the stern, staring at Anita. After that he took in the surrounding fishermen, but this time he seemed to be sizing up his situation differently. He dropped the tiller, and stepped forward. In one motion he picked up Surya's body, balanced in on the gunwales, and tipped it into the ocean. Anita screamed as she stood up in the catamaran, balancing on the logs. She tore off the dupatta and dove into the water.

Down and down and down she went into the darkness, her hands outstretched, feeling for anything in the cold and blackness. How could a body disappear so fast, so completely? Down and down she went, swinging one way then another, seeing nothing. Her chest began to feel crushed, her head ready to explode. She couldn't hold her breath any longer. She felt something on her wrist, her hand, and felt herself rising.

She broke through the surface and again felt the tug on her hand. Beside her a man pulled her to the catamaran, putting her hand on the side. Anita gasped for air. Grateful to be able to breathe again but torn apart that she was above water and Surya was still down below, she was slow to notice the boatman trying to get her attention. There, filling the little canoe, lay Surya's wrapped-up body. Anita held on while the boatman paddled them back to shore.

Behind her shouts from the boatmen filled the night. Circling Braj, other boats pulled away but the men continued to yell at him. He yelled back, revved his engine and turned the bow seaward. The boats closed in ahead of him. He revved his motor again and turned south. Again, the boats closed off the avenue of escape. Angry, he tried to charge through the boats, looking for a breach in their line. As one, the fishing boats fell back. And then, kerosene lanterns flew through the air, crashing onto Braj's boat. A second later it exploded.

The boat shattered into a thousand bits rising into the predawn sky, flames shooting up into the air, the screech of wood breaking and fire sizzling. A second explosion brought a wrenching sound as though metal had been torn into fragments. Ash and slivers of wood rained down on them, but Anita could already feel the sand beneath her feet as she and her partner pulled the catamaran onto the beach.

Anita couldn't take her eyes off the flaming, burning mass out on the water. But as she felt the boat begin to drift, she turned back; her partner had pulled the boat only partly out of the water.

"You must help!" he said to Anita. She turned to ask him what he wanted when she saw him pulling on the fabric wrapping Surya's body. "This is not a corpse."

"Not a corpse?" For a second Anita couldn't think. How did he know? Who was it? Was it Surya? Alive? She grabbed one end of the parcel and helped the boatman carry the heavy body up to the dry sand. They laid it down and he cut away the cloth as fast as he could, with three swift slices of a knife. The plastic wrap and cloth fabric folded back and the face that emerged was luminescent, benign, radiant, the sweet, innocent face of Jesus as a young man, his right hand raised in benediction, his head surrounded by a golden halo. The painted wood figure in seventeenth-century garb gazed up at her, his soft pink cheeks spotted with flaking paint.

The boatman crossed himself and muttered a prayer.

Anita leaned against the vellum, staring at the crowd of villagers hovering around the wood image of Jesus, exclaiming the love of Jesus for its recovery and planning its return to the small chapel from where it had disappeared days ago. The men and women, children and grandparents, had materialized out of the darkness as soon as the boatman stepped back and exclaimed at what he had found.

Anita was too stunned to speak, but as the bubbling joy around her penetrated her shivering limbs and sodden brain, she began to feel it made sense after all. Smugglers want anything expensive, including Christian images — they're nondenominational offenders — but that thought had never occurred to her. She was only looking for her cousin and her own family's images.

Anita had caught an even bigger fish than she'd expected — the police would be delighted — but that didn't help her. She had been so sure the large parcel was Surya's body that she didn't stop to think any further, not a step beyond that. And here she was — wrong, totally, completely, horrifyingly wrong. This wonderful image of Jesus had been rescued, but Surya was gone

— somewhere, somehow. She had landed in Kerala, left the airport, and simply disappeared.

Anita was so absorbed in this startling turn of events that she didn't hear the motorcycle coming across the sand. She turned only when the Catholic villagers grabbed her attention and pointed to something behind her.

"Anand!" Anita was taken aback by his sudden appearance as he coasted to a stop in front of her. Dressed all in black, riding a black motorcycle, Anand could fade into the night. "You know what has happened?"

Anand nodded as he took off his helmet. "You're not the only one chasing smugglers, it seems. The police were poised in the small cove near your hotel, just waiting for that motorboat to pass by."

"It was a Christian image the villagers were trying to rescue." Anita turned her gaze to the growing mass of men and women now on their knees praying. "I had no idea it was such a big operation."

Anand shrugged. "It's a big market — stolen antiquities."

A sudden flush of joy overwhelmed Anita. "I'm so glad for them. I felt exactly the same way when I knew I held our Ganapati. That's what was going on in the kavu —

they were hiding stolen images where they knew no one would find them. It's a very smart idea. And they almost got away with it." She smiled, then grew worried. "But we still don't know anything about Surya."

Anand shook his head. "She landed at the airport and disappeared."

"It's not possible," Anita said, looking up at the night sky. She closed her eyes and let the emotions fall away, trying to think clearly. "Wait! Wait!" She paused. "There's one more possibility. After what I heard tonight, listening to those men talking while going in and out of the kavu, I have one idea left.

"I didn't think anything of it at the time," Anita continued, "but I found a button near the house — not one of mine." Anita glanced at the praying villagers, the cruise ship resting quietly at sea, the men on the fishing boats pulling scraps of wood from the sea, the divers searching the ocean floor for the lost bundles, the line of police cars coming across the sand. "All the pieces are coming together," she said. "What time is it?"

Surprised at the question, Anand turned toward the horizon behind them. "Almost dawn."

"The boatmen came to the kavu near

three and again near four this morning, didn't they?" Anita seemed to be speaking to herself as she repeated this observation. "It's all been in the nighttime — the river travel and moving things about, hasn't it?"

"From what you are telling me now, yes. Everything under cover of darkness," Anand said as he watched her.

"Including Surya's arrival — in the dark to a household sound asleep, thanks to a glass of lassi." Anita grabbed Anand's arm and climbed onto the back of his motorcycle. "I think I may know where she is."

The motorcycle sped past awakening neighborhoods — streets filling with early morning workers, baskets of fresh fruit and vegetables to be delivered to hotel dining rooms, maidservants waiting for the bus that would take them to the first part of a long day, children hurrying for their early morning tutorials. Anand swerved and sped, and turned down the driveway to Muttacchi's house before Anita's salwar was dry. He pulled up in front of the main house and cut the ignition.

"Well?"

Anita clambered off the back seat. "Surya arrived in Trivandrum on the late night flight, but Gauri said she would never visit here again. Both are true. But I took the prediction to mean that Surya was dead, so I was hunting for a corpse — or someone about to become one, and so someone who needed to be found and soon." Anita turned around and studied the land between the house and the road, then turned and began walking inland. Along the road the forest grew thick, some parts protected by a stone-wall and others open to meandering cows and goats. Anita picked her way through the brush, Anand following.

"Surya arrived and made it all the way to the house — that button is hers. But some-one stopped her."

"You're thinking Veej?" Anand asked.

Anita paused, and her smile was sad and wry. "He doesn't seem strong enough, psychologically, I mean, does he? But that's because I don't think I ever really saw him. But he was part of it. He ran when he saw I was getting close." She plunged ahead through the trees.

"Do you know where you're going? Or are you just looking?"

"When I was a child, my mother told me about a kavu that had a small stone cave in it. She said it had been carved by invaders centuries earlier, and when the family established their center in another part of the property, they left it to be concealed by the kavu." Anita walked on, passing the back yard of a small house close to the road, not stopping to speak to the somewhat surprised woman brushing her teeth near a water spigot.

They walked on in silence except for the thrashing against branches and shrubbery, Anita a few feet ahead, Anand following behind. After they came to a marshy area that seemed to spread deep into the woods, Anita stopped and looked around her. "It should be here," she said, "the altar." She pushed past another shrub and came into an open, sandy ground about five feet by five feet square. At the far end, shrouded by thick growth, stood a tall, black-encrusted oil lamp with a dozen small leaf-shaped miniature trays for oil and wicks.

"I think it's here, back in there." Anita pulled the dupatta from her shoulders and draped it over her hair, both still damp.

"It's possible," Anand said. "The rulers of the Pallava Dynasty extended their rule this far over a thousand years ago and left some sculpted caves. There could be one here."

Anita stepped over a dead tree trunk and stood, one hand steadying herself against a palm tree. Once again she was defying every rule she had ever been taught about kavus, and once again she felt she had no choice. "Well, I'd better get it over with." Anita glanced at Anand over her shoulder. "I'm in so much trouble offending Bhairava in our kavu that I might as well not worry about one more deity, whoever it is."

Anita pulled the dupatta down over her forehead, doing her best to feel respectful, and plunged into the kavu. She already knew what Muttacchi's kavu was like, so she was ready for the lianas nearly strangling her, the roots tripping her, the branches blocking her way, but this was much worse than her own family's kavu. Still, she pressed on, peering through the growth for any sign of a cave.

"Over there." Anand's voice came from behind her.

"I didn't think you were here."

"I've always wanted to see the inside of a kavu, but with the family I have, especially my brother, I would never have the chance. I'm afraid I have my father's irreverence." He grinned and pointed again. "Over there, I think."

Anita followed his directions and found the traveling easier — branches and shrubbery were already broken, a rudimentary path laid out. The large rock outcropping loomed up among the trees, but rose little more than fifteen feet. Anita knelt at the mouth of the cave, perhaps four feet high, and peered in. There, in the darkness, lay a figure, trussed and still.

The figure moved.

"Surya! She's here, Anand!"

TWENTY-THREE

Dr. Premod stood in the doorway, one arm stretched out blocking access as she leaned against the doorjamb. The neatly pressed green sari, the uniform of women doctors here, draped beautifully across her body; no one would ever know just how angry she was — except Anita. The silence between Anita and the doctor grew almost unbearable but the doctor continued to frown, her large brown eyes barely focusing on the woman in front of her. Anita began to feel invisible, or at least ignored.

"Just for a minute." Anita took a step to her right, ready to push past the doctor.

"I have heard you say this before, many times. She has only just arrived here — she must rest." The doctor's Malayalam was tinged with an American accent, just as her English was tinged with an Indian enunciation, but clearly, to anyone with a practiced ear, she had lived for some time in the

424

States. Anita admired her for many reasons, not the least of which was her decision to return to India to treat her own people, even if the hospital where she worked was among the most expensive in the country — at least for Indians. The doctor lowered her head, apparently consulting with something deep within, before looking up. "She has been heavily drugged. It will take her some time to recover fully. She is greatly disoriented."

"She's my cousin-sister. I have to know she's all right. Her grandmother will not rest until I can reassure her. Please."

The silence lengthened. "All right. Two minutes." Dr. Premod waggled her head, lowered her arm, and walked away. Over her shoulder she called back to the nurse, "Two minutes only!"

Anita was beside the bed before the doctor finished speaking. "Surya? Can you hear me?"

The woman lying among the white sheets was as still as death — until her eyelashes fluttered. She opened her eyes and looked up at the ceiling, to the walls, and down until she seemed to see Anita.

"Hmmmm." Surya smiled weakly and closed her eyes.

"Surya, Surya. I'm so glad you're all right." Anita squeezed her cousin's hand lying on the sheet, then turned and pulled a stool up to the bed. She sat down and rolled the stool closer to the bed. "I have to ask you. Please, can you tell me what happened? Just what you remember?"

Surya's eyelashes fluttered again and she opened her eyes and stared at Anita. The women were almost the same age, and Anita thought they had been more sisters than cousins. The phrase "cousin-sister" had depth for her, delineating more clearly the close relationship of two women who had grown up together as though in one family. Surya was her cousin-sister, and Anita had barely been able to think straight all the while she'd been worrying about what had happened. But even now, she wondered if Surya was really all right. Her gaze was so vacant, so lost, and then so absent and seemingly foolish — that look that comes over the very sick when they have lost the psychological strength and edge that tells you someone strong resides within.

"Surya, do you remember anything, anything at all?"

"Hmmmm. It was awful — I don't know what was happening — it was like being dead, only being able to know that I was dead and hear the living all around me."

Anita felt a chill all over her body and gave

an involuntary shiver. She squeezed Surya's hand. "Just tell me what you can, Surya."

"That's enough," Dr. Premod said, marching into the room.

"That's not two minutes." Anita leaned over to ask Surya again, but the doctor tapped her on the shoulder.

Twelve hours later, as the sky turned pink and day turned to night, Anita nodded to the nurse and walked once again into her cousin's hospital room. Anita smiled down on Surya, then pulled up a stool. Her cousin let her head fall more to the side so she could look directly at Anita. "I can't believe it's over." Surya smiled easily, warmly.

"You seem much better now," Anita said.

"Oh, I am, I am. I'm warm and well fed and comfortable."

"Do you mind if I ask you some questions about what happened? The night you were to arrive at the airport. What happened? Did you fly into Trivandrum? Not into Mumbai?" Anita leaned closer.

"Oh, yes. I came into Trivandrum on time. I had my luggage — nothing lost or delayed this time. I got a taxi — I went to the prepaid service — very safe, you know. I got my taxi and off we went. It was lovely — I was so glad to be home. I love to ride through Trivandrum at that hour — like a secret for a very few."

Anita waited while Surya caught her breath and picked up her story.

"No one knew you were here. Why didn't you call?" Anita spoke slowly, carefully; she wanted answers to specific questions.

"My mobile phone card. I changed my mobile phone cards on the plane but my Idea card died before I could finish even one call." Surya sighed, as though exhausted by even those few words.

"You could have used a pay phone."

Surya smiled. "I was tired, Anita. I get stupid when I get tired. And you know how lazy I am. I just wanted to crawl into my own bed."

"So you hired a taxi."

Surya nodded. "I got home safely. The taxi stopped halfway down the driveway — I didn't want to wake everyone. I thought I'd just speak to whoever was awake and then he or she would tell the rest of the household as they awoke later. You know how it is? I knew the servants would be up soon — it was nearing four o'clock."

"So who was awake? Lata? Sett?"

"No, not them." She paused. "A man I didn't know was there."

"Who else, Surya?" Anita hadn't meant to speak sharply, but Surya's head jerked back and her eyes focused intensely for a moment.

"Ah, there was Veej. He was there with someone else, some other man. I could barely see them in among the trees, but Veej was there, and he was holding something, some kind of parcel. You must ask him what he was doing." Her eyes grew dull.

"What do you think they were doing?"

"I don't know, but they came at me with the oddest expressions on their faces. When they got about ten or twenty feet away they looked at each other. And then Veej hit me. And the other one, too!" Surya began to cry.

"It's all right, Surya. It's all over." Anita leaned closer to her, soothing her as best she could. Great gasps of fear and pain seemed to well up inside the injured woman, and her whole body began to shake and tremble. As the tears flowed she grew easy, and her ragged breath grew evener.

"What's the next thing you remember?"

"The cold — I was so cold — and the dark. And the damp. I couldn't tell where I was." Surya began to tremble.

Anita was ready to start shivering herself as she thought about what this meant. She'd been mere feet from Surya the entire time she was missing.

"Yes, that part was real — too real. You could have died there," Anita said. "Do you remember the kavu that belonged to the neighboring property and the family sold the land and the old owner comes once a year to do a puja? Otherwise, no one goes near it. Do you remember there's an outcropping in the center, with a small cave? My mother told us about it."

"Oh! That's why it was so cold and dark." Surya closed her eyes, as though she could shut out the memory of her recent agony.

"It was the perfect hiding place. No one, but no one, would even think about the kavu and its cave as a place to hide someone — except smugglers. No one would even think to look there."

"I thought I was going to die," Surya said.

"And all the time I thought you had passed through the other kavu, taken down to the coast to be carried away on the cruise ship and dumped at sea." Anita told her of the events of earlier that morning on the coast, the images hidden in the kavu, and the flight of one boatman and the death of the other.

"I had no idea," Surya said, growing paler.

"It's all right. You've told me what I needed to know."

"It's all over?" Surya looked up at her

430

cousin with such a plea in her eyes that Anita could feel herself caving in, but she pulled back.

"No, not yet."

Anita pushed the stool away and walked to the window. Outside the palm trees hung in the gathering evening. Beyond the grounds stood the compound wall of a small temple — where Anita had taken refuge. Was it only two days ago that she had been here?

"I was bitten by a snake," Anita said, turning back to her cousin.

"Oh, I'm sorry. You are all right?" Surya seemed confused by the direction the conversation had taken.

"Yes, yes, I'm fine. I recognized the snake." Anita walked to the end of the bed and grabbed the footboard. "But only the one on the ground, if you will. Tell me, Surya, when did you start corralling old murtis and selling them to smugglers?"

"Me? How can you say that to me?" Surya's face flushed as she tried to sit up and protest. The day's rest had done her good, and her voice was stronger, strong enough to protest with passion. Anita recognized the familiar rebellious streak in Surya's eyes.

"You asked Gauri if she had any images

she wanted to sell, didn't you?"

"Well, sure, but —"

"And you asked Muttacchi what she did with her old images." Anita gripped the railing tighter, trying to keep her voice level. The more she discovered, the angrier she had become — especially with someone who should have honored these customs as she did. "They're not like a pair of old shoes, Surya."

"But they're just old murtis, Anita. She said I could have a couple to take back with me. For godssakes, Anita. No one wanted them." Surya grabbed at the sheet and tugged it up closer to her chest.

"And the Ganapati! The family image! Are you saying no one wanted that? What were you thinking?"

"They were never supposed to touch the Ganapati! I swear!" Surya raised herself on her elbow, and jabbed at the air for emphasis with her other hand. "It was only supposed to be the little images that no one cares about anymore."

"How do you know no one cares about them?"

"They were just stuck in a cupboard, Anita." Surya grew angrier. "No one cared."

"But you managed to think up an excuse, just in case someone did care. You came up with that bronze disease business." Anita wasn't sure how much to believe of Surya's protestations. "And you dragged Veej into it — you corrupted a servant!"

Surya gave an ugly laugh. "I assure you, Anita, he was way ahead of me. That's why he hit me — I caught him in the middle of the night handing off images."

"But the Ganapati!" Anita still couldn't believe anyone in her family would touch this murti. Surya was surely smart enough to know that stealing an unused image was one thing, but the family murti, the ancient Ganapati, was something entirely different. "Who got you into this? Or was it all your own idea?" Anita picked up the delicate wristwatch lying on the bedside table; she turned it over and whistled when she read the name. "Are those real diamonds?"

Surya twisted around in her bed and reached out to take it from Anita.

"You're lucky the others didn't steal it from you."

"They're not thieves, Anita."

"They're not?" Anita almost burst out laughing.

"Well, it would give anyone away. That's five thousand dollars you're holding."

Anita stared at the watch again, then laid it back down on the table. "So why would

Veej attack you, if you're one of them?"

"Stop talking like I was part of some great conspiracy," Surya said. Her face grew hard, an expression Anita recalled from their childhood, whenever Surya's stubborn streak emerged.

"But you were, Surya. That's the point."

"It wasn't like that at all, Anita." Surya paused, relaxed as she seemed to come to a decision. "I met this man at a shop. A year ago, two years ago, I don't remember."

"How can you not remember?"

"Don't be sarcastic, Anita. He said he'd pay top dollar for anything old I brought him, especially images. And big ones were especially valuable. I told him I only had a few small ones. But he said fine."

"Who was he?"

"I'm not sure, but another man in the store called him Mootal. He's a money-lender, I think."

Mootal again, thought Anita. "Why would he offer to buy anything from you?" Anita said.

Surya scowled at her. "I was trying to bargain down the shopkeeper — a pair of gold earrings. He bought the earrings."

"He just — a stranger who's a money-lender — just bought a pair of earrings and gave them to you?" Anita couldn't believe

434

what she was hearing.

"Just one."

"Just one what?"

"One earring. I was to get the other one when I delivered the murtis."

Anita couldn't bring herself to speak. She opened her mouth, closed it, couldn't swallow. She let the explanation hang in the air between them, like the fish stinking in baskets at the end of the day, waiting for the late buyers. "What happened then?"

"London is expensive, Anita." Surya glanced at the watch. "I think he guessed I needed money. I was supposed to leave the images in a parcel where Veej could get it. That was all." Surya closed her eyes.

Anita felt the rumblings of rage in her chest. "How many of our family homes have you raided for old murtis?"

"Look, Anita, I'm sorry. I really am. Okay?"

"No, Surya, it's not okay. I risked my life for you."

"Don't be so melodramatic." Surya scowled and looked around the room with disapproval. Anita felt a stillness grow in her, and a sadness.

"The police will want to hear your story." She turned toward the door.

"The police! Anita!" Surya struggled to sit

up in the bed, but Anita glanced back at her once as she left the room.

TWENTY-FOUR

The doorman pulled open the glass doors to the hospital to allow Anita to pass through. She gave him a kindly nod as she flipped open her mobile phone, took one look at it as she was about to tap it to jog it into life, then remembered where it had been — fifty feet under water. She flipped it shut and slipped it into her pocket.

"Try this one!"

Anita raised her hands to catch the mobile phone flying through the air toward her. Clutching it to her breast, she spotted Anand leaning against the hood of his white Mercedes.

"You look like you're off for a game of cricket." Anita strolled up to him. "What have you been doing today?"

"Explaining to the police why I was on that beach at that hour. And soon, very soon, they will want to talk to you — again.

"Again?" Anita thought back to the early

morning interview that seemed to consist entirely of two police officers staring her down and muttering between themselves and ordering in tea or coffee. That and calming down Auntie Meena had taken up most of her time that day. Anita leaned against the bonnet. She was just starting to admit how worn out she was.

"Right now they're scouring the cruise liner for stolen images and chasing down the men I saw on the headland."

"Do you think Muttacchi would offer me a meal if I drive you there?"

"I'm sure she would, Anand." Anita pulled open the passenger side door, but instead of sliding onto the seat, she looked over the roof of the car. "How did you know where I was? You just drove up across the beach, out of nowhere."

"Everyone knows where you are," Anand said. Anita winced. "Sorry, I couldn't pass it up. But it is sort of accurate. After all, you disrupted the entire coastline, a night of fishing, the sound sleep of dozens of foreigners visiting here for their health, and the peace of mind of one tour guide in particular."

"Now, such pleasing news you are giving me!" She grinned and gave the roof a celebratory slap. "But how did you know about the fishing fleet and all the rest of it?"

"How else? Gauri raised such a ruckus — waking up the entire household. At least, that is what I was told." He slid into the driver's seat. "Come along. I'm confident the entire household is waiting for us."

"You mean she woke up Muttacchi? Did she tell her everything?" Anita slid into the seat, subdued. She hadn't planned on having to face the old woman just yet. She had spent the day talking to the police, soothing Meena, and hanging about the hospital, waiting for Surya to get strong enough to talk. Anita needed time to plan her approach to Muttacchi — and her confession. But at least she had rescued the Ganapati — that should count for something.

"Gauri told her enough to get her on the telephone to me and everyone else." Anand put the car in gear, pulled out of the parking space, and turned into traffic. "She told me you went off on the motorbike, so I tried to catch up with you, but you were long gone. I didn't know those things could go so fast."

Anita slid lower in her seat. She didn't have to tell him everything.

Muttacchi's household was in disarray when Anita and Anand finally arrived. She could see that the minute she stepped over the threshold. Lata was bickering with Sett, who was cursing her barely underneath his breath. Auntie Meena was apologizing profusely to Muttacchi for everything and anything that came to mind, in a robotic effort to minimize the catastrophe that seemed to be building around her. Muttacchi seemed to be in something of a stupor. The only normal one was Gauri, who was humming happily to herself as she went about her tasks.

Both relations pushed themselves out of their seats the minute they saw Anita, running toward her with their arms outstretched, babbling their relief. They hugged her, shed tears over her, and then, just as passionately, realizing she was safe and sound, they began to chastise her for scaring them half to death and taking foolish, dangerous risks.

"The police have come — a second time!" Muttacchi drew herself up to her full height, which wasn't much, but her entire bulk seemed to be aimed at intimidating Anita.

"For the boatman?" Anita asked.

"Boatman?" Meena stuttered, turning to Muttacchi.

"That man that Gauri scared half to death — he fled but not far. He is lying wounded with snakebite even as we speak in hospital." The old woman glanced at Gauri, still humming away to herself. "She was possessed again."

Anita nodded. "I saw her. She was terrifying." Anita drew the other women to the table under the pergola and settled them again in the seats. "The boatman was part of all this business."

"What business?" Meena started to get up again, but Anita rested her hand on her aunt's shoulder, and the older woman subsided into her chair.

"Smuggling murtis out of the country, stealing murtis to sell to collectors, and getting rid of anyone who gets in the way." Anita sat down, and a moment later Gauri placed a cup of tea in front of her. Anand was directed to a small separate table also under the pergola, butted against the main table, and Lata began serving him *dosas* and sambar while Gauri served Anita at the larger table.

Between mouthfuls of dosa Anita explained about Surya and her untimely arrival at the estate, her near tragic end in the cave, and the network of men and women, Indians and foreigners, making the removal of murtis large and small possible. As she spoke, she tried to gauge Muttacchi's reaction and how much of this sordid tale she had already surmised herself from Surya's peculiar behavior. If Muttacchi were still more innocent than not, Anita knew she'd skirt the truth to save the old woman's feelings.

"Tell me who would do such a thing?" Meena asked, clearly disheartened by Anita's summary of the smuggling operation. Muttacchi gave her a pitying look, and Anita had her answer to the nagging question of how much she would have to spell out.

"Veej, for one," Anita said. "He needed money for his family and had access to lots of old family homes. Konan was deeply in debt to the moneylender Mootal. The newsagent knew everyone and coordinated the links. He set up Mootal, I think, about a year ago, perhaps as a way to draw in more people for his scheme. The boatmen smuggled the images down the river, storing them in kavus where no one would ever find them." Anita wished she could stop talking and eat — Lata was so overwhelmed with relief that she was cooking up a storm of tasty dishes to go with the dosa.

"Veej has been with us for years," Muttacchi said, more hurt than surprised.

"But what has this to do with Surya?"

Meena asked. Her eyes could barely focus, and she looked from one to the other, around the estate, as though she were herself wandering lost in the forest.

"I'm sorry to say it, but Surya likes nice things and nice things cost money," Anita said.

"That is what she said to me once," Muttacchi said.

"I think it began rather simply, when she asked Gauri if she had any murtis she wanted to sell," Anita said, thinking back to Gauri's impoverished home. "And it sort of got out of hand after that."

"She once said she wanted a murti or two to take back with her to London." The old woman shrugged. "I was overjoyed that she would have such an interest."

"And the next thing you know," Anita said, "Surya was visiting relatives and pilfering old images put away for special occasions that might never come."

The women fell silent, each one imagining the thefts in her own way — as an outrageous act in another's home, as a violation of the rules of hospitality, as a sacrilege, as an unbelievable charge that might yet be somehow, miraculously, disproved.

"She was always such a welcome guest,"

Meena said, her jowls sagging under the news.

"She will never be invited again," Muttacchi said, in a quiet but resolute voice. Both women turned to her.

Anita was shocked at how hard the old woman could be — she had expected some sense of how long it would take for the old woman to forgive, but this judgment was entirely unexpected.

"Gauri's vision was prescient, of course — Surya will never come here again. I feared Gauri's vision meant that Surya was dead, but for this thievery she is as good as dead. She will never attend here again."

In near silence Auntie Meena rose, leaned over, draped her arm around Muttacchi, and laid her own cheek against hers. They held each other quietly, without tears, for a minute, before Meena returned to her seat. "Yes, it is to be thus." Meena gave a deep sigh. "But I don't understand why you had to take to the water, Anita." Meena looked incredibly tired, as though she hadn't slept in days.

Anita paused to absorb the image of Meena comforting Muttacchi. Auntie Meena so often came across as hysterical, maneuvering, naïve, and lost, but in a true crisis she never failed to do exactly the right thing, and Anita never failed to admire her for it.

Meena gave Anita a smile and said, "Go on. Tell us the rest."

"This is where the impossibly demanding tour guide comes in." Anita shut her eyes as she conjured up the image of Sophie, the woman who just had to have a private tour of Trivandrum from none other than Anita. "Once the murtis were on the cruise ship, she carried them back with the tour luggage."

Meena gasped, as Anita knew she would. There was a part of her that still harbored a belief that foreigners had some special virtue about them, and to see their feet of clay crumbling like a mud wall in the monsoon was shocking and disorienting.

"Sophie was also part of the plan to make sure that I take the tour to the temple on the river. The beggar woman was undoubtedly paid to send me along the path. And one of the smugglers provided the snake." The memory still made Anita wince. She knew she was lucky to have escaped with her life.

"And Gauri?" Auntie Meena suddenly had tears in her eyes, which didn't surprise Anita. For all her aunt's crustiness when it came to the servants, she considered them part of her family, and to confront the possibility of Gauri being in league with crooks and killers was more than she wanted to believe. "It was all a distraction — all those trances, to keep us away from the truth?"

Gauri jumped up from where she was squatting near the kitchen. *"Ayoo!"*

Anita began to laugh. "Oh, no, Auntie, just the opposite. Gauri went into a trance every morning after someone had violated the kavu. The boatmen and the moneylender were terrified of what they thought she'd figured out or what Bhagavati was telling her."

"She knew?" Muttacchi said, her hand moving to her chest as she gazed at the maidservant. "But she didn't know what Bhagavati was telling her?"

"Something like that," Anita said. She wondered what the real truth was and how everyone would take it. "The possessions are genuine, I think. Bhagavati chose her to make us look at what was happening. But I think it's permanent." Anita almost didn't want to look at the expressions around her — not everyone was pleased with the prospect of Gauri falling into a trance any time something went awry.

"But the exorcism," Meena said, looking askance at Gauri.

"Mostly legitimate, except for the intent," Anita said. "The assistant priest was part of the network — he knew which temples he could steal from — but Konan told the priest to really go at it."

Muttacchi's hand clenched and un-clenched in her lap, and Anita could feel several of the others shrinking from what they knew could be an explosion of anger at the injustice that was done. Konan's future was on the line.

"But you, Lata. I couldn't figure you out." Anita turned to the cook standing nearby, swiftly changing the subject. "Your so-called relation. What was that all about?"

"That man saying he is my relation. He is not my relation." Lata sneered. "He threatens me so I must say he is my relation when he comes to see Veej so no one will suspect anything." Lata started to return to the kitchen.

"And you must give the lassi with something in it," Anita said.

"And why would you do that?" Muttacchi asked in a voice so soft Anita wasn't even sure she heard it. But Lata did. She turned around, a look of deep anguish on her face.

"Thief is why!" Sett grumbled from the kitchen veranda.

"Shut up, Sett!" Muttacchi's harsh tone

startled everyone. "Tell me, Lata."

The old cook looked at each one in turn, the color draining from her face, then she turned bright pink. "I have assisted my sister's child."

"Stealing," Sett said, spitting out the words.

"No, Sett, not stealing, not like you, pilfering from the kavu to sell to ayurvedic shops." Muttacchi stared hard at him.

"All three are stealing?" Meena said, too stunned to do anything but stare at Sett and Lata. "And you know this?"

Muttacchi brushed aside Meena's comment. "Now I understand why Lata is not telling me what I am suspecting. I could forgive Lata — a woman who does not do everything she can for her family is not decent." Her voice had an edge that could split rock. "But now that I know, you, Sett, cannot stay here. You have betrayed me and my family. You have stolen from the kavu — for money!"

Anita gazed at the old man, wondering if everyone else felt as awkward at this dismissal as she did. Sett, for his part, stiffened, his face contorted, but as he opened his mouth to speak, Anand stirred in his chair. Sett glanced at him, lowered his head, and walked away, hunching his shoulders, his head jutting forward.

"Lata!" Muttacchi called out, and everyone around her cringed. "You should have come to me if there is need. But while I think, you will go to your sister's." The old cook sighed, resigned to the gradual separation from the family she had served for many years.

"May I ask a question here?" When Anand spoke, the other women looked at him as if they had no idea where he had come from. "What about the explosion?" he asked. "The boat sank and the murtis with it."

Anita nodded, thinking of the figures lying at the bottom of the ocean, with fishermen and police divers trying to recover them.

"Oh, no, Anita. Not our Ganapati!" Meena clasped her hands over her mouth and began to cry. Muttacchi sighed and tears welled up in her eyes.

Anita immediately rested a hand on her arm. "No, Meena Elayamma, not our Ganapati."

"Not our Ganapati?" The chorus was loud, ecstatic, disbelieving.

"No, not our Ganapati, I am relieved to say." Anita reached for her tea.

"Ganapati is safe? Where?" Muttacchi leaned forward, her fingers tightening around Anita's wrist.

"Ah, well, that's a bit of a problem," Anita said.

An hour later Muttacchi, Meena, and Anita assembled in front of the kavu, Anand standing a few feet behind them. Anita was so tired that all she wanted to do was crawl onto a bed, no matter how hard, and sleep for hours, maybe even days. Right now she didn't care how anyone felt about her crossing the line into the sacred grove, crawling among the trees and shrubs and lianas and flowers, scattering birds and wildlife from their sanctuary. She didn't care if no one ever permitted her into a temple again — she was that tired.

Meena was so horrified at what she had learned that she could barely choke out her words. Muttacchi stood transfixed in front of the image of Bhairava — she could not bring herself to step foot into the kavu, no matter how strong the temptation, and the temptation was the most powerful of her lifetime. If the Ganapati was almost within reach she was torn in two between the two deities. After several minutes of silence, Muttacchi began to weep.

"The murti is lost to us, gone. But he is safe where he is, I suppose." Muttacchi turned to Meena. "Do you agree?"

The look on Meena's face suggested otherwise.

"You might still be able to get it back," Anand said.

Everyone turned around and stared at him. Quiet throughout Anita's recitation except for one or two questions, he was pretty much forgotten. But now, everyone knew he was there.

"How?" Muttacchi grabbed his arm. "No one can enter the kavu. How can anyone do this?"

"You're right. No one can enter the kavu because the ground is sacred." Anand rested his hands on his hips, nodding as he spoke. "But the air above is not." Anand looked up at the patches of sky visible through the trees. Everyone else followed his gaze upward, and there they stood, three women and one man staring up at the sky.

The following morning a tall cherry picker trundled around the side of the house, over the sandy courtyard, and through the trees toward the kavu. Behind it came a gaggle of boys cavorting like gazelles, a number of neighborhood women, and a crowd of men — all out to enjoy the spectacle at Punnu Chellamma's house. The owner of the machinery motioned the driver forward as though he were a mahout guiding his elephant, and it almost might have been. But in this case modernity won out over tradition.

Anita pointed to the general area where she believed she had left the Ganapati in its wrapping. The crowd drew closer, moving as a single organism. "Yes, right there," Anita said, waving for the driver to halt. The owner also waved, and the driver slowed and squeaked to a stop.

"We need someone to help," Anita said.

"Not Kedar," Muttacchi said. "He would do it if I asked, but he is of a delicate nature. He has sensibilities. We cannot ask him."

The women studied the cherry picker, a new device in their experience.

"How about Gauri?" Anita said. "She's certainly attuned to Bhagavati's desires."

Again Muttacchi shook her head. "This one must touch plants in the sacred grove, enter the sacred space even if it is only air. No, this one must be pure."

"I suppose we could get a priest to come and purify her," Meena said. She still had reservations about Gauri.

"No," Muttacchi said, turning around swiftly and grasping Arun by the shoulder. "No, it is Arun. He is a child still and pure like a child. If he enters the kavu by some mishap, he is to be forgiven because he is yet a child. He goes."

Everyone turned to stare at Arun. Was he lucky, unlucky?

By the expression on his face, Arun seemed to think he was unlucky, but before he could say or do anything, the owner grabbed him by the arm and dragged him over to the bucket. He picked up the boy and dropped him into the bucket, banged on the driver's door, and stepped back. At the last minute, the owner jumped in too. The bucket trembled, then lifted off the ground and rose up in the air. The villagers proved to be worthy of their participation and cheered loudly. Arun sank down in the bucket, disappearing from view. Anita couldn't tell if he was wildly excited or bursting into tears from fright.

The bucket swung up and out and over the kavu, brushing between branches and vines until it was several feet into the grove, hovering well beyond the image of Bhairava. The owner swatted flies and branches, clearing a path for his carrier.

"Farther back," Anita said, waving at the bucket. The driver shifted gears, the bucket jolted and swayed, and the machine inched closer to the trees.

"Look down, Arun. Look down!" Anand called out. "Do you see anything?"

The boy's head appeared over the edge of the bucket as he peered down. The owner leaned over, tipping the bucket precariously over the jungle. Meena gasped and all but fainted. Gauri began to sway, her eyes rolling back into her head. Muttacchi took a step closer to the grove and stared upward.

"There! I see it!" Excited, Arun leaned over the edge and the bucket tipped even farther, to the great delight of the villagers.

The owner directed the driver and slowly he lowered the bucket into the jungle. When they had gone as low as they dared, careful not to damage any growing thing to the extent possible, the owner tied a rope around Arun's waist, wrapped the other end around a makeshift cleat, and lowered the boy into the jungle.

"Don't touch the ground!" Muttacchi called out.

Anita crouched down and peered through the growth. Deep into the grove she could see Arun dangling from the rope a few feet off the ground. Just as he reached down, he swung himself and his legs went out and up and down. Again he reached. On the third attempt he lifted the parcel from the ground and held it up.

"I've got it!" Arun called out. "I've got it."

Arun clutched the parcel to his chest as he rose through the jungle and back into the sunlight. The villagers cheered.

Gauri was well into her trance. Bhagavati reportedly was pleased.

Meena decided not to faint. Instead, she turned to Anand and smiled. Anita saw that smile and groaned inwardly. She knew that smile, knew what it meant, had dreaded it for years. But before she could rescue Anand and distract her aunt, she heard Meena's soft words.

"Yes, Anand. I am seeing so much help you are offering to us." Meena moved closer to the young man. "I have misjudged you. I have not shown you proper appreciation. Yes? Your family. You have grandparents, yes? And what would be their names?"

The matchmaker had begun her work.

ABOUT THE AUTHOR

Susan Oleksiw is the author of the Mellingham series featuring Chief of Police Joe Silva, who was introduced in *Murder in Mellingham* (1993). Oleksiw first introduced Anita Ray, an Indian-American photographer, in a series of short stories and later in *Under the Eye of Kali* (2010).

Also known for her nonfiction work, Oleksiw compiled *A Reader's Guide to the Classic British Mystery* (1988), the first in a series of Reader's Guides. As consulting editor for *The Oxford Companion to Crime and Mystery Writing* (1999), she contributed several articles. Her book reviews, articles, and short fiction have appeared in numerous journals and magazines.

Oleksiw received a PhD in Sanskrit from the University of Pennsylvania, and has lived and traveled extensively in India.

Oleksiw is a co-founder of Level Best

Books, which publishes anthologies of crime fiction by New England writers.